To Alicia,

R S Leyse

Self-Murder

Self-Murder

Robert Scott Leyse

SHATTERCOLORS PRESS
NEW YORK, NEW YORK

Cover illustration by Mark Edward Leyse,
courtesy the collection of Jim Cleveland
Photographed by Hugo Kobajashi

Book Cover Design and Layout
by Cathi Stevenson / Book Cover Express

ISBN 978-0-9821710-2-8

Library of Congress Control Number: 2009904592

First Edition

ShatterColors Press
New York, New York

To the memory of my aunt, Angie Esther Ella Leyse

ACKNOWLEDGEMENTS

Profuse gratitude to the following people: Angie Leyse and Chloee Murphy for their reading and critical commentary of early drafts of *Self-Murder*; Mark Edward Leyse likewise for reading and commentary, and for the cover painting; Jim Cleveland for the loan of the cover painting and Hugo Kobajashi for photographing it; Jane and JoAnne for the adventures in LawFirmLand; Don Robin for the wild dogs; and, as always, my parents for their unwavering and selfless love and support. I would also like to thank Omar, Lulu, Byron, and Zuke for the animal energy; Central Park, NYC, for being my favorite playground on the face of the earth; and Paris, France, for kick-starting *Self-Murder*.

Self-Murder

Opening:
Ensnarement in Recollection

Dearest reader, I'm not facing this blank page willingly; not addressing you willingly; not commencing this recollection willingly. Believe me, I'd much prefer to have succeeded in returning to the stable manner of life I enjoyed previous to when the experience I'm going to recount shattered that life; much prefer to have succeeded in reassembling the pieces of that life, assimilating the experience which troubles me; much prefer to remain unknown to you, pass my days in obscurity, be as silent as the grave. But the fact of the matter is that, even though the events I'll be describing transpired over three years ago, the unanswered questions connected with those events continue to distract and disquiet me, swathe my thoughts and dreams in oppressive shadows, transform all efforts to sleep into cold-sweat-anointed ordeals. The fact of the matter is that time, instead of healing this wound, has further opened and infected it; that time, instead of inducing merciful forgetfulness, has seen fit to prod and sting me with unceasing speculations as to what actually occurred during those tumultuous months; that time, instead of restoring me to a manageable frame of mind, has brought about a degree of mental distress which is more impossible to force into the background—lose in any amount of mindless diversion or conscientious effort to resurrect a professional life—than the searing pain of a knife-thrust. So yes, I'm facing this page because I need to wrestle with the memory which haunts me, transfer an unnerving experience onto it and those which will follow; because I hope to purge myself of my past, rid myself of it once and for all.

I've been attempting to avoid this moment—I've fought it off for as long as I possibly can. Because, dearest reader, to repeat something already stated above in a slightly different manner: if you're inclined to suppose I've commenced this reminiscence because I feel writing's a fine thing and that it would be commendable to frame a past sequence of bewildering events in the form of a novel for the edification of others (demonstrate that one can, indeed, exert oneself to rise above suchlike events and, perhaps, succeed in doing so), then you're wrong. The only reason I'm going to complete this paragraph and begin another one is because there's nowhere else for me to run. If, for one moment, I could believe suicide was a solution; if, for one moment, I could believe the act of shooting myself would instantly liberate me from this present which is a ceaseless accumulation of distress fueled by a memory that steadfastly refuses to declare itself, resists all my efforts to get to the bottom of its stranglehold upon me, then I wouldn't hesitate to point a pistol at the side of my head and pull the trigger. But, although I wish with all my heart I could believe otherwise, nothing will ever convince me that the next world is strong enough to serve as a refuge from inner conflicts left unresolved in this one: a persistent inner whisper—which, try as I might, I can't shout to silence—informs me that discharging the pistol would be nothing but a futile, naive and misdirected, postponement of the cure and that, like it or not, I'd eventually find myself—in some future equally unsettling life—right back to where I am now: being under the necessity of coming to terms with a disquieting past.

I well know what I want from the next life: complete and ever-lasting annihilation. That's right, no memories, no sensations—not the slightest trace of thought in my head, most infinitesimal flicker in my nerves. But, again, the inner whisper informs me that such an afterlife—hardly-to-be-hoped-for state of permanent insentience—must be *earned*; yes, informs me that such an after-life is beyond one's reach as long as one's in a condition of dis-unity with oneself; that all inner rifts persist into the next world, and must be resolved in the present before one can hope to attain to the state of deep dreamless sleep one craves. So there you have it: a resolution of inner differences is what I'm endeavoring to ac-complish by penning these words, the sole reason I'm bothering. And I'll say it again: if I thought I'd instantly be propelled into everlasting silence by the act of discharging a pistol aimed at my temple, I'd do it this moment without hesitation and this sentence would never be completed, the words you're reading wouldn't exist.

And now, dearest reader, I ask: do you dare to fall in love? I no longer do! What's love? It's the sudden seizure by unfamiliar emotions which delight and frighten in equal measure, subordi-nate one's will and personality, transform one into someone else. What's love? It's the hunger which increases with one's every at-tempt to sate it until one's adrift in it, being whirled and knocked about, like a leaf in the frothing water of a swift stream. It's a sure thing the sun will set in the west every evening; it's also a sure thing, as regards love, that there will come a point when the woman with whom one's captivated will begin to dissolve and vanish from under one's caresses, provide not relief from but added temperature to the fever which is burning one up; a point when one will find oneself engulfed in surge after insatiable surge of roiling desire, desperate for a means of calming oneself all but impossible to find. Too much is never, ever, enough. "More! More! More!" is the one and only thought buzzing in one's head.

Yes, love—wonderful love! What does love do? It carries one outside the established boundaries of one's existence, uproots one from one's accustomed manner of life. What does love do? It does away with all points of reference, guidelines of conduct, and rules of convention. Is this a good thing? a romantic thing? Not if one suddenly finds oneself helpless to resist impulses one was formerly rightfully wary of, begins to recoil before the possibility of committing unforgivable acts!

It's a fact that checks and balances no longer exist when the sight of the face of one's beloved—vertiginous plunge into the bottomless brightness of her eyes—is one's reflection as one's never seen it before, an onslaught of churning dreams one never knew one had. It's a fact that the inevitable outcome of love which refuses to compromise and suppress itself—become habitual, submit to the impositions of civilization—is a state of sensory overstimulation that begins to isolate one from not only the object of one's affection but from the world at large, and cause one to blankly stare in response to all words, rituals. What follows? There's no telling what the state of isolation, intensity of thought-dissolving desire, brought about by love may compel one to do; no telling what one may resort to in efforts to be liberated from one's affliction, set free.

So I ask again: do you dare to fall in love? dare to permit unbridled love to run its full course within you? And further: have you ever fled from your loved one at the very instant you were craving her embrace because you knew a few more moments in her vicinity might be enough to inundate you with sensations you'd be unable to reliably regulate—perhaps propel you towards loss-of-self-moderation-engendered criminal behavior? I have! That's right, I fled from my beloved—my endlessly doted upon one-and-only—because her mere presence was convulsing my senses, obliterating my thoughts, eroding my personality to such an extent I was fearful of losing every trace of inner stability, tasting of urges sane individuals avoid. Yes, I fled from her even though she was the beginning and end of everything that meant anything to me—fled from her while soul-alteringly in love with her!

But flight from one's beloved, the permanent removal of oneself from her physical proximity, is one thing; flight from the love one feels for her, the persistent effects of that love upon one, is something else altogether. Because love doesn't relinquish its claims, permit itself to be relegated to the sidelines, without offering resistance. So yes, although I saw no more of my beloved, the love I felt for her continued to generate itself within me and I was unable to distance myself from it: an understatement if there ever was one. That's right, I did my best to run from love without looking back—without remembrance, reflection, regret, any thought whatsoever; but love continued to flare within me and, deprived of its usual outlet, forced me into prolonged periods of sleeplessness during which increasingly vivid and attention-monopolizing waking dreams reined unopposed; yes, gave birth to an uncontrollably excitable imagination which steadily substituted itself for the world about me; an imagination which laid claim to my mental and sensory faculties to such an extent it soon began to affect my feelings, determine my actions.

And it was in that atmosphere of love's aftermath; atmosphere of perceptual distortion and emotional disarray, nonstop abrupt mood shifts, unceasing swings from one extreme of behavior to another; atmosphere of imagination-inundation, such that I was incapable of believing I was able to determine if I was actually feeling a certain way or only imagining I was... But why am I acting as if this love-aftermath atmosphere is a thing of the past? It continues at this very moment—it's the reason I'm writing this introduction, commencing this reminiscence. That's right, dearest reader, it's the memory of that love which haunts me; it's the tumult-obscured events of that love which afflict me with devouring doubts; it's the unabated influence of that love which undermines my every attempt to think clearly, get to the bottom of how I could've possibly acted as I did, determine in exactly what manner I did act; it's that love which both forms the subject of and forces me to pen the pages that follow. But, enough—no more procrastinating! My reminiscence begins on the following page...

PART ONE:
SELF-TRANSFORMATION'S SIREN SONG

I'd just turned off of the main boulevard, and was strolling up the slight incline of an easily overlooked side street when I saw her in the window of a cafe; saw the pale oval of her face, pitch black cascades of her hair! Everything about her—the inward smile of her expression, tense placidity of her manner, charge which her mere presence lent to the atmosphere! was an urgent invitation, out-and-out command! My right foot (and I swear it's true!)—my right foot, I say—while still off of the ground, suspended in mid-stride! abruptly—without awaiting my consent! jerked itself in the direction of the cafe with such force I nearly tripped over it, fell! And before I was fully aware of what I was doing—with the suddenness of a light aimed in one's eyes in the dark! I was crossing the street, stepping inside the cafe, standing on the slick surface of its polished hardwood floor—blinking at the brightness, wincing at the noise! without the remotest idea of how to conduct myself in a matter which in-stantly struck me as far surpassing all others in degree of difficulty and danger; without the remotest idea of how to extricate myself, escape!

Ha! Not above a minute previously I'd been sauntering about the streets with nothing of greater import in the forefront of my thoughts than a slight consciousness of boredom; but the moment I stepped into that cafe, I was in the grip of a violent anxiety attack! Did I say "anxiety attack"? Say rather: sensory seizure! Say, rather: emotional convulsion! Say, rather: an onslaught of terror such as I'd seldom, if ever, experienced before! And I attempted to about-face, flee the cafe, resume my nighttime wanderings, but couldn't do so—couldn't do anything but continue to stand immobile, like a deer transfixed by headlights, while the terror continued to mount inside me with such force I was certain I'd soon lose my footing, fall to the floor!

And yet I somehow managed to remain standing; somehow managed to will myself to cross to the bar, order a cup of tea! God! I was shaking to the joints of my bones while clinging to the edge of the counter with white-knuckled hands, endeavoring to discount—distance myself from! the impression I was being stared at by the people at the tables; stared at by the tables themselves, every object in the room! And the lights were becoming brighter; the mixture of conversation, shuffling chairs, clinking glasses was becoming a deafening din; the air was suddenly a thick agitated liquid which was quivering against me, spreading a faintly stinging flush over the surface of my skin; the entire room was suddenly rushing at and racing away from me at one and the same time—dipping, rising, turning inside out! while becoming overheated, suffocating! I was struggling to continue to cling to the counter-edge; struggling to appear as calm and unconcerned as possible—steady myself, stop shaking! while wondering what was happening to me, why I was there! Because I could no more account for my being in that café, comprehend why I'd been compelled to enter it, than I would've been able to account for myself had I suddenly found myself without a stitch of clothing on: so acute did the disturbance become within me—so absorbed did I become in my efforts to subdue the havoc in my senses, prevent it from thoroughly shoving rationality aside! I forgot about she who was responsible for it!

Forgot about her? Not for long! Suddenly I was under the impression I was being watched by one portion of the cafe; suddenly I was aware of an electric jab in the pit of my stomach which was distinctive from—stronger than! the state of uneasiness I was already in! I glanced up involuntarily, met her eyes in the mirror on the wall behind the bar, was again made to understand why I was there! Yes, I recollected—for a split-instant! how I'd first glimpsed her, but three or four minutes previously, while still outside; how her face had immediately crowded all else out of my field of vision, caused the whole of my body to tighten with tension; yes, how I'd been yanked from my carefree frame of mind, delivered over to tumult! This business of dashing inside the cafe before having the time to orient myself, be fully conscious of what I was doing; business of seeming to act in obedience to a will not my own, as if I'd been invaded by another being... When I say I recollected it for a split-instant, I mean it! Because, by the time a full instant had transpired...

And disbelieve—laugh! to your heart's content; inform me again and again that Dark Mistresses—sirens, sorceresses, succubi! are but figments of the imagination, mythical personifications of subconscious urges and obsessions; inform me they've never existed but in allegorical form, been anything but the means by which men have externalized and sought to overcome impulses unsettling to them: I counter by asserting that the sight of her face in the mirror did things to me nothing had ever done to me before! I was standing there, staring; was... The noise of the cafe was suddenly a hissing silence, as of trees rustling in the wind; the counter before me, walls about me, ceiling above me receded into the distance, and... God, I was all alone with her face which was leaping off the silver of the mirror, burning its image—fiery brand! into the center of my head; all alone with her beauty which was inundating me with a sensation of explosive paralysis, scintillant vertigo, euphoric dread!

Listen: the expression of her face; the contrasting qualities which were depicted upon her facial features; the mixture of savagery and kindliness, world-weariness and childlike wonder, erudite sophistication and animal disregard: it all swirled before me, stirred and churned within me, merged with the reckless—the serene—the cruel—the gentle—the forbidding—the inviting! brightness of her eyes, became a sense-scattering blast of revelation! God! The floor was sinking; I was swaying, on the point of swooning! I jerked my head down and shut my eyes in order to gain a respite from the unendurable stimulation of the sight of her, was—for how many seconds? staring inward at a blazing wall of silver, being assailed by waves of flaming—spine-electrifying! shivers: it was as if my flesh was dissolving, metamorphosing into fiery mist!

I don't know how I managed to hear—comprehend it was I who was being addressed—but someone was saying, "Sir! Your tea, sir!" I opened my eyes without daring to glance up; I placed money in someone's hand; I picked up a small pitcher and cup; I turned about to face the room, and locate a seat; I... I'm not stretching the truth when I insist that being forced to acknowledge and respond to the words of others while I was in that state was almost too much for me to bear; that the physical movements involved in paying for the tea and then turning to face the room were almost impossible to execute; that it was necessary for me to instruct myself every step of the way, as in: "Whatever you do, don't reveal the state you're in! Above all, seek to appear as natural as possible: conceal your trembling, introduce smoothness into your gestures! And of course it's attracting attention, the way you're staring at the counter, refusing to look up, meet anyone's gaze; but... Alright, you can't remedy that: your head's on the point of uncontrollably twitching; if you attempt to move it independently of the remainder of your body, deprive it of the support of an immobile neck, then it certainly will begin shaking and attract even more attention! Just make the best of it: better to be thought somewhat odd than to succumb to a shiver-fit, make a humiliating spectacle of yourself! That's it, try to place the money in the hand in a casual manner—don't drop it on the counter! Good, now make a gesture indicating he should keep the change; now pick up the pitcher and cup—don't spill the water! Ok, now turn your body towards the left, and keep turning it until you're facing the tables—try to raise your eyes far enough to enable you to survey the room, and..." Yes, as difficult as it may be to believe, I was obliged to carefully consider every movement of my body, no matter how slight, before venturing to execute it; and, once resolved to execute a given movement, obliged to do so with the utmost caution: only by so doing could I continue to monitor the disturbance within me, hope to prevent it from surging to the surface, depriving me of what little self-control remained.

But, to resume: I was facing the room, raising my gaze just far enough to enable me to discern the location of the nearest vacant table, and... Well, the distance from where I was standing to that table wasn't far but I was still inwardly shuddering, caught in a vise of movement-inhibiting tension, and it seemed as though I'd never manage to cross that distance; as though the table was getting further away with my every step towards it. Yes, I was struggling to make my body obey me—consciously placing one foot in front of the other, instructing myself, "Now the right, now the left!" while staring at the floor, not daring to raise my eyes again, sensing rather than actually seeing in which direction I was proceeding. I've no idea how I managed to reach that table without dropping the tea; or how I managed to seat myself without missing the chair...

Be that as it may: the moment I was seated, I was pressing my elbows hard against the tabletop and pressing the heels of my hands hard against my cheeks; yes, shielding my eyes with my fingers, deliberately restricting my field of vision, staring straight at the tabletop while endeavoring to imagine I was somewhere else, anywhere but there. In vain! There was the matter of the twin spots of insistent silver which were glowing in the corner slightly to the left of directly in front of me: they were her eyes and, try as I might, I couldn't stop being aware of the fact they were continuing to stare straight at me; couldn't stop feeling them bore through the fingers of my left hand, penetrate below the contours of my face: it was as if they were peeling away the successive layers of my psychic armor, bringing my secrets to the surface, leaving me no place to run or hide!

Yes, she was summoning my glance, demanding my undivided attention; she wasn't going to take "No!" for an answer, be content with less than unqualified compliance! God! To even attempt to meet her glance again, let alone actually do so! I couldn't! One more link-up with her eyes, one more exposure to the blinding lightning bolts which lurked therein, one more instance of being inundated with their electric fire, and... I wouldn't be capable of enduring it; and God only knows what the end-result would be, into what sort of seizure I'd be propelled! All I could do was remain seated, continue to seek to pretend she wasn't there; all I could do was hope she'd be moved to pity, walk out the door, and that I'd never see her again!

I found myself staring at my reflection on the smooth black marble surface of the tabletop in yet another effort to distract myself from her influence, become oblivious of her gaze... Ha, my reflection began to spin in the brightness of the overhead lights which were also reflected thereupon—shortly became a whirlpool of blazing silver, leaped at my eyes, all but blinded me! at the same time that the chair upon which I was seated grew uncomfortably warm and the air began to crackle, hiss! And I'm not exaggerating when I insist it was as if stinging needles were being shot into the pores of my skin, turning every cell of my flesh into a white hot jolt; when I insist I couldn't so much as twitch one of my fingers, move the smallest muscle of my face; when I insist I was authentically fearful of succumbing to a violent seizure, being knocked to the floor!

And she was still sitting there! Or was she? Was she still over in that corner or not? Because, as incredible as it may seem, I didn't actually know any longer! I was far too preoccupied with the excessively draining task of holding myself together—clinging to some remnant of self-control, keeping some small amount of rational self-direction intact—to be capable of detecting if she was over there, distinguishing the fiery feeling of her eyes upon me from the fire which had blazed into being within me. Listen: I was continuing to stare into the blinding scintillation of the tabletop; to hear the sharp hiss of the air; to feel I was being displaced in every nerve by hot electric chills, and... Oh, suddenly dark shapes were hovering before my eyes; suddenly my body was racked with spasmodic twitches; suddenly my head jerked itself free of my hands, and I was glancing in her direction—towards the palpable intensity of her eyes! without being able to stop myself, and... Ha! *She was no longer there!*

A surge of relief instantly swept through me; the tension of my muscles subsided to the degree that I was again capable of executing voluntary movements. Had I so desired, I would've been able to raise the cup of tea to my lips—something I'd, until then, been unable to think of doing. But did I, really and truly, wish to experience relief? Did I, despite the excessive discomfort of the state I'd been in moments previously, wish to be deprived of its cause? Ha, it's a fact: no sooner was I safely removed from what I'd considered a great danger and restored to a certain amount of self-control, than... Well, more pronounced than the sense of relief was regret on account of having missed an opportunity, allowed her—the unprecedented stirring-up of emotion, intensification of experience, that she represented—to slip through my fingers, disappear! That's right, I was cursing the fear which had interposed itself between us—the fear which had behaved like a jealous third party, assumed the duties of a jailer, cruelly prevented me from coming to any amount of understanding with she who'd affected me like none before!

Yes, once she'd departed, all I could think about was when, if ever, I'd see her again: was it possible? or an illusory hope which would yield nothing but disappointment and depression? Ha! Already, I was wishing I could relive the past ten minutes; that the clock could be turned back to when I was strolling on the sidewalk outside; that I could enter the cafe for the first time again, be given another opportunity to overcome my fear, master the upheaval within me. I was certain that, given another chance, I'd not squander it; certain I'd manage to meet her glance head on, unflinchingly hold it; certain I'd succeed in approaching her, introducing myself, seeing to it we ceased to be strangers. But, as matters stood: she was gone, and all I could do was inform myself again and again that the chance had been offered to me in good faith and that I'd behaved in the most inane manner conceivable; that a door on a new, indescribably vital, life had swung open and I'd been invited to enter, but had stupidly thrown the opportunity away! Christ! All I wanted to do was pick up my chair and wreck the place with it!—smash the windows, dishware, mirrors—especially the mirrors!—kick over the tables, slash the wallpaper to tatters, yank down the overhead lamps—destroy it all! And it suddenly seemed to me the other people, customers and employees alike, were regarding me sarcastically; that they were openly snickering and laughing at my expense—making unflattering comments, cracking unkind jokes! Additional anger rose within me: I was silently informing them they didn't know with whom they were dealing; that, although I'd been unnerved while in the presence of the bewitching beauty, I was otherwise a capable individual who wasn't in the habit of tolerating insults! Yes, I was thinking they shouldn't be too smug, conceited, and self-assured; thinking how fragile contentment is, and that those who take it for granted, assume it has no price tag, are fools; thinking how gratifying it would be to make them regret their unkind remarks, suffer for the mockery in their eyes! I was close to resolving to confront them...

But the interior of the cafe was changing: suddenly the walls, ceiling, floor—tables, chairs, all near and distant objects! were advancing towards me as with intent to smother, crush! Yes, suddenly the dimensions of the cafe were obscured by dense dimness-suffused air; suddenly there were shadowy flittings—black wings! in the air; suddenly I was up on my feet, racing for the door—the promise of open space, unhampered movement! without being able to stop myself!

But no sooner had I put a reassuring amount of distance between myself and the oppressive claustrophobia of the cafe; no sooner was I beginning to detect solid ground beneath my feet, find my stride; no sooner was I again capable of being conscious of my surroundings—noting the names of streets, ascertaining which area of the city I was in—than my bewitching beauty returned to my awareness with a vengeance, expelled all else from my thoughts, sent shock waves through my nerves! The spaciousness of outdoors instantly disappeared; the storefronts, signs—anything by which I might orient myself! were replaced by blurry shifting shapes, whirling mist! Yes, the city which I knew like the back of my hand vanished amidst—was flung into formless anonymity by! the tumult within me; I was being chased—whipped, stung! through the streets by a barely containable amount of inner excitement!

For the remainder of the night I was racing about the city in any and every spur-of-the-moment direction—going nowhere in particular, simply making certain I continue moving—while seeing nothing but my spellbinding beauty's face; her face which was a visual embodiment of everything I longed for and couldn't define—unshakable as a delirium-inducing vision, dream one's unable to determine if one had while awake or asleep. Ha! Did the face that I'd seen in the cafe actually belong to her? or had I greatly embellished the features of her face, emotion of her eyes, tone of her presence with my imagination? and, if the latter, then why had I never before embellished another woman's qualities as I had hers? More to the point: how had she managed to disorient me to such a degree, inspire such sensory and emotional havoc? Our encounter had been no more than ten minutes in duration and we hadn't exchanged a word; the closest we'd come to direct communication had been a brief touch of our eyes; and yet I was aroused—dizzyingly restless, boundlessly energetic, on full-scale alert! as I'd never been aroused before! I was blazing with an intensity of desire I hadn't previously believed I was capable of enduring, as if in danger of forgetting my name!

I recall returning to my apartment shortly after dawn, falling onto my bed without undressing, sleeping until early in the afternoon; recall awakening to find that the picture of my bewitching beauty's face was still with me—still bringing about urgent sensory shimmerings, washing through me in sigh after electrified sigh! Listen: it being a weekday, I'd been expected at the office in the morning, over five hours previously; ordinarily, I would've reported to work with a handy excuse, then stayed late to make up for lost time; I would've done so without thinking twice, with the attitude of detached professionalism which had become second nature to me. But on that afternoon it was suddenly a fact that reporting to the office was out of the question; a fact that I no longer inhabited the same world as my co-workers; a fact that I had no choice but to keep my own company while the aftershocks of my experience in the cafe continued to accumulate and flare inside— disorient, frighten, excite, and delight! me, carry me towards I knew not what...

Yes, suddenly it was impossible to report to work, communicate with others; impossible to do anything but pace about my apartment in a state of stunned bedazzlement, race about the city in a state of euphoric dread. I lost all grasp of time; I'd awaken in the dead of night, collapse in the late evening; the days spun together, became intertwined; I didn't know if it was still yesterday or already tomorrow: the one constant in my life was the condition of bewildering arousal into which my bewitching beauty had propelled me. Always, her face was aglow in my mind's eye; always, her beauty was stirring disturbance into my nerves; always, her eyes were piercing me through and through, turning me inside out—awakening aspects of myself I was unfamiliar with, maintaining me at a barely endurable level of fascinated fear.

I'd awaken and she'd be hovering in the drawn-shutter darkness of my apartment—there: brushing her hair away from her face, staring straight at me, speaking to me in an undecipherable language of her eyes—there: thoroughly disorienting me without departing from, sending the slightest ripple through, her flawless composure—there: aglow with the mesmerizing vitality of a different world, flaunting the fact she was intimate with an uncountable amount of sensations far outside the sweep of my own experiences. On these occasions I'd become rigid with tension while seeking to unravel the mystery of her eyes, probe the depths of her equanimity, speak to her—reply to her! in her own language... And then it would seem to me I was no more than a moment away from seizing ahold of her riddle, pinning the answer down; but that moment wouldn't arrive—would remain maddeningly near, just out of reach! and... Oh, I'd be gasping while stretching and twisting—arching my back, flexing my shoulders, extending my limbs—in the thick steamy air, wet pungency of my bed; would be flowing about in my feelings like water gushing over the top of a dam, melting and dissolving in waves of icy hot sighs—all but swooning—while still vaguely aware of continuing to see her face...

There arrived a point at which I virtually ceased to venture from my apartment on account of not wishing to disturb the manner in which my spellbinding beauty was monopolizing my attention, stimulating my imagination, bringing on states of excitement in which I'd become unrecognizable to myself. I'd lie awake in the reverberant silence, awaiting the special moments when enthralling inner upheavals would occur. To wit: her face would appear before me, and I'd instantly be coiled tight inside— skittish, hyper-alert, impatient—to such a degree it was as if another being was blazing under the surface of my skin; and I'd be *this* close to leaping to my feet, racing out the door, walking off my excitement in the streets; but would remain motionless, continue to contemplate her face, and... Well, I'd be struggling to mentally keep abreast of and continue to monitor the changes taking place within me, but they'd be occurring too rapidly—the current would overtake me! Her face would become a cloud of glowing mist—blast of blinding silver—and I'd suddenly be incapable of so much as locating myself in my body, much less of formulating an opinion about what was happening to me; yes, suddenly be gripped by a sort of blissful agony while (I'm at a loss of how else to state it) *seeing* an endless expanse of dimensionless vastness; *seeing* a representation of desire which knows no limits; *seeing* my most unrestrained flights of hope and fancy descend to earth, become tangible possibilities. I've no idea for how long

I'd be engrossed in the vision, absorbed in the sensory storm. All I know is that, once the vision departed and my normal eyesight returned, I'd find myself lying on the bed or the floor and be uncertain as to whether I'd been awake or asleep; as to whether the vision had visited me in an open-eyed trance or in my dreams. I'd remain where I was, lie there seemingly for hours while preoccupied with the thought that there was a vast undiscovered world of emotional possibility simmering inside me and that I was only now beginning to come into contact with it. I'd picture myself wandering the streets of unfamiliar cities, entering nondescript buildings, strolling down dim hallways, entering bright rooms; and it would instantly be understood that all taboos were ignored within these rooms; that these rooms were exempt from society's prohibitions, outside the jurisdiction of courts of law; that they were places where one could safely surrender to impulses which were flagrantly at odds with the established order; further, it would be understood that I was being invited to participate—invited to shed the trappings of the familiar, abandon my present life, embrace the unknown. Yes, I'd be lying there with those pictures, thoughts, and fantasies representing themselves to me as my unavoidable future, and... But how am I to make myself understood? How am I to make myself believable when I insist that the fear I felt was inseparable from some of the strongest sensations of joy I've ever known? How communicate that a wonderful sense of liberation accompanied profound unease when I became convinced I was being forced to abandon the only manner of living I'd ever known?

Yes, it was as if she was a fiery phantom which had taken up residence within me, commenced an extensive renovation; as if she was tunneling below the foundations of my personality, rearranging the building blocks of my psyche; with the result that I was set adrift in a sea of sensations, thoughts, and desires which were openly hostile to the manner in which I'd always lived, relentlessly eroding my ties to—isolating me from—the world I'd always known. There was seldom a moment when I wasn't under the impression that my ingrained habits, convictions, and aspirations were being inundated by attacks of restlessness—surges of longing—too strong for them to withstand; when I wasn't under the impression that I'd become fuel for a hungry fire but, instead of being consumed, was metamorphosing into that fire. And I only wanted to blaze brighter, be pushed to the furthest limits of endurance, have my utmost capacity for survival amidst emotional extremes put to the test! Yes, I prayed that my bewitching beauty would continue to consider me worthy of habitation; continue to keep me tense, quivering, eager; continue to acquaint me with, balance my fear of, the unknown...

But without the means of seeing my bewitching beauty again and renewing her influence upon me—without the knowledge of who she was or where she lived—how could I expect my condition of arousal to last? One random encounter was far too finite to sustain continued journeys outside of my accustomed psychic boundaries! Which is to say that the inevitable moment arrived when her influence began to diminish; when the longings she'd stirred to life began to die; when I found myself emerging from her spell, awakening from the dream—stranded in a void of unrealized anticipation, stalled desire.

Listen: suddenly it was difficult to picture her clearly—suddenly her face was blurred of outline, unfocused—and I was struggling to reassemble the sum total of her features, recreate the full impact of her beauty; struggling to mentally revisit the cafe where I'd glimpsed her, again undergo our encounter, reexperience the euphoric disorientation, tantalizing turmoil, irresistible fear. Yes, I was doing my best to create a permanent picture of her in my head which possessed the full radiance, hummed with the same focused energy, of the original—a picture that would continue to unsettle and inflame me regardless of whether I saw her again or not. But her picture was eluding all my efforts to retain it, steadily disappearing like mist into dry air; and the more indistinct her picture became, the more I became a stranger to the feelings she'd inspired—found myself susceptible to bouts of emotional inertia, desolate resignation, indifferent boredom.

Yes, my attempts to prolong my spellbinding beauty's influence—renew the shock of our encounter in the cafe, keep the reverberations alive—was a losing battle, and all too soon the state
that she'd placed me in was little more than a hypothetical situation: something I was capable of conceiving of but incapable of
experiencing. And to round off my defeat the former routine of
my life began to return to my awareness and reinstate its claims
upon me to the degree that I found myself beginning to dwell
upon the length of my absence from work and wondering whether,
if I stayed away for much longer, my job would still be there when
I returned. And of course I was berating myself for such thoughts,
infuriated that they were occurring to me, but... Well, it would be
more accurate to say that I was attempting to berate myself and be
infuriated because, in truth, I couldn't manage to cut myself to
the quick—rally my will, be anything but a helpless observer—
while watching myself steadily be reclaimed by the stifling regu-
larity of a nine-to-five existence. What a situation!—loathing my
return to normalcy but unable to act upon, be animated by, the
loathing!—unable to do anything but become resigned, devoid of
responsiveness and empty of fight, against my fondest wishes!

Yes, the bewitching beauty had, for an infuriatingly brief interval, injected me with new—all but uncontainable—vitality,
transformed my mundane rationality-framed existence into a nonstop waking dream of electrified senses, explosive hunger, delirious aspiration. She'd made it possible for me to believe that a new
untamed world of self-transcendence, magic, and mystery was
near at hand. But by the time of which I now speak (when nearly
two weeks had transpired since I'd first detected the waning of
her hold upon me), I couldn't bring the faintest approximation of
her face to mind, much less feel the slightest spark of what I'd
felt while under her influence. That's right, a new sense of purpose—enthralling glimpse of the possibility of shedding my accustomed personality, being indoctrinated into a new order of
intensified experience, emotionally heightened living—had possessed and animated me for a short while, but had then vanished:
nothing more, nothing less. Ha! Perhaps the episode had never,

so to speak, sunk its claws into authentic experience? perhaps it had been little more than an instance of self-delusion, wishful thinking? perhaps the spellbinding beauty was in actuality an un-remarkable woman of plain appearance with next to no capacity for strong feeling? God! I ended up believing that and doubting the significance of the entire episode, from beginning to end. Yes, that's the state to which I was brought; that's what became of my new sense of purpose, unbridled aspiration...

*   *   *   *   *

But then late one night, two or so months following the en-counter in the cafe, I was waiting at a red light in my car—think-ing about nothing in particular—when I was suddenly ill at ease for no apparent reason; suddenly overcome with a feeling of trans-parency, as if my secret thoughts and dreams had chosen to rise from within me, plainly stamp themselves upon my face for all to see. What could bring about such sensations at such short notice? Before having the opportunity to clearly formulate the question, I knew that a pair of eyes were fastened onto me from my left—intently observing, probing, analyzing. Annoyance seized me in addition to unease: I abruptly turned towards the passenger win-dow of the car which had, at some point, pulled up alongside me; yes, turned to confront—vanquish, stare down—the offending eyes, and... God! I found myself face to face with my bewitching beauty, gazing straight into her eyes which were in every respect as focused and fiery—blinding, disruptive! as they'd been in the cafe previously, if not more so! My muscles instantly tightened—throbbed! to the point of pain; a white hot surge of panic inun-dated—stabbed! the center of my chest; my head violently twisted and I found myself facing forward again: I didn't waste a sec-ond—quickly fastened my eyes onto a point of brightness (the glass face of a building?) ahead of me, mentally clung to it for dear life!

Yes, I was seeking to banish all except that point of bright-ness from my awareness, forget she was watching me, pretend she wasn't there: was I succeeding? Ha! The touch of her gaze was far stronger than any amount of contrary concentration I could muster! I couldn't escape the feeling I was being turned inside out; that my most scrupulously guarded secrets were being conjured into the light of day; that I was being subjected to a thorough examination, judged wanting in all respects! Nor could I prevent panic from continuing to tie searing knots in my chest— prevent terror from accumulating! I swear I was *this* close to slamming my foot down on the accelerator—propelling the car into crisscrossing traffic! in order to escape her eyes; swear the urge to do so quickly became a shrieking "Now! Now! Now!" in my head; swear it required all the will at my disposal, every last spark of the survival instinct, to fight off that urge! And who knows if I would've succeeded in fighting off that urge for much longer had the traffic light not turned green, allowed the car in which she was seated to advance? Yes, thank God the light turned green and that I became aware her eyes were being pulled away from the side of my face! Thank God for the slight amount of relief I experienced as a consequence of that awareness!

But no sooner did the tension within me subside to the point of marginal tolerability—no sooner was I again able to, however feebly, see outside of the disturbance within me—than I saw the car in which she was riding pull to the curb before making it halfway down the next block; saw her, I kid you not, emerge from that car, stroll up the walkway of an apartment building, insert a key in its door, step inside! "No! No! No!" I silently yelled as the dashboard began to spin, yanked the windshield—full extent of the view outside! into its whirling motion, swallowed all in hissing light!

I don't know for how long I sat there as if paralyzed: all I know is I became aware that horns were honking; that a battered car had pulled up alongside mine and a woman was leaning out of its window, putting on an angry face, making unkind gestures: what could it mean? I finally realized I was the object of her anger; that the honking was originating from the cars behind me due to my having detained them by not heeding the green light, and... Ha, the hostility of the motorists, when contrasted with the

violence of the disturbance within me, barely seemed to exist: I
was far more conscious of the fact that the unease brought about
by this new encounter with my bewitching beauty was regather-
ing itself, threatening to again tear me from all cognizance of my
surroundings, utterly immobilize me! I had to get out of the car,
escape the whirling dashboard—had to surround myself with open
space, move my body, break the tension's grip!

The traffic light had turned red again and the honking was
continuing to reach my ears as if from far away; oppressive
buzzing noises were also reaching my ears, seemingly from inside myself; the windshield was still vanishing in the brightness
of the dashboard: I don't know how I managed to detect that an
opening appeared in traffic while the light was still red. God, and
what was I thinking when I allowed my car to dart across the intersection, in disobedience of the light, and pull to the curb on the
opposite side of the street? when I exited the car, recrossed the
intersection on foot, came to a stop on the sidewalk alongside the
motorists—still being detained by the red light—that I'd infuriated? But that's the point: I wasn't thinking, I was blindly fleeing
the maelstrom within myself!

Listen: several of the motorists were shouting abuse and the
abuse was music to my ears—a life raft keeping me afloat in the
rough waters of my disordered senses, just the amount of contact
with the outside world I needed to forestall succumbing to the full
fury of the upheaval inside me. It's all a matter of perspective and
comparison! The motorists—some of larger physique than myself, not to mention that I was greatly outnumbered—were informing me I deserved to be throttled, have my head torn off? I
don't mind admitting that ordinarily I would've exercised due
caution, not hesitated to make amends with some well-placed respect, an apology or two; not thought twice about making myself
scarce! But that night was far from being ordinary and I was disregardful of threats of bodily injury; not merely disregardful, but
oblivious—not courageously, cavalierly, recklessly oblivious,
simply... It's just that *anything* was preferable to being forced to
turn my attention inward, realize what was brewing inside me!

What I wanted from those people was for them to hate me twice as much, and show it—to froth at the mouth, shriek their throats bloody, rain a steady stream of virulence upon my head! What I wanted was for them to continue to be capable of capturing my attention, providing me with something to do!

And is my memory being honest with me? did I really...? Yes, I began screaming back at the motorists, so anxious was I for something to preoccupy my thoughts which were threatening to splinter into formless noise! I recall the ovals of their faces striking me as being bland, nonsensical, idiotic; the flailings of their arms as being clumsy, fruitless, absurd!—can see myself laughing in mockery, derision! shouting louder, howling! seizing an object from a trash can, throwing it! daring the nonentities to come for me: why do they hesitate? Cowards! Drop dead, the whole worthless lot of you! And then I lift the trash can over my head, watch it clang onto the pavement, strike a fender of one of the cars: does the recipient of this gesture emerge to challenge me? No! I recall seeing skittishness and alarm burst onto several faces, watching the cars depart rather quickly; recall suddenly finding myself alone!

And it wasn't the fear of being held to account for having flung a trash can at a car which forced me to commence dashing down the sidewalk; wasn't the fear some of those involved might have second thoughts about having retreated—remind themselves I was but one person—and feel compelled to return, teach me a lesson; wasn't the fear they might encounter a cop on patrol, provide him with enough information to hand me a night's lodging in jail: not at all! Be it remembered my car was parked across the street and the keys were in my pocket. If I'd been fleeing from possible consequences of my confrontation with the motorists, the most effective means of doing so would've been to drive off. But I can assure you I was incapable of giving the said confrontation another thought—that it would've been a godsend had I been able to be alarmed concerning trivialities such as possible consequences. Indeed, I would've welcomed the return of the motorists: they would've been resuming their useful function of providing me with a means of orienting my thoughts in the physical world, standing between myself and full awareness of what was surging to life inside me.

Listen: the moment the motorists departed, I was alone with my bewitching beauty again; alone with her face which instantly blazed bright in my mind's eye; alone with her eyes which were informing me I'd not merely crossed paths with her for the second time, but discovered her place of residence. The mere fact of having encountered her was traumatic enough; to ask that I also be required to comprehend what the discovery of her place of residence meant—comprehend it would unfailingly influence the future course of my life, whether I wished it to or not—was asking far too much. And so, at the same time that the recently witnessed scene of her being dropped off at her building was coming into focus in my awareness, I was doing all I could to blot it out, refuse to admit it had anything to do with me; yes, was dashing down the sidewalk—all but tripping over myself in my haste to get somewhere, anywhere! while all too aware that an unsettling realization was close to kicking down the doors of my consciousness, gaining possession of me from the ground floor to the top...

For the remainder of that night, until sunrise the following morning, there wasn't a moment when I wasn't in motion, zigzagging this way—that! in a hyper-animated twitch and jerk—kick kick kick! of my feet which were suddenly possessed of a bottomless well of stamina—as if sheathed in the red shoes that danced the girl to death! All to no avail, however: I could've walked every square foot of the city—flung myself into the darkness of every alley, climbed the walls of every dead end! and, still, I wouldn't have been a hair's breadth closer to where I wanted to be! After all: how is it possible to escape inner havoc which is being wrought by an unsettling discovery? How is it possible to shed disturbed senses, inflamed nerves, flayed flesh? How is it possible to erase memory, arrest chain-reaction compulsiveness, undo the weavings of fate?

When sunrise arrived following what must have been at least six hours of unbounded exertion—of, as I've stated and not exaggerated, constant frenetic movement—I was thankful for the numbness of my feet, pinching tightness of my calves, aches shooting up my back. At last it was an ordeal to haul my body about, resist slumping onto the nearest doorstep; at last drowsiness was undermining my panic, mitigating my fear. I can barely recall recovering my car, returning to my apartment, collapsing without bothering to undress...

I'm certain I managed to descend into the echoless silence of a deep dreamless sleep, but I've no idea for how long it lasted. I remember I was later tossing and turning in a state of agitation situated somewhere between sleep and wakefulness; remember being vaguely conscious that daylight was streaming through the windows I hadn't had the presence of mind to shade at the same time that I was experiencing what I can only describe as being dream-reenactments of the events of the previous night—dream-reenactments in which I'd see the face of my unsettling beauty, experience the shock of recognition, again and again; in which I'd flail about on the car seat in a state of seizure, wrestle with the temptation to slam my foot down on the accelerator, again and again; in which I'd repeatedly watch her be discharged at the curb, walk up those steps, enter that building; repeatedly watch the windshield fall into the dashboard, spin into hissing light. I also remember that, while these dream-reenactments were occurring, it was as if I was being wrapped tighter and tighter in heavy folds of hot wet movement-inhibiting cloth until I could no longer move. Yes, I remember ceasing to toss and turn, lying on my back in a state of tense immobility while sticky with icy sweat; remember the dream-reenactments became more vivid and that the more vivid they became, the stronger was my sense of being pinned to the mattress; remember I could neither return to the sanctuary of sleep nor fully awaken...

When I finally did awaken in the early evening... Ha, I didn't awaken by degrees—crack open my eyes, lie abed for a spell, ease my feet towards the floor, stand and stretch... What happened was that I was jolted to my feet—landed in the center of the room in what seemed to be a single leap—while full awareness that I'd discovered my turmoil-engendering beauty's place of residence forced itself into the forefront of my thoughts, demanded my undivided attention. Yes, the building that she'd entered was crystal clear in my mind's eye—the intersecting streets which marked its location were shouting their names: I could neither blur the pictures nor train my thoughts upon anything else. I would've liked nothing better than to permanently strike that discovery from memory, be released from the course of action it had imposed upon me. Because now that I knew where to find my spellbinding beauty, I realized I'd be unable to prevent myself from seeking her out; that, unlike in the instance of our first encounter in the cafe (when limits had been imposed upon my condition of excitement by the fact I hadn't possessed the means of seeing her at will), I was no longer safe from an unrestrained eruption of the feelings she'd engulfed me in. Yes, the discovery of her place of residence had reenlisted me into the service of my obsession in a manner which greatly trivialized my previous stint; this time around, I'd be forced to pursue my obsession to its utmost limit— fully undergo the personality-rearranging experiences which had only been hinted at before—regardless of whether I was prepared or willing to do so.

And once I saw my unrest-inducing beauty again: what then? Would I succeed in getting to the bottom of the mystery—unraveling the witchery—of her effect upon me? Would I be liberated from the state of sensory disorder she'd placed me in? Would the gnawing longing I was under the influence of instantly subside? Would...? Oh, such questions relentlessly taunted me in flagrantly sarcastic tones of voice! What did I want from her? Did I know? Did the self I'd always known, personality I was accustomed to, exist any longer? Did anything exist outside of this violent attraction? Hadn't the other people in my life as good as dropped off the face of the earth? Hadn't my work, social routine—everything that linked me to the outside would—vanished as if none of it had ever been? Wasn't I now—literally overnight! alone in the world, with no one and nothing but my obsession to cling to? Simply put: I had to see my bewitching beauty again and had no choice in the matter and that was that! Any rationalization I might seek to attach to it—speculation as to the result! was useless bluster and the only thing remaining was for me to shut up, collect myself, and attend to business!

And, yet... Ha, it's only natural to seek to resist something one's being forced to do! "No choice but to turn up at my spellbinding beauty's door?" I asked with a mixture of fear, wannabe-disbelief, and helpless fascination. "No choice?" I repeated as I began pacing about my apartment, darting from room to room, in repetitive desperation. "That I'm overcome with the compulsion to turn up at her door, I don't deny; but why not impose limits on this compulsion? I certainly ought to have some say in the matter—be able to choose when to surrender to the compulsion, or decline to do so altogether!" What self-delusion! The walls were beginning to sway—reel, dance! about me; a steady rasp—as of sandpaper on wood! was beginning to sound in my ears; the lights were beginning to dart—stab! at my eyes; and... God, the walls were pressing up against my face! the sound in my ears was an unbroken scream! the lights were glaring to the point of displacing sight! I had no choice but to race for the door, get out of there!

Ha! Had I come outside in the hope of being calmed by open space, soothed by the swish of breeze upon my cheeks? in the hope of finding solace in the pulse of the evening crowds, being drawn into the laughing exhilaration, blithe anticipation, of those in search of amusement? If so, I'd been more than naive! Because I was instantly under the impression that the sky was bearing down upon me; that the breeze was a steady slap in my face; that the passersby were seeking to restrict my movements, drive me over the edge of the curb! Yes, suddenly my every step seemed to be executed in an overly anxious manner which was radiating dissonant vibrations, attracting alarmed and hostile glances: I wished to slow my pace, adopt a more natural stride, blend in with the others but couldn't convince myself I was doing so while watching the shop windows flash silver—melt! about me; watching the cracks in the sidewalk rapidly approach—slide under! my feet; watching intersection after intersection race forward to meet me!

I've no idea for how long I walked or which route I took: all I know is that one of the intersections suddenly froze before me, and the streets lost their anonymity: the names of two of them were echoing in my head. Then I realized I'd found my way back to the location of my second encounter with my bewitching beauty and that I was staring across the intersection at her place of residence, situated halfway down the next block...

But no sooner did I realize where I was and why I was there; no sooner was I on the point of crossing that intersection with the intention of entering her building, finding out who she was and in which unit she resided; no sooner was I certain I'd soon be gazing upon her again, than I was uneasily—violently! self-conscious, unable to lift either foot from the ground! God! It was as if the passersby were pausing to turn and glare at me; as if the nearby objects—lamppost to my left, mailbox across the street, bus stop shelter to my right! were advancing towards—threatening to crush! me; as if the air was gathering itself about—applying pressure to! my skull! My thoughts went blank: I was seeing silvery brightness again! hearing hissing crackles again! sensible of having hot—excruciatingly tight! knots in my chest again! of... Oh, was vaguely conscious of spinning about and dashing in a direction opposite from that of her building; of being engaged—yet again! in the all too familiar pastime of moving for the sake of moving...

When I returned to myself in sufficient degree to be aware, however sporadically, of my surroundings I was in a different section of town; was standing on the landing of a building, grasping the cold iron of its railing, shaking and kicking it with such fury I was tearing the skin of my palms, causing my ankles to ache. I was enraged on account of the fact I'd been incapable of crossing that intersection, entering my spellbinding beauty's building, seeing her again—incapable of carrying out the course of action which I absolutely had to carry out. I was eager for someone to become annoyed at the racket I was making, and request me to stop;

eager for the opportunity to tell that someone to drop dead, goad him into attacking me; eager to mock, curse, scream—strike and be struck, kick and be kicked! I had a string of sarcasms, insults, and taunts at the ready; I was fully prepared to start—and finish! a violent altercation! I was picturing the said altercation in my imagination—anticipating it in my taut muscles, coiled nerves! with such vividness I was on the point of behaving as if an adversary was already standing before me! Yes, I needed an enemy, someone besides myself upon whom to vent my anger—someone to draw my rage away from myself! But no one stepped forward to answer my challenge, and I therefore remained at the mercy of my self-contempt—at the mercy of...

Suddenly the railing slipped from my grasp and landing vanished from under my feet: I was racing down the sidewalk again while aware that, even had an enemy advanced to confront me, it would've been nothing but a thoroughly ineffectual temporary solution; aware that no amount of external conflict was capable of sparing me from the conflict within myself, mitigating it in the least degree, and... Well, it's not difficult to understand that one's seldom more susceptible to dismal moods than during the period immediately following one's failure to capitalize on an expectation which has seized ahold of one's entire being; that a state of desperate depression is often the consequence of one's inability to achieve the object of an all-consuming desire; that self-destructive tendencies are most likely to infect one in the hours after one's missed an opportunity to rid oneself of an obsession which is gnawing at one's every thought. But it's one thing to comprehend the phenomenon, experience it solely on a mental level; quite another thing to sense the phenomenon brewing inside oneself and know that no amount of comprehension is going to spare one a full onslaught! And I could certainly feel the force of thwarted desire churning in the pit of my stomach, contracting my muscles; feel it pulling me into a tightening web of tension, casting a murky pall upon my interpretations of my surroundings; feel it infecting me with melancholy, hopelessness, and dread!

Listen: suddenly the streets were more desolate—stripped of warmth of feeling, leached of all trace of comfort! than I'd previously believed possible—saturated with a dreary fog which seemed to be seeping into me via the pores of my skin! No escape! The gutters were filled with motionless—oil slick befouled! indigo-black water which was staring up at me coldly, unpityingly—with utter indifference, unresponsive deadness! at the same time that the tops of the buildings were curling over me, blotting out the sky, shoving thick shadows—more and more shadows! onto the sidewalk at my feet; yes, wrapping black crepe about the street lamps, placing a dark pane of glass in front of my eyes! And all sounds were distant echoes distorted beyond recognition; objects which had formerly been composed of solid matter were insubstantial gatherings of mist that slid about me like sheets on clotheslines in a strong wind! I began walking with unaccustomed slowness—walking slowly while staring at the black water in the gutter without wanting to, and... I paused, came to a stop; was standing on the edge of the curb, observing my reflection on the black water's surface: the water began to spin—faster and faster! until it was sucking the oval of my face into its vortex, engulfing the light of my eyes in darkness—obliterating the entirety of my image! and... God, I was sinking—further and further! into the tumult within me, becoming increasingly entangled in the intensity of my unexpended excitement!

I remember I began to cross the streets far more frequently than the end of each block required, repeatedly stroll towards and unduly linger about the center lanes; yes, remember being compelled—again and again! to see double yellow traffic direction dividing lines at my feet even though my vision was still obscured by gloom-crippled senses; even though the headlights of oncoming vehicles appeared as little more than blurred patches of glowing haze in omnipresent dimness—blurred patches which alternately faded into and out of brightness, shrunk and expanded, in such a manner that it was difficult for me to judge how near or far away they were. And, while indulging in this reckless behavior, it seems to me I was also hearing whispers in my head, as in:

"What if I underestimated the distance and speed of approaching traffic, then dashed towards the opposite side of the street? What if I slipped on wind-flung litter and didn't have enough time to scramble to my feet, get out of the way?" But why did I say, "it seems to me I was also hearing whispers in my head"? There's no "seems" about it, I recall it for a fact!—recall informing myself, each time I wandered into the street, that death might be only a misjudgment of twelve inches away—only a miscalculation of two seconds away—only a slip of the foot away! Yes, recall informing myself that, if I continued to incautiously stroll into the street in my disordered state, perhaps a misjudgment of distance—or miscalculation of timing—or slippery surface! *would* materialize, with the result that I'd be killed. Killed? I recall picturing myself lying inert on the pavement, going into shock, becoming numb; recall seeking to imagine life steadily ebbing from my battered body, finally departing altogether; recall wondering what would follow, where I'd be! At the same time, I was wondering why we insist upon clinging to this life when we could be off to elsewhere, liberated from the confinement of our bodies—liberated from the emotional upheavals which strain our muscles, rack our nerves, disorder our thoughts; especially, when we could be liberated from the self-disgust, desperation, and fear which seizes ahold of us the instant an all consuming desire's deflected from its object, denied an outlet! Yes, I was wondering why we resist being torn from this life even though we be gazing upon our surroundings from the end of a long narrow tunnel, enveloped in an awful inner night; resist it even though we're being wrapped tighter and tighter in dense coils of painful tension, fighting the downward spiral of an inner whirlpool!

But was I truly crisscrossing the streets in a reckless manner, deliberately placing myself in peril? God, I sincerely don't know if I was or not! Perhaps I was, somewhere in the back of my thoughts, far more aware of the margin of error than I was giving myself credit for. Yes, it does strike me as being possible that I was taking care not to be struck by the vehicles, but doing it in such a manner—cutting it close enough—that it would appear to me I was in danger; as being possible that my senses were remaining alert and reflexes remaining quick without my knowledge; in short, that I was clinging to life without my knowledge. Or is this train of thought delusional?—an attempt to avoid admitting it was entirely on account of chance that I avoided being injured or killed? As I've said, I sincerely don't know! And, moreover, I probably never will know how close I came to ending up underneath one of those cars, entangled in its axle; to what degree I was seriously considering ridding myself of myself; whether the idea that I was subconsciously mindful of my safety is far-fetched or not! All I can be certain of is that the extent of my distress was such that it was threatening to dispossess me of my instinct for self-preservation, drag me to the level of doing violence to myself; but, again, as to how close I came to succumbing to that threat...

Nor do I know for how long I was flailing deep inside myself, separated from my surroundings by a veil of gloom; for how long I was being compelled to bring death into the forefront of my thoughts, wonder at the ease with which one may depart from the physical fragility of this life, and why so many more—myself most of all! don't elect to do so; for how long I was, so to speak, being repeatedly led to the edge of a precipice—tempted to fling myself off! by the disturbance within me...

What I do know is that, at some point, I became aware my seizure-inducing beauty's face had reappeared in my mind's eye, and... Oh, I instantly passed, as a result of that awareness, from the above-described state of thwarted desire's vengeance into the state of once again being actively engaged in the pursuit of that desire! That's right, the moment her face reappeared... Ha, steady flashes of lightning wouldn't have inundated my surroundings with more illumination! In seconds the black crepe unwrapped itself from about the street lamps and the dark pane of glass before me became transparent; in seconds I was blinking my eyes, glancing up and down the street, as if emerging from the influence of a baneful spell!—yes, shaking my head in disbelief at finding myself in a section of town far removed from her place of residence, asking myself why I'd wandered astray—why I wasn't already inside her building, standing on her landing, knocking on her door! But these questions slipped from consciousness almost at the instant of being posed because I was already racing through the streets again, making a beeline for her address, with the luminous loveliness of her face—vertigo-instilling depths of her eyes! shimmering in my nerves, whipping me into a dizzy fever!

I can assure you that when I again found myself standing at the fateful intersection—gazing upon my mesmerizing beauty's building for the second time that night—I was reeling with impatience to get my visit over and done with; can assure you the only thing I wanted on earth was to be standing face to face with my obsession as soon as possible. So why, then, wasn't I proceeding to cross that intersection? Why did I suddenly, for no ascertainable reason, feel as though I was being led to my execution? Why did I rapidly become a panic-stricken wreck who could barely remain standing for as long as it took me to about-face, flee? Why was I unable to prevent myself from repeating the ordeal of desire-denial-generated self-loathing I'd already undergone on that night? from again descending into a state of explosive depression in a far-flung section of town? again being compelled to view self-immolation as a possible exit, solution?

Listen: for the duration of that night I was being whipped towards my spellbinding beauty's door by an all-consuming urge to see her only to be turned away, forced to flee, by a violence of inner upheaval I couldn't master! That's right, several times I underwent the experience of being afire with deliriously eager expectation one moment, tumbling into dread-saturated despairing rage the next! I literally wasn't able to face her; literally didn't possess the amount of mental, emotional, and physical stamina which would be required to surmount the wall of fear that was thrusting itself between us, keeping us apart! The result of that first night was that I returned to my apartment shortly after sunrise in a state of stressful excitement more pronounced than that in which I'd departed from it, with the thirst to pay her a visit continuing to tear at my nerves, drive all else from my thoughts! Her face was the last thing I saw before falling asleep, the one and only subject of the recurring dreams which wouldn't permit me to rest easy in my sleep, and the first thing I saw upon awakening in the late afternoon...

And, upon awakening on that second day, it was again in vain that I struggled to think of something besides my unsettling beauty, resist reminding myself I'd discovered her place of residence; in vain that I sought to rebel against the compulsion to turn up at her door, stop longing for the moment when I'd once more be gazing upon her face; in vain that I endeavored to prevent myself from exiting my apartment, returning to the street on which she lived...

What was the outcome? As I'd passed the first night, so I passed the second; and likewise did I pass all the nights of the following week or so. Time and time again, I'd find myself standing at that intersection, and be resolved to enter her building; time and time again, I'd find myself being flogged in the opposite direction by panic attacks pronounced enough to blur my vision, make my body shake; time and time again, I'd find myself staggering about in distant sections of town, absently staring at my surroundings from out of the depths of a tumultuous state of gloom; find myself struggling to hold my own against the fury of the unsated craving within me; struggling to resist the urge to dwell upon death—extinguish my future days! and... Ha, time and time again, my spellbinding beauty's face would reappear in my mind's eye, recall me to myself; time and time again, I'd find myself blinking my eyes in bewilderment, erratically glancing about, as if I'd awakened from a trance; find myself unable to believe I hadn't, as yet, managed to see her—wondering why the delay, why I'd run away; find myself vowing to get the visit over and done with sooner than soon! So I'd return to that intersection again; return to that blockade of fear again—repeat the cycle of expectation/devastation again! Time and time again...

And this condition of not being prepared for the journey to her apartment even though I was ceaselessly being prodded—whipped, stung! towards her apartment; this condition of having an urgent—devouring, inescapable! need to fulfill and, at one and the same time, being prevented by my panic attacks from beginning to scratch that need's surface; in short, this condition of being simultaneously thrust in two emotionally opposed directions, endlessly going nowhere in a racing forward/retreating backward frenzy: there *had* to be a means of extricating myself, an exit! Because if I continued to accumulate unspent energy—lack an outlet for the ever increasing amount of unfulfilled desire within me—then it might result in a degree of sensory overload I'd be incapable of emerging from; might result in a state of irreversible mental collapse! What, however, could I do about it?

Yes, I was all too conscious of the fact that my condition couldn't continue; fact that I was rapidly running out of what little inner stability remained to me; fact that I had to reorient myself—find a new direction to flow in, obtain an outlet for the hunger churning within me! if I wished to remain among the sane...

Suffice to say matters came to a head on the morning after I'd spent about a week and a half's worth of nights attempting to cross that intersection and visit my beguiling beauty and failing to do so; on the morning when, instead of managing to obtain a small amount of relief from the turmoil of the night by drifting into a vague approximation of sleep for a few hours (as I'd somehow always done previously), I was flat on my back on the hardwood floor of my apartment, staring at the bright white of the ceiling, while stinging heat forcefully pulsated throughout my body and steadily accumulated, gained strength. No, I couldn't escape the inflammation of my senses, cease dwelling upon its cause: the night after night that I'd spent repeatedly coming up against the impassable wall of fear, being hammered back on myself, delivered over to the claws of deflected desire; spent repeatedly wrestling with the temptation to surrender to self-destructive impulses while fearing, every second, that the temptation would best me. Above all, I couldn't prevent myself from becoming convinced I'd just spent one suchlike night too many, crammed far too much blazing overstimulation into already overstrained nerves, and was in imminent danger of succumbing to an irreversible breakdown.

Listen: on that morning while lying electrified on the hardwood, wincing at the ceiling's glaring white, I was suddenly afraid to shut my eyes; afraid because I was certain I'd instantly see a blinding inner light and that, the moment I saw this light, my head would begin to hiss, buzz, vibrate; and, further, that this hissing, buzzing, and vibrating would increase until my awareness was submerged in a senseless din of gibbering voices, endlessly shattering shrieks. What could have induced me to entertain such a fancy, if fancy it was? It was the amount of stimulation I was under the influence of which was to blame! I could feel hot tingles gathering themselves under the surface of my skin, scampering about like swarms of agitated ants; feel waves of excitation lapping against one other—churning, foaming, breaking! from my fingertips to my toes! And these sensations, in turn, had seized ahold of my imagination, forced me—from out of nowhere! to conceive of the notion that, if I dared close my eyes, I'd be staring at a blinding inner light emitted by the amount of disturbance within me; likewise, it had occurred to me that the act of gazing upon this light would immediately allow its energy to surge unhindered into the center of my forehead, grip my skull in a paralytic vise, bring about a seizure! Yes, that's the fancy which seized ahold of me, why I was afraid to shut my eyes!

But keeping my eyes open was little better because the white of the ceiling was steadily becoming brighter, beginning to sparkle—writhe! in the air in front of my face, dart at—flash within! my eyes to such a degree it was displacing the dimensions of my apartment from my field of vision, blinding me to everything but itself! God! It was as if I was gazing upon the dangerous illumination of my inner disturbances even though my eyes were open! I couldn't help but flinch in expectation of the hissing, buzzing; couldn't stop myself from jumping to my feet, flailing my arms, racing about; from leaping onto the bed, pounding the mattress with my fists, tearing at the sheets, biting the pillows; from shaking my body—twisting, thrashing, kicking! as vigorously as I could! Anything to distract myself from my sizzling nerves, splintering thoughts, predatory imagination; anything to erect a barrier of activity and exhaustion between myself and direct apprehension of the breakdown which I couldn't help but believe was brewing inside me! No use! My body was refusing to be worn down; my senses were refusing to be dulled; my fear was refusing to flee! The bright white was still dancing on the ceiling, shimmering on the walls, sparkling in the air, slamming into my eyes!

I recall that, at some point (I'm not certain how much later), I was face-down on the bed—pressing my eyes into the mattress while squeezing the back of my neck with both hands, biting down hard—such that my jaws ached! on a sheet wadded in my mouth; recall I was bracing myself for a renewed attempt—an attempt I was certain was seconds away! on the part of the hissing, buzzing, and vibrating to seize ahold of me; recall that bright patches began to appear on the surface of the mattress—blaze in the darkness I'd sought to shroud my eyes in! and that my body was instantly rigid to such a degree I couldn't so much as twitch my fingers, take a breath! Yes, I'm telling you there was a moment when I implicitly believed—with all my being! that the horrors I'd concocted in my imagination were but a half-instant away from seizing ahold of me in actuality; a moment when all the hope, wonder, desire, euphoria, fear, rage, and despair that I'd experienced on account of my bewitching beauty flashed before me and I heard myself say to myself, "So this is the fruit of my labors! This is my glittering prize!" and forcefully shut my eyes; a moment when I was seeming to rapidly spiral down inside myself while surrounded by splintering silver, sharp hisses; when I was gripped by a close to unbearable crescendo of terror, and resigned myself to oblivion—surrendered! and...

Ha, will I be believed? It was at that moment of relinquishing all hope of emerging from my ordeal—moment of ceasing to struggle against the everlasting night which I was certain would soon engulf me—that the tension inside me subsided and all trace of distress disappeared; yes, that I was inundated with gentle ripples of calmness, a feeling as of pristine spring water flowing throughout and cleansing me! I rolled onto my back, opened my eyes, was gazing upon a room aswim in soft luminescence; was stretching my arms and legs, flexing the rigidity from my fingers and toes, arching my back while awash with waves of joyful relief—seeming to float above the bed on a cushion of happy sighs! And it wasn't long thereafter that I slipped into just the sort of dreamless sleep I'd given up hoping for, found myself cradled in benign silence such as I'd despaired of ever experiencing again...

And upon awakening shortly past midnight after having enjoyed my first untroubled interval of sleep in nearly two weeks: it's true my unsettling beauty instantly became the sole preoccupation of my thoughts, crowded all else from my mind's eye, in the manner I'd grown to expect; and equally true that these thoughts and pictures on her behalf inundated me with a violent surge of excitement, tore at my chest, turned my stomach inside out, immobilized me on the edge of the bed. But I'd, as it were, been enlightened by my harrowing experience of the morning, freed from delusion by the fancied moments of near-breakdown (In fact, my clarity was such that it amazed me: it was as if I'd been spoken to in the silence of the slumber which resulted from my ordeal, enlightened by upwellings of my subconscious; as if constraining perceptions had whirled away like cobwebs in a strong wind, and a fresh ability to apprehend a greater whole had taken their place.); and so, in place of the blind compulsion to dash across town to her apartment building (which, it will be recalled, had also been characteristic of these attacks), there was suddenly the understanding that the necessity of confronting her was the requirement that I first undergo such preparations as would increase my emotional stamina, immunize me to the panic which convulsed me the instant an encounter with her became imminent; the requirement that I first overhaul my personality, overcome my limitations; in short, the requirement that I embark upon and successfully complete a rigorous program of self-transformation. And the longer I sat there with her face ablaze in my mind's eye and my body coiled tight as a result, the more it became apparent that the task of overcoming my limitations—acquiring a stronger, more mentally and emotionally resilient, self—would involve delving into realms of experience I'd never delved into before; involve seeking out and uninhibitedly entrusting myself to shades of sensation, casts of feeling, and frames of mind I was unfamiliar with; involve probing the darkness-enshrouded areas within me, exploring the aspects of myself I knew nothing about. Therefore, my journey to my spellbinding beauty's apartment, far from being a mere thirty minute dash across town, could very well turn out to be a matter of months, depending on how long it would take for me to effect the amount of inner transformation necessary to enable me to cross that last intersection, enter her building, and knock on her door.

I also remember being struck by the fact that my newfound approach to my predicament was, quite simply, an instance of becoming fully conscious of something I'd been semi-conscious of for days; struck by the fact that my inability to, as it were, yank the solution into clear awareness—unite my impulses with it, sink my nerves into it—had resulted in my being hounded by the specter of psychic collapse; resulted in my being pinned face-down on the bed, paralyzed with terror, while convinced my last moment of sanity had arrived. Yes, it occurred to me that the smallest recalibration of one's nervous system can mean the difference between being at the mercy of one's impulses and developing a viable plan of action for dealing with those impulses; mean the difference between recoiling from a hostile imagination and disarming that imagination; mean the difference between succumbing to madness and obtaining a new lease on sanity. And then I was shivering at the thought of how fragile mental stability is, *so* thankful I'd managed to cling to mine...

As I continued to sit on the edge of the bed I gradually became aware that my usual apprehension with regard to venturing into the domain of the unknown had vanished; that thoughts which had formerly inspired me with a distrust of myself, set off warning sirens in my head, no longer made me uneasy; that inclinations I'd always recoiled from, suppressed on account of believing them detrimental to my mental and emotional health, were striking me as being no more harmful than a stroll in the park; yes, that I'd not only obtained the courage to chart new emotional territory, negotiate new avenues of desire, but was thirsting to do so! What delight it was going to be to do away with the boundaries I'd habitually imposed upon my behavior, turn the reins over to those aspects of myself which had previously bewildered and unsettled me!

Waves of warm, comforting, invigorating joy commenced to well up within me, counter the tension which had immobilized me on the edge of the bed; I was able to move again, rise to my feet, and... Ha, I hardly knew what to do with myself, so giddy was I becoming as a consequence of my newfound alternative to the searing frustration of the past fortnight! What a wonderful adventure, orgy of self-exploration and -transformation, lay before me! Yes, I was fortunate to be under the influence of an inescapable need to visit, gaze deep into the eyes of, she who inhabited a realm of existence which was far removed from my present capacities of endurance; fortunate to be forced to undergo unfamiliar experiences—overwhelm myself with revelations of sensation, feeling, and thought—which would strengthen me, allow me to gain access to her world; fortunate to have met up with she who was the living personification of my hidden desires, unsuspected dreams!

I was soon pacing about the apartment, seeming to float above the floor, while drunk with exhilaration—reveling in my eager animation, boundless energy! I was informing myself no man's more worthy of envy than he who finds himself swept away—severed! from his customary manner of life by a violence of desire which awakens him to the fact that the dissolution of his familiar personality will bequeath him far more than it will deprive him of; informing myself only a fortunate few ever find themselves cut loose from engrained inhibitions and to be contemplating a magical new world of limitless possibility which has materialized in their place! Yes, I was the one worthy of envy! I couldn't wait to taste of the fruits—soar to the heights, descend to the depths, savor the pleasures, withstand the pains! of the new world which lay before me!

The night sped by in happy delirium, as if in minutes, and daylight seemed to spring upon me. I remember glancing up as if from a dream to see that sunlight was setting the edges of the window shades aglow; remember checking the clock, laughing when I saw it was nearly eight. Almost as if acting under hypnosis, I packed a couple changes of clothes, unplugged appliances, and emptied the refrigerator. Soon I was stepping into the hallway, casting a last look about my apartment, locking the door for what I felt would be quite awhile...

PART TWO:
THE MESMERIZING MIRAGE
OF SENSUAL SATIATION

Where do I begin? Ha! The events of the first month or so of my program of self-transformation are far too jumbled in my memory for me to believe myself capable of presenting all of them in their correct sequence! Some preliminary information—an effort to set the stage, outline a few generalities—is therefore in order.

First, it should be stated that I immediately developed a pronounced aversion to the daytime, and fell into a routine which permitted me to experience as little of it as possible; in other words, I generally rose in the late afternoon or early evening and retired three or so hours after sunrise. Why did I wish to avoid daylight? Need I say that, the moment the sun sets, one ceases to be oppressed by readily discernible surroundings? ceases to be at the mercy of the sharply delineated foregrounds which hem in one's senses, strangle one's imagination, curb one's desires? Need

I say that, the moment the sun sets, one finds it easier to become oblivious of the fact that disheartening things such as tiresome duties, insipid routines, sterile acquaintanceships, and dead-end relationships exist in this world? easier to become aware of various blood-stirring inclinations, impulses, and yearnings which have lain dormant, bided their time, within one? Need I say that, the moment the sun sets, one finds oneself surrounded by shadow-swathed uncertainties of outline—expansive depths of indistinct background—which invite one's imagination to run riot and invite one's desires to keep pace with one's imagination until there's nothing one can't conceive of oneself doing, nobody one can't wish to become? Need I say that, in my own case, it was necessary that I turn to the night in order to undergo the sort of experiences which would transform me into a stronger person? turn to the night in order to rehearse the journey to my seizure-inducing beauty's door? Oh, and the way the multicolored beacons of the neon sizzle and blaze in the night; the way the flushed faces of the hungry pass to and fro among the beacons as the air hums, crackles; the way the swirl of boldly advertised desire reverberates in one's nerves, jumpstarts one's pulse, whispers, "Surrender! Surrender!" Yes, channels of communication which are closed during the day are open at night; gestures confirm mutual preferences and glances seal pacts with stunning—effortless—clarity and, before one knows it, one's strolling down the sidewalk in the company of a stranger who's become closer to one than one's most intimate friend; a stranger to whom one will reveal secrets one wouldn't dare reveal to anyone else; to whom one will entrust one's very life for the duration of the night in some room somewhere where the torrents of desire will race unimpeded regardless of one's yea or nay as one reels before and disappears in the mirror of her eyes!

But I'm veering off the track, getting ahead of myself, carried away! Ha, and (as long as I've become tangential) here's another aside: dearest reader, I hope you'll appreciate the concern for restraint and clarity I'm exhibiting now, as opposed to instantly plunging into the melee of my initial adventures. Because, if I was

eager to begin accumulating novel adventures from the moment
of bidding farewell to my apartment, I'm no less eager to begin recalling them now. But, again, because my adventures followed
thick and fast during the opening weeks of my orgy of self-exploration and I'm unable to vouch for their order of occurrence,
it's important that I devote a few paragraphs to providing helpful
generalities before communicating specific examples. And so, to
resume:

First, I'll repeat that I avoided the daytime as much as possible, and devoted virtually all of my waking hours to the night.
Second, I'll state outright what I've already hinted at: I was sin-
gle-mindedly engaged in the pursuit of women, compelled to
begin with them as a means of flinging myself into new experiences, basking in the glow of unfamiliar emotions. And, mind
you, it wasn't that I'd never pursued women before, strung one-
night flings together; it was that I'd always erected an inner barrier between myself and these women—been compelled to keep
a fair amount of myself out of the picture, under wraps—and that
it was now time to do away with that barrier, abandon the manner
in which I'd always held myself in check; yes, time to get myself
alone with a woman—any woman—and conjure forth various
pent-up inclinations which lurked within me; time to embrace the
new shade of boldness which had crept into my desires—the new
hint of (dare I admit it?) rage which had crept into my desires—
as a consequence of my infatuation/obsession with my bewitching beauty. And I'll state, yet again, that my bewitching beauty
never departed from my thoughts and that her picture was always
crystal clear in my mind's eye; that it was as if she knew something about myself of paramount importance of which I was ignorant and that I had to discover what it was; as if she was aware
of the underlying motives of my actions, could effortlessly plumb
my innermost recesses; as if she wasn't merely aware of what it
was that I was seeking, but possessed of the capacity to give it to
me—if only I could learn how to ask for it, prepare myself for receiving it.

But I could spin in my thoughts *ad infinitum* and I'd still get no closer to an all-encompassing description of my spellbinding beauty's effect upon me; no closer to pinning either her or myself down! All I can do is state once more that she was governing my desires, directing my actions, dictating my thoughts with inflexible rigor and that I had no choice but to take to the night, search for women with whom to pass a few hours; no choice but to charm, captivate, cajole these women into permitting me to set the stage for the enactment of rituals outside the limits which had formerly characterized my associations with them; no choice but to maneuver them into permitting me to indulge the new aura of audacity which was beginning to hover in the background of and infiltrate my every feeling; which, with each successive day of my adventure, I couldn't help but sense was increasingly altering my glances and gestures, affecting not merely my perceptions of others, but others' perceptions of me. Because I'm telling you that the features of women's faces—not to mention the lissome curves of their bodies, sultry purr of their voices, sly sparkle of their touch—acquired a vividness they'd never possessed before, incited me to do things I'd never done before—things which were beginning to scare me in earnest, but which I still couldn't help but do! I didn't dare remain with the same woman for long, for fear my newfound audacity would grow too comfortable in her company and express itself too unrestrainedly for the good of either of us! I'm almost positive I never spent two consecutive nights in the same place, slept with the same woman twice!

But let the examples speak for themselves. Yes, let me turn to the task of sifting through my memory for those episodes of the first month or so of my program of self-renewal which have survived intact, seek to present them their order of occurrence:

*   *   *   *   *

Hail the kiss in greeting, blithely planted on one's cheek, which leads one to seek out the moistness of the lips that planted it there; and the kiss on the lips which shiveringly lingers and soon results in an insistent entwinement of tongues; yes, hail the electric exchange of breathlessness—exquisite tease of suffocation! which forces one's hands to explore the contours of the woman's face, slide through her hair! There's nothing like running one's ten fanned out fingers up the back of the woman's neck, through the crackling curls of her hair; nothing like gathering the curls above her head and one's own, letting them fall, feeling satiny gossamer swirl against—seem to shimmer under the surface of! one's flushed cheeks! One can't help but clasp the woman tighter, thrust a leg between the two of hers, wind it tight about one of them; can't help but reach up her dress, dance one's hand up and down her thighs, thrill to their softness; can't help but lower her towards—stretch her out upon! the floor!

So there we were: she was underneath me, on her living room carpet, but a few feet from the front door, and... The lily white smoothness—supple cream! of her neck, shoulders, and upper chest was aglow—rippling! in my eyes—engulfing me in gasp after tingling gasp! and, before I half-realized what I was doing, I was tugging at the buttons of her dress, exposing—smothering my face in! the round ripeness of her breasts—gently nipping the aureoles! while yanking her hemline to her waist! Ha! No sooner revealed than attended to! In a flash I was snuffling at the pungent wetness of her panties—avidly licking silk friction! while raising her behind from the floor—seeking to pull her panties down, have at the fountain of life!

We didn't hear him on the stairs, didn't hear the door open; but I heard the shout, felt the boot—pain-surge! slam into my ribs; felt the rage—choking disbelief! get caught in my throat, contract every muscle! I jerked towards the right, rolled onto my back and then onto my hands and knees—was scrambling with him in pursuit! I seized a small table by one of its legs, swung it behind me at his legs while rising to my feet, running to the far wall, turning! The table had missed, he—bigger than I! was nearly upon me! I darted to the left—shoved a dresser over! as a fist—to the sound of hissing air! barely grazed the back of my head! I leaped over the fallen dresser, had an unobstructed path—open diagonal! to the door, and didn't hesitate...

Seconds later I was in the street with the sequence of the altercation—shout, kick, fury, flight—sliding walls, clashing angles, overbright lights—hammering at my temples, along with the thought that I might be pursued by the offended party. I ran for a block, walked very fast for another, darted into a cafe, found I couldn't sit still on account of the high level of excitement within me. High level of excitement? Ha! My nerves were bursting at the seams!

I exited the cafe, was on the sidewalk again: doing what? going where? I no longer cared if the slob caught up with me; was no longer able to preoccupy myself with anything besides the state I was in! I was seething with unspent energy, interrupted desire; with the remembrance—lingering resonance! of the woman's shiveringly anxious—breathlessly anticipative! body, a thousand charged pictures of what would've transpired had it not been for that worthless animal, interfering lout; with unadulterated fury at the thought of such a clown's existence! I just wanted to locate a stupid-looking face—any stupid-looking face! in the crowd and smash it; yes, knock it to the sidewalk, kick it, stomp on it, crush it, annihilate it! Because when I go gate-crashing—force open a back door, locate the key to a chastity belt! the husband—the boyfriend—the whatever! is less than nonexistent: I don't care what he does, what he looks like, what has passed or will pass between him and the woman I'm undressing; the only thing that matters are the moments I'm with her—the now, right now! and for the other—the nonentity, less than zero! to appear unannounced, and distract us from our proceedings... God, no run of bad luck—onslaught of misfortune! is too awful for such a meddler, obstructing pest!

I glanced down at the former location of the lone button she'd had time to tear from my shirt, was instantly beset by another surge of anger at the thought of the ridiculousness of it—the unbelievably shoddy pranks that chance is willing to lower itself to play! Christ! I kicked an overflowing trash can over: so what? Did I really believe antics becoming a child were going to turn off the excruciatingly vivid pictures which were continuing to race—one batch after another, several batches at a time! through my head? continuing to unsettle me with their depictions of what would've unfolded had not the oaf appeared? which were alive with the caress-hungry contours—flushed suppleness, electric fluidity! of the woman I'd been forced to abandon? which were blazing snakes writhing under the surface of my skin, in my veins? No, I couldn't shut the pictures off, escape them; they were rapidly overtaking—drowning out! my awareness of everything else—enveloping me in a state of explosive obliviousness, leaving me nothing but stabbing irritability for company; they were an onslaught of maddening nerve-pricks which wouldn't stop reminding me—every increasingly unbearable instant! of the necessity of following through on what had commenced in her apartment!

Yes, I'm telling you I needed to sigh and dissolve in a flurry of tension-dispelling caresses, bury my face in cascades of crackling hair, thrust my tongue between tremblingly parted lips, slide my hands—icy hot hands! up and down the aroused agility of a pair of breath-stealingly sleek thighs! I was—I'm not exaggerating! ready to rub up against buildings, twist and thrash on the sidewalk, lash out—scratch and bite! at anything—everything! like a cat in heat! Ha! My hands began—of their own accord! to thrust themselves under my shirt, stroke the sides of my torso: I couldn't stop them! Nor could I prevent myself from entering the dim corridor that lead to the courtyard of a large stone building, pulling my shirt up to my neck, unzipping my pants; from pressing my naked back against the cold wall behind me, taking deep breaths, closing my eyes...

Listen: the tingling stiffness between my legs was forcing my right hand to seize it, alternate between tightening and relaxing its grip, slide up and down; and then what vibrant visions of fabulous heights of bliss and delirium swirled in my head!—what a kaleidoscope of luminous glimpses of lithe curves, creamy skin, luxuriant hair, loving lips! Yes, the more I stroked the more I was enrapt by imagined instances of poise, facial expression, and gesture which were larger than life, stronger than life: no woman of flesh and blood ever possessed such hypnotic beauty; no woman

of flesh and blood was ever ripe with a like promise of unsur-
passable delight!—nor ever blazed thus in my skin, raced thus—
like hot liquid light! through my veins, pulsed thus—in steadily
stronger throbs! between my legs, surged thus—in gushes of gasping incandescence! up my belly, onto my chest! The wall behind
me was no longer there, the concrete below me was mist in the air!
I took leave of myself for an all too brief instant—became an electrified absence, united with my dreams! before easing myself to
the ground...

Moments later I was sitting with my back to the wall—drifting with the lull in the tension, ebb of the tide—without it occurring to me to put my clothes in order, apparently unconscious of
being exposed to the gaze of anyone who might enter the corridor...

* * * * *

I passed through the scarlet curtains at the entrance of a strip
club, located a center seat a couple rows from the stage. A single
unoccupied wooden chair was upon the stage, surrounded by
snaking wisps of tobacco smoke which drifted to and fro, alternately coiled and unwound, under the spotlights as if drawn to
them from the surrounding dimness like moths. I'd been on my
feet since awakening over six hours previously, exuberantly
strolling about the city at random without feeling any need for a
rest. And now that I'd, on less than a whim, come in from the
street and sat down—deprived myself of freedom of movement,
forced my body to be still—I was uneasy, jittery, annoyed like a
wildcat when shut in a cage: itching to spring to my feet, race out
the door, resume wandering.

Yes, I was unseeingly staring at the empty chair on the stage,
wondering how I could have permitted myself to trade the windy
sidewalks—open vistas, emotional free-flow—outside for the
stagnant air, stifling confinement, maddening pent-upness of an
overheated room. Well, however the situation had come about—
whatever momentary lapse of sound judgment, instance of off-
guardedness, had made me susceptible to the ill-considered

impulse on which I'd entered the place—I wasn't going to endure it for a second longer. So I raised myself from my seat and turned towards the exit, was on the point of taking my first step towards it...

But then the curtains to the right of the stage emphatically swished apart and I heard the piercing clatter-clack of high heels, saw the fluid sheen of a sapphire dress—saw a white hibiscus bouncing amidst tumbling curls of pitch black hair, the radiant oval of a cheerfully mischievous face! Ha! All desire to depart instantly disappeared on account of the sparkling gasp which engulfed me; on account of the manner in which the expansive vitality—sense of inner boundlessness—that I'd enjoyed during my wanderings outside was restored to me; manner in which the star attraction's every facial expression, gesture, and shift of pose was reuniting me with the avenues of feeling I'd momentarily lost!

She wasted little time in placing one of her feet on the chair, grasping the hem of her dress with both hands, flicking it up and down her raised leg such that the white cream of her thigh's naked skin, above the top of the bronze-toned stocking which sheathed her leg, rapidly appeared and disappeared—and, of course, she was smiling one of those sly, lascivious, all-knowing inward smiles!—and, of course, I was following the rhythm of her hands with unblinking eyes, pouncing upon every glimpse of the contrast between the stocking and her skin—inwardly pouncing upon it with my entire body, the muscles of which were tightening with excitement, impatiently aquiver!

But no sooner was I wholeheartedly flinging myself into unreserved admiration—surrendering to the ebb and flow of her excitement-engendering gyrations—than she abruptly removed her foot from the chair, smoothed her dress to her knees, made a scissor-movement of her hands to indicate that the performance was over, and stomped towards the curtains with a look of annoyance. What? Was I to be led to believe a door on inner free-play had been opened only to have that door slammed in my face? Was I to be moved to trust only to have that trust betrayed? Was I to be drawn towards bliss by succulent curves only to have the owner of those curves succumb to offended moodiness or outright capriciousness and rudely take her leave? Was that her game? to set stimulation in motion, then abandon it to gnawing frustration? to make a joy-inducing promise, then break it—strand me in a void of choking disillusionment, violated need?

What was I to do? race out the door, find another show in order to finish what had been irreversibly started? Damn! I wanted to leap on the stage, storm through those curtains, seize ahold of her, drag her out, compel her to resume! Anger was rising within me, threatening to break to the surface; my heart was pounding in my ears, muscles were inundated with sharp biting heat, vision was fixed at the blankness of the air! I could feel my face twitching; was afraid my ire was becoming obvious to others, beginning to think it might be advisable to leave before an altercation ensued...

Well, I was certainly overwrought; and, being overwrought, was temporarily a stranger to the obvious. But when the obvious became clear to me, how quickly my anger-surge fell out from under itself in waves of dissipating tension, and allowed me to laugh! More to the point: how could I have failed to realize her departure was but a mock-departure, coquettish tease-ploy, part of the act? Hadn't she (only now did I recall it) smilingly turned her head at the moment before disappearing behind the curtains, made an unmistakable "I'll be back!" sign with an upraised finger? Amusing how the state of rapidly increasing excitement I was in had temporarily obliterated that pertinent fact from awareness, blinded me to the blatant evidence of my eyes; how I'd momentarily gone off on a tangent of mistaken assumption, annoyance, and unease; yes, amusing how readily sensory stimulation toys with perception, reaction, and resolve!

I was still shaking my head in amusement when she reemerged from the curtains with a lip-licking smile of mischief, began to pirouette until her flawless legs were flashing in and out of view amidst the rapidly rising and falling ultramarine of her dress. Twirl, whirl! All extraneous thought dissolved; I was instantly measuring my breath to the rhythm of every hissing furl of her dress, swift dark blur of her hair, and high kick of her legs as naturally as if she'd never left the stage and there hadn't been a break in the action...

She stopped dancing, came to a standstill; but gave me no time to catch my breath—adjust to the dizzying acceleration of my response in her favor—before sitting on the chair, turning to face frontward, raising both of her feet to the edge of the seat, spreading her legs, inviting my gaze to plunge into the space between her parted thighs, and... Well, her white silk panties were right there, not more than twelve feet away—staring me in the face, laughing! but I could do nothing about it, neither place my hand upon them to caress the mound—thrill to the sensation of moist warmth! underneath nor pull them down her legs!

Doubtless the goal of one who makes a habit of frequenting such spectacles is to be overcome with the desire to seize ahold of the woman in front of him—clasp her volatile body close, quench his thirst in the breaking waves of emotion within her—at the same time that he's being prevented from doing so—being compelled to swim against the tide of his need; with the result that desire builds up inside him like floodwater behind the wall of a dam. Yes, instead of appeasing desire the moment it tugs at him, such a man wishes to resist it—hoard it—in order to propel himself into stronger states of excitement. And, whether I wished to do so or not, I was certainly undergoing such an experience at that moment, as she continued to face me with legs spread and panties laughing: I definitely wanted to climb onstage, ease her to the floor, and thrust myself inside her!

And then she, in another demonstration of her consummate ability to tease, abruptly turned to the right and reclined onto her back on the seat of the chair—lifted her chest towards the ceiling, mopped the floor with her hair—while pumping her belly up and down and slowly unzipping her dress from neckline to waist: the white of her skin slid inside my eyes, surged in my veins, inundated me with sensory vertigo, inner swirls of electricity! God! The way the muscles of her stomach were alternately expanding and contracting—quivering, rippling! The rhythm of life itself! I was tingling between my legs and could almost feel myself entering her snug glove—almost feel her slipperiness undulating in response! even though I was still in my seat, immobile! Yes, what a rich wild—sensation-dense! immobility it was! I was rapidly losing the boundaries of my body—my skin was flushing into throbbing heat, seeming to exchange places with the air!

Nor did she relent: after unzipping her dress, extracting her arms from its sleeves, pulling it from under herself, and draping it on the back of the chair she brought her knees up to and pressed them against her breasts until the latter were swelling towards her throat and shoulders, on the point of bursting from her brassiere. She held the pose, tightened her muscles while drawing deep measured breaths—hummed with coiled immobility, radiated sharply focused need! It was as if sparkling electric mist was inundating the space of air between us, passing through the pores of my skin, fluttering and swirling in the center of my chest; as if I could feel her smooth, flushed, taut skin rubbing against my own!

And I ask: was she raising her knees from her chest, extending her legs towards the ceiling, spreading and closing them, while removing her panties and stockings with deftly gliding—slyly pausing—hands? Was she running her hands up and down her thighs, all about her belly, under the cups of the brassiere? Did she—while arching her back, twisting her torso! push the brassiere towards her shoulders until her breasts burst free, quivered in sync with the rhythm of her breathing? Was she taking increasingly deeper breaths while easing her hands—all ten eager fingers! back down her belly, burying them in her black fur, stroking? Was she shivering, shuddering? Were the lines of her face—delineations of self, personality! running together, blurring? Was she sighing, melting, dissolving—swimming, flailing about, willingly drowning! in waves of euphoric surrender? Was she? Or was it a dream-sequence in my head?

What I know for a certainty is that the lustrous white of her curves was suddenly trading places with the brightness of the spotlights—blurring into an increasingly shapeless glow! despite my most strenuous efforts to remain intent upon every detail of her body, keep her in focus; and, also, that I was trembling—shaking! despite (or perhaps on account of) the muscle-straining rigidity of my body, and... God, why did fear accompany this loss of visual focus? Why was it that, the more her body became lost in the brightness of the lights, the more panic churned in the pit of my stomach, stabbed at my chest? So distressed did I become I started to scrape the palms of my hands with my fingernails and bite the inside of my lips—as well as curl my toes in my shoes until they ached—in an effort to maintain ongoing perceptual interaction with the outside world, remain in touch with identifiable sensations; yes, in an effort to prevent my awareness from being engulfed by the uneasiness which was streaming through my nerves like liquid ice, chilling my spine!

Why were my perceptions slipping away from me, being stolen from me—such that the discomfort I was seeking to induce in my palms, lips, and toes soon became a flat sensation of numbness and left me nothing to cling to, cast me adrift in the swirl of dread? What was happening? The woman onstage was now a formless silver white glare: was it the same bright light which flickers in one's forehead when a seizure's imminent, warns of danger?

God! In a panic reaction I jerked my eyes away from the bright glare she'd become, stared at the floor! I shut my eyes tight, pressed the heels of my hands hard against them, so as to escape the unsettling light—engulf my vision in darkness! Searing seconds passed—or perhaps minutes; then a curious thing occurred: the woman onstage reappeared, in sharp focus, in my mind's eye! What was she doing? She was lying on her back on the polished hardwood of the stage in a state of sleepy languor with her arms flung out to her sides, chin pressed against her right shoulder, eyes gazing into the vacancy of the air, mouth wide open; lying there as if undecided whether she wished to recover from an excessive amount of exertion and resume that exertion or resign herself to savoring the sensation of being physically and emotionally spent.

Innocuous enough, right? So why, then, was my uneasiness increasing?

Listen: it suddenly became firmly understood that the star attraction wasn't exhausted, but in shock; that she wasn't lying on the floor by choice, but because she couldn't move; that her chin wasn't pressed against her right shoulder because she found it comfortable, but because it had been twisted into that position by a broken neck! God! Regardless of this unpleasant interpretation of the mental picture, it was still *only* in my head, a concoction of my imagination! So why, then, did an unmanageable burst of terror tie searing knots in my chest, all but paralyze my breath, shove me towards the edge of a swoon? Why—a shattered instant later! did I spring from my seat as if yanked by puppet-strings? Why did I stumblingly flee the place—on legs which threatened to buckle! without a backward glance?

Then I was slumped on a doorstep somewhere outside with breeze on my face, chatter in my ears, and headlights in my eyes without comprehending how I'd come to be there: it was as if I'd just awakened from a tooth-grindingly stressful nightmare, and was staring at a street in a city I'd never been in before...

* * * * *

A large red and black sphinx moth was sipping nectar from the flowers in the box outside the window and I was watching it with my face pressed against the glass, doing my best to hypnotize myself with the spiraling blurs of its rapid dartings from flower to flower—drift into a daze, waking sleep—while the girl of that night lay stretched out on the bed on the far side of the room, contemplating herself in the circular mirror on the ceiling. Days? How many days had elapsed since I'd first seen her? Where had I first seen her, and why hadn't I escorted her home on that occasion? How had I known how to find her again? Why do I ask?

We'd been together for nearly three hours, since shortly after midnight; we'd been exchanging light, quick, teasing, noncommittal caresses with the aim of prodding rather than calming—fanning rather than quenching—the stirrings within us;

deliberately drawing one another into a state of unsettledness, hypersensitivity, irritability; infecting one another with hot shivers, icy flushes, blazing chills. We'd soon enough reached the point at which it had become all but impossible to prevent warmth and sincerity from creeping into our caresses—expressing itself via lingering pressure, ardent clasps—and, as a consequence, had decided to keep our hands away from each other and to only touch ourselves. There were moments following this hands-off policy, as we stared at each other while stroking ourselves, when I was following the movements of her hands with such unblinking concentration that it was almost as if I'd traded places with her and it was my hands which were squeezing her thighs, fluttering across her ribs, stroking her throat; almost as if it was her body which was shivering and tensing in response to the wanderings of my hands upon myself.

That's right, she'd been squarely in front of me, a mere yard away, ceaselessly informing me—via the glow in her eyes, quiverings of her lips, jitteriness of her gestures—that she was for the taking; she'd been blossoming—unwinding, turning inside out—with every flinch and blush in response to my gaze, steadily pulling me into the waves of attraction mounting inside her. Naturally, I'd yearned to seize palmfuls and lick mouthfuls of her creamy contours, clasp her panting body tightly, salve the jagged edges of my nerves with the balm of her skin. Nevertheless, I'd always managed to honor our agreement and remain on my side of our self-imposed partition by the simple act of plunging my face into a pillow, placing my hands over my ears, and blanking my thoughts. I'd had to resort to the pillow routine a number of times and, in each instance, it had been more difficult to do so. I'd come very close to pouncing on her—breaking the spell, tumbling down from the heights of my hunger.

But I'd succeeded, if not easily, in resisting the urge to fling myself onto her; which is to say I'd continued to fuel my craving while denying it an exit, thereby inducing novel sensory distortions in myself. For example: I recall instances of falling backwards onto the mattress, stretching and taking deep breaths, while relishing the tingling vibrations which were cresting and dipping inside me in wave after dizzying wave; recall instances of lying there with eyes shut as pictures of her agile voluptuousness blazed in my head, brought about surges of excitement strong enough to overwhelm my limbs with invigorating rigidity, semi-paralysis— surges of excitement which would crackle in my nerves like imprisoned lightning, harnessed violence, an explosion-to-be. I also recall instances of opening my eyes following the above-described phenomena, seeing a pair of white ghosts floating in silver above me, and of not immediately realizing it was the two of us reflected in the mirror on the ceiling: for a minute or so, I'd watch the ivory mirages continue to ripple in mercury; watch the dimensions of the room alternately loom large and shrink in the light-warping opaqueness of the air; watch sheets of liquid glass undulate on all sides of me, iridescence fan out across the ceiling, brightness engulf the bases of the walls; and I'd be hard pressed to determine where my flushed skin ended and the charged atmosphere began, whether I was lying upon the bed or suspended in the air above it. Yes, what interesting sensory fireworks result when desire's willfully stockpiled within one! What waking hallucinations one witnesses when one holds firm against the urge to pull an aroused woman close at the same time that the said urge is attaching itself to one's every thought, flaying one from the inside out!

I'd lie there while under the influence of the above-detailed perceptual distortions until, at some point, those distortions would begin to waver in strength and give ground to the familiar, thereby allowing me to become aware of rustlings of the sheets, tremblings of the mattress: I'd involuntarily glance towards their cause, and... Well, the effect of the sight of her upon me, far from being diminished by my interval of absence, would be more pronounced: I'd instantly be drawn into a flurry of inner gasps— surges of pulse! on account of the beauty of her excitement-altered face, struggling to keep my distance from the magnetic field of her hungering eyes! It was as if our shared unrest was darting back and forth between us, being simultaneously transmitted and absorbed by our nervous systems: I could feel the exchange taking place as palpably as if it was electrified dust-particles entering the pores of my skin; feel us both being overtaken by the delicious unease—euphoric disorientation! of the procreative fire! And it's true that a man and a woman are two separate dwelling places of a primal urgency which brings them together—obliterates their individual identities, robs them of themselves—in order to unite with itself; then, during the interval of this primal urgency's union, one feels superfluous, helpless, nonexistent at the same time that one feels more whole, united with life, and fulfilled than at any other time! Ha! Studies pursued, careers nurtured, money accumulated; and, in the end, it's all done for handfuls of blushing skin, earfuls of slurred moans, eyefuls of supple curves, mouthfuls of sweet wetness, nosefuls of pungent sweat—soaked sheets, cat scratches, achingly blissful exhaustion! But I'm getting carried away...

And so I'd reached the point at which I could no longer count upon myself to abide by our pact, resist seizing ahold of her. Still wishing to delay the moment of release, I'd fled the bed—retreated to the window on the opposite side of the room, commenced watching the sphinx moth dart among the flowers in the box outside. So there I was: doing my best to forget she was lying on the bed in a state of readiness, stroking and priming herself before the mirror on the ceiling. But then the moth flew off in a swift streak and I was left without a means of preoccupying my attention; and, before I was half-conscious of what I was doing (before I could think to avert my eyes, or look beyond the glass at the city outside), I was staring at her reflection in the window, plainly seeing she was both aware of and responding to my stare. Ha! She immediately sat up, slid to the edge of the bed, seized ahold of my eyes with her eyes, and smiled! What an inner pull her smile was! I couldn't help but turn away from the window to face her: her smile, in acknowledgement, instantly brightened—animated her body from the tips of her curled toes to the topmost ringlets of her hair, invested her curves with a tone of playful insistence, sparkled in my spine before I had a chance to breathe twice! She had me and knew it, but was taking nothing for granted—I wasn't going to escape again! So she shiveringly stretched her arms above her head, fell backwards onto the mattress with her knees in the air, writhed among the sheets while continuing to keep her eyes upon me: I was as good as being yanked across the room!

A moment later I was standing beside the bed, watching her hands slide about the rippling tautness of her body; watching her dig her shoulders into the mattress, arch her back, breathe deeply; watching her eyes become brighter, dart at me from deep inside themselves, surge! Ha! My knees were sinking into the mattress, I was falling forwards; and her breasts were swelling against my chest, heaving; her lips were quivering at the tip of my tongue, parting; her thighs were wrapped about my waist, squeezing; I was... I believe I remember passing my fingers through her hair, licking her neck (or was it one of her arms? or the symmetry of a leg? or first her neck, then her arm, then her leg? or...?)—well, forget particulars! My tongue was zigzagging across her white-ness; I was lightly scraping smooth contours with my teeth— mock biting! while the room was spinning, ceiling trading places with the floor; yes, rolling about the bed—now on top of her, now below! as her arms, legs, and hair alternately imprisoned me, re-leased! And was I repeatedly yanking her to her knees, giving her a push, watching her fall onto the softness of the mattress— bounce, twist, stretch, laugh? Was she repeatedly scrambling to right herself, retaliate with tickles, pokes, shoves of her own? Ha, not likely I'll ever be able to recollect—reassemble! the correct sequence of what was seen, seized, savored: it all ran together— blurred! as if seen in an unfocused magnifying glass, heard and felt in a swiftly shifting dream! I was under the influence of a thirst seemingly impossible to slake, growing more excited with every attempt to abate the excitement; only clearly aware of over-whelmingly wanting to slip under the surface of her skin, unite with the uncoiling tightness, enthralling ebb and flow, inside her...

I ask: can one be certain how one will behave when desire— hoarded to the point of stinging in one's extremities—finally bursts its bonds? Does the act of swimming against the current of desire produce an inner counter-movement, such that subconscious impulses are stirred from their places of concealment, and begin to overflow into—surge unchecked in—the realm of enactment? I pose these questions because at some point later that night (following I've no fixed idea of what variety of exertion) we were lying side by side on our backs, apparently catching our breaths, while observing ourselves in the mirror on the ceiling, and... Listen: I swear I saw (in the mirror) a hand emerge from under one of the rumpled blankets, glide towards the nightstand, grasp a heavy ashtray of clear glass, then return with it to its place under the blanket. Moments passed: I was staring at her face in the mirror, seeking to decipher its expression: why? I was under the impression she was making a conscious effort to veil her feelings, become inscrutable: why? I was holding my breath to heighten the silence, better listen with my every nerve: why? I... God, I saw (again in the mirror) an abrupt movement of the same blanket beneath which the hand had retreated; yes, saw the hand reappear with the ashtray, become a swift blur as it released it! Then I heard glass break, spun from the bed just in time—landed on the floor lopsidedly, with a jab of pain in my right ankle! When I glanced up, the mirror was still falling: jagged chunks were wrenching themselves loose from the stainless steel frame, dropping straight down, hitting the mattress, smashing into their predecessors! I couldn't believe it: she was lying belly-down on the far side of the bed, just out of range, with a light dusting of silvery flecks on her shoulders and back; was warily lifting her head from between shaking arms, raising herself to her elbows, turning to meet my gaze!

I recall staggering to my feet, being close to falling back onto the floor, with an empty space of fear in place of where my stomach should've been; recall gathering clothes—franticly shoving arms and legs into sleeves and pant legs, yanking on shoes; recall locating the door, exiting without a word or glance good-bye...

* * * * *

Was I speaking aloud when I heard my voice intone, "I want to drink your death!"? In other words, did I whisper it into the ear of she with whom I was spending the night or silently recite it to myself? I wouldn't bother to ask had I not suddenly become aware that her hands were pressing against—slapping at—my chest in a manner which seemed more strident than playful; aware it was almost as if she was insisting I raise myself off of her, bring the proceedings to a halt. But, then again, perhaps I only imagined anxiety temporarily contracted the smooth oval of her face; only imagined agitated shadows briefly scattered the glow of her eyes. After all, she neither cried out nor persisted in exhibiting indications of disquietude; and so, assuming such indications had actually manifested themselves instead of being a creation of my fancy, they hadn't managed to take root within her, accelerate to the point of influencing her actions.

All the same, regardless of the quick passing of her attack of doubt (and an unconfirmed attack of doubt at that), I was instantly recollecting the crowded club in which we'd met, informing myself it's not always possible to appraise with a critical eye, make a well-considered decision, on the dance floor; that, as soon as one's carried away by dancing—swept into the collective surge of vanquished frustration, giddy release—it's possible for a woman to strike one as being unabashed, daring, and fearless when she's nothing of the kind; possible for one to select the wrong partner with whom to spend the night and not discover one's mistake until well after the music's ceased to echo in one's ears. Oh, had I made such a mistake? Had the throb of the music, flicker of the lights, abandon of the crowd distorted my judgment, caused me to bring the wrong woman to the hotel? Was there a chance she'd succumb to distrust and worry, gather her belongings, flee before the night was over? a chance I'd be sentenced to a night alone on account of the fact I was already far too excited to be capable of returning to the streets, searching for another woman, repeating the getting-acquainted ritual—proceeding from glances to words to caresses again? a chance I'd end up pacing about the hotel room with no one to share my hunger with, expend it upon?

Listen: suddenly I was second-guessing my caresses almost to the point of being unable to begin them—close to being afraid to touch her at all—on account of the fear of frightening her, being abandoned, stranded in a state of unappeased yearning. And I knew only too well that such uncomfortable self-consciousness wasn't likely to inspire her with confidence, put her at ease; knew that the more I allowed apprehensive constraint to affect me, the more likely it was she'd succumb to the same; knew that my fear of frightening her might very well frighten her into subjecting me to my worst-case scenario; but I still couldn't banish the picture of myself pacing about the room alone in the dead of night from my head, prevent that picture from undermining spontaneity—afflicting me with self-censorship, awkward hesitation. And, worse: soon it was as if I was gazing upon her from behind an opaque pane of glass; soon the features of her face, though they were but inches from mine, were losing their lines and definition, blurring into unfocused planes of haze; soon it was all but impossible to read her responses, discern where I stood in her eyes. As a result of this perceptual disunity, additional anxiety gripped me—such that I couldn't help but suppose my face was tightening, becoming angular and unfriendly; that my eyes were hardening, becoming cold and distant; that warmth of feeling was departing from my touch, being supplanted by insensitive abruptness, irritating clumsiness; that she'd very soon, indeed—and justifiably! be whipped towards the door by worry!

But I additionally remember that, even while I was recoiling at the thought of being abandoned, there was a budding urge to spring away from her, scamper from the bed and dress myself, although I'm not certain why: was it because I was beginning to seriously doubt I'd be able to salvage the situation, starting to ponder whether it was better to outright accept that I'd be spending the night alone—prepare myself for spending the night alone—than further frustrate and annoy myself with vain attempts at postponement of such? or...? Oh, is it possible that, unbeknown to myself, I was more afraid of what might transpire if she chose to remain than I was of being abandoned? more afraid of permitting our activities to pursue their course than I was of passing the night in lonely insatiety? Yes, is that why I at one point found myself poised to race to my clothes, exit the room: because I was afraid she might not get around to doing it herself? On the other hand the fact is that, to however great an extent I became convinced I was about to call it quits, I did nothing of the kind... Ha, so why pose these questions? Why wonder who was afraid of whom? or who was afraid of what? or which fears eclipsed the others? or whether there was, in fact, a single fear which had a firm grounding in actual perceptions and existed independently of my imagination? Because, for all I knew, I'd been unwaveringly going through the motions of an exemplary lover while playing out a scene of incompatibility, suspicion, and anxiousness in my head; for all I knew, my outward behavior hadn't at any time mirrored what was going on inside me. But that's the point: I didn't know whether I'd been behaving well or badly, hadn't a clue as to what her true frame of mind was.

I've no idea for how long the above-described uncomfortable interval lasted: all I know is that I—in an eventual hands-flung-up-in-futility frame of mind—gave up attempting to discern if there was discomfort in the situation or not and simply surrendered, collapsed onto her with my head turned to the side; that, although my eyes were still open and I was aware of the brightness of the overhead lamp, all thought was erased from my head; that, following what must have been a couple minutes of blankly staring into the air, I gradually became conscious of the steady rise and fall of her chest, soft breeze of her exhalations upon my cheek. I raised myself to my elbows, gazed upon her: the pane of glass which had separated us was no longer there; the pale oval of her face was crystal clear, with a look of smoldering delight and trustful submission plainly stamped upon it! Ha! Ticklish tingles spread over the surface of my skin, relief and joy pulsatingly surged in my veins—I was instantly dizzy with eagerness to resume our activities! Yes, I wanted to make amends for the interval of unease I'd undergone, and possibly imposed upon her—caress away every last pocket of tension in her muscles, uncoil every trace of wound-tightness in her nerves!

Within seconds I was stroking her chest, throat, cheeks—licking her lips, thrusting my tongue between them! without trepidation, any remnant of self-accusatory caution; yes, unhesitantly squeezing, slapping—lightly scratching, nipping! her undulating body in response to the smile of encouragement upon her face—unflinchingly greeting the radiant accord of her eyes with my eyes! and... I couldn't say when it was that I became aware I was actively listening to the rhythm of her breathing (which was becoming more audible by the moment, beginning to rise and fall in seductive oscillations of cadence like gusts negotiating a narrow alley's sharp twists and turns); aware I was redoubling my caresses and kisses, rubbing myself against her more insistently, with the aim of increasing the force and depth of her breathing—duration of her sighs, moans! and... Ha, the deeper the breaths she drew, the deeper the breaths I drew; and, before I half-realized what I was doing, I was covering her mouth with mine, sealing both of our lips, while holding my breath—holding it up to the moment when she expelled hers through her nose! Yes, before I half-realized what was happening, we were drawing increasingly deeper breaths together—holding them for longer intervals! and...

Listen: during those intervals in which we held our breaths together, I'd feel the taut urgency of her muscles ripple—twitch! against my skin; feel her inner vitality quiver—throb! in my veins; feel the electric warmth of her yearning crackle—seethe! in my nerves; yes, feel it all with a vividness I'd seldom, if ever, experienced before; feel sensation intensify—the very pulse of life accelerate! in a manner deliriously magical, and... All I can say is that I wanted those intervals to last longer; that, each time we held our breaths together, I'd feel her exhale from her nose—break the spell, end the intensification of sensation! before I was ready to do so myself; that, as a consequence of my sense of deprivation, I found myself pinning her wrists to the mattress with my elbows, winding my legs about her legs, grinding my belly into hers, immobilizing her. Then, as soon as we drew another breath together, I seized her hair with one hand, pinched her nostrils shut with the other, and sealed her mouth with mine—held my breath while preventing her from breathing! and... Oh, I'm telling you I couldn't stop pressing myself against her harder, winding my legs tighter, grasping her hair more firmly; telling you that, even had her eyes been frozen in an expression of stunned bewilderment, shocked disbelief—even had she been struggling to twist from under me, kick me away, reclaim her right to breathe at will—I would've been incapable of perceiving it; telling you I was sensationally blind to all but the shimmering friction of her skin, vibrant hum of her nerves! God, and forceful sparkles were swirling and rushing throughout me, accumulating to such a degree (far quicker and with greater intensity than when she'd been free to exhale and inhale on her own) that they were overspreading my skin with hot chills—engulfing me in prickly numbness, fiery anesthesia! I lost the ability to localize sensation, distinguish one portion of my body from another, determine where my body ended and hers began; was only aware of euphoria unlike any I'd previously known, and of wanting to prolong and increase it!

Ha! All too soon I became aware portions of my body were shaking off the numbness, announcing their discomfort; aware I was beginning to want to tear my lips from hers, inhale a breath of air; beginning to see flicker-flash pictures of myself falling into a faint! Instants accumulated: the urge to seize a breath became stronger, all but unbearable! But then: I swear something else suddenly slipped inside my body, froze every muscle, and prevented me from taking the breath I needed; swear the something else was savoring the sensation of hovering on the edge of a swoon at the very moment my fear of swooning was at its height; swear the sentiments of the something else and myself intermingled and that I was seized with what I can only describe as being upstaged fear, eclipsed terror; yes, that I was, indeed, afraid but that the joy of the something else—the other! was meeting my fear head-on, balancing it, propelling me into a state of explosive equilibrium where the very stream of time was as if doubling back on itself, uncertain of how to proceed! But no sooner did it flash upon me— in a millisecond burst of blinding white! that I was only now beginning to experience what I was truly seeking—on the threshold of grasping a precious secret, being propelled into a magical realm of inner-clash resolution! than I was in the grip of sharp vibrations, shaking without being able to stop; than both of our bodies separated—erupted! as if stung by whips! Yes, her mouth violently jerked in a streak of red towards the right—hissed, gasped! at the same time that bursts of air rushed down my throat so forcefully I could barely feel the arms which were striking my shoulders, face—barely feel the slapping hands, clawing nails!—just manage to discern the agitated face, heaving chest, flailing legs on the bed below me; to hear a muffled stammer, shout—hear, "Not again! Do you understand? Don't you *ever...*!"

When my breathing stabilized and the beat of my heart was no longer thumping in my temples; when my senses cleared and I was again able to place one thought in front of another... I found I was on my hands and knees above her, restraining her arms and legs as gently as I could (grasping the wrists of the former, pressing my ankles against the calves of the latter) while softly saying, "I'm sorry the game got out of hand, it won't happen again. Don't worry—I'd rather die than make you afraid..."; yes, found I was bringing my face close to hers, smiling into her angry eyes, kissing the frown on her brow; found I was atremble with sympathy and regret, worried in earnest. And, before too long (following another two or three minutes of caressing words, tender kisses, and kindly looks on my part), her efforts to extricate herself—the indignant twists of her torso, resentful jerks of her limbs—began to seem half-hearted; yes, soon the angry angles of her features began to smooth out, relax, capitulate; likewise, the hard glint in her eyes began to fade. And then she ceased resisting altogether, became limp, sighed; albeit, in a shrug-shouldered manner...

I remember releasing her wrists, raising my ankles from her legs, sitting beside her, questioningly seeking her eyes with mine; remember she was regarding me with a look which I can only describe as being unwilling resignation, self-critical submission; yes, as if she was attempting to convince herself I wasn't to be trusted—inform herself she was still too close to danger for comfort, warn herself our activities must cease—at the same time that her still hot and bothered body (for how could it be otherwise?: neither of us had yet turned inside out in time to the upwellings of procreation) was distracting her from those attempts, undermining the workings of her reason, compelling her to remain. No, she couldn't prevent sweet encouragement from smoldering amidst the uncertainty in her eyes; prevent a flush of pleasure from intermingling with the trepidation upon her face; prevent her posture from suggesting surrender more convincingly than it suggested recoil. Nor could she prevent herself from suddenly grasping the bedposts behind her, pressing the back of her head into the pillow, widening her eyes—staring straight at me! in a manner which caused every muscle in my body to twitch with excitement as I gasped for breath!

God! Her pale face was framed—set in relief, made even more radiant and vivid! by the glistening black of her disarrayed hair; her delicate chin and full crimson lips were invitingly—hungrily! lifted upwards; her throat—smooth, supple, slender, unblemished throat! was right there, in front of me—stretched to its full length, quiveringly taut! and... Oh, I recall being enthralled and frightened in equal measure as I abruptly sat atop her belly, grasped both sides of her torso with my thighs; recall a sensation as of claws scratching my skin from the inside—a sensation at once unpleasant and beguiling! as I watched my hands jerk towards her face, pause near her chin for an instant, before descending towards her throat... But then strident shrieks stabbed at my ears—filled the air with jagged angles, shattered light! as she pushed me off of her, scrambled from the bed, dashed to the far side of the room! For a few moments she was a blur of frantic gesticulations, rustling clothes; then she vanished through the door...

* * * * *

Was I toying with a knife in response to a girl's eager encouragement? Ha! Why bother to ask? I remember, for a certainty, that I was holding the flat side of the blade—long, gracefully curved, gleaming—against her milk-white cheek; remember being captivated by the contrast between the inanimate steel and her living flesh; by the thought that a simple rotation of my wrist would bring the cutting edge of the blade into contact with her skin—that a subsequent two or so inch downward movement of my arm would instantly convulse her lovely face with desperate fear, unendurable pain; and, more, I remember reciting the thought aloud to her and watching mischievous delight further animate her features, set her eyes alight, as an apparent consequence of the recitation; remember hearing her giggle slyly, sensing a surge of lascivious vitality in the electric softness of her body; remember her arousal darted into the tautness of my muscles, joined me to its magnetic field!

Who was leading whom? I couldn't help but set the knife atop the nightstand in order to have both hands free; couldn't help but grasp, squeeze—caress, tickle, slap! her thighs, waist, shoulders; help but rub my belly, chest, cheeks against the fluid shudderings of her muscles; oh, help but do anything and everything I could to reach into her secret tensions, bring any remaining guardedness, distrust, and rebellion to the surface—transform it into flushed excitement, dissolving sighs! Nor was she slow in responding in kind, doing her best to duplicate—or surpass! my efforts; as I felt her fingers—sparklingly intuitive, electrically all-knowing fingers! conduct exploratory tap dance after tap dance from my ankles to my temples, strum the strings of my nerves, coax—prod! the eddies of my desire into full-fledged waves!

Yes, one moment I was lying atop her, easing my face into her creamy breasts such that they were heaving against my cheeks, inciting me to plunge my face deeper; and the next moment—suddenly, somehow! I was on my back as she straddled my thighs, pressed on my shoulders with her palms, swished her hair across my face and chest; then in another moment—abrupt twist of my body, blur of my vision! she was stretched full-length on the mattress and I was lying alongside her with my head at the opposite end from hers, kissing and nipping her calves, running my hands up and down—seizing, kneading! the silkiness of her thighs, aware she was equally as enthusiastically wrapping her arms about my legs, sucking—here, there, everywhere! for all she was worth; then, in some other dizzying moment—with the sequence increasingly difficult to follow! she was cooing sultry nothings— interspersed with erratic gasps! into one of my ears while flutter- ing her fingers about my throat, tickling it—as well as my shoulders, back! into warm tingles; shortly chewing upon the said ear while slipping her fingers inside my mouth, lightly scratch- ing my tongue; followed by... I was caressing her *somewhere* while inhaling nosefuls of lilac-scented sweat, watching her eyes widen, cheeks quiver; watching her auburn-copper hair thrash among the silver sheets; watching the silver of the sheets leap into my eyes, become bright fog, and my vision blur: where was I? I was only able to perceive her as being a flurry of swift white un- dulations; was no longer fully certain as to whether a given move- ment or sound—clasp, caress, shiver, or sigh! originated with her or myself; aware of little besides becoming increasingly inundated with sparkling heat, pulsating electricity...

Listen: I was soon backing away from her in order to escape the self-restraint-eroding stimulation of her fingers and tongue; soon running my fingernails up and down my legs and about my chest in an effort to dilute the flush of arousal with a trace of irri- tation; soon shaking my head and blinking my eyes in order to clear my clouded vision, reobtain depth perception; yes, doing anything and everything I could to impose distance, reinstate boundaries, reobtain the ability to distinguish my body from hers. Then I was watching myself sit atop her belly, grind her arms into the mattress with my knees; watching myself seize ahold of her hair, immobilize her head, with my left hand while picking up an object from the nightstand with my right; watching myself re- peatedly pass the object across her throat until her throat was red, bright red!

Several seconds later my arm came to a rest and I was staring at the object in my hand, and I wonder: was I immediately aware that the said object was a tube of lipstick? or did I half-believe I was holding the knife? Was I immediately aware that the red on her throat was lipstick? or did I half-believe it was blood stream- ing from a wound? And when I finally did clearly and distinctly inform myself I was, indeed, holding a tube of lipstick and that the red on her throat had been placed there by the same: why did I ask myself whether I'd intentionally grabbed the lipstick from the nightstand in place of the knife? Was it because I was genuinely in doubt about the matter? or because it was a means of sending shivers up and down my spine, placing myself in an absorbing state of ambiguity? Ha! What was being playacted and what was being sincerely felt? Where did the posturing end and authentic emotion begin? To what extent, if any, did I believe I'd approached the point at which it would become possible to employ the knife instead of a harmless substitute?

However much I may have wished to remain in the state of ambiguity (sit there shivering, trembling, shuddering in a state of icy joy while half-persuading myself it was by the slimmest of margins that I'd avoided crossing the line between mock and actual perpetration of murder), I wasn't permitted to do so for long. Why wasn't I permitted to do so? Because I became aware that she was laughing, squealing with delight even, and involuntarily glanced at her face—whereupon I saw that the look of mischief hadn't left her features; that her amusement was as pronounced as ever. Then I distinctly heard her say, "Silly boy!," and felt her fingers grasp my right hand: she was seeking to seize the lipstick...

I remember yanking the lipstick away from her, transferring it to my other hand, in a resurgence of lightheartedness and gaming in which the ambiguity vanished as if it had been little more than a dream; remember she was soon shouting, "Tickle! Tickle!" while pushing me onto my back, poking at my ribs; remember I dropped the lipstick and that she instantly grabbed it, began crisscrossing my chest with red streaks while yelling, "Take that!"; remember we were thereafter rolling about on the mattress —flinging blankets at one another, pummeling with pillows— and... Well, it was then—at the moment when we were at the height of riotous fun and my sides ached with laughter—that I began to miss the sensations I'd felt immediately after painting her throat red; that I was suddenly annoyed at how quickly I'd been swept out of the tantalizing state of ambiguity, propelled into frivolous frolic by the sight of her amused face. Yes, it was clear that she hadn't, for an instant, considered the matter of the lipstick in any light other than that of innocent play and I was resentful of the fact, determined to see to it she experienced the same ambiguity—suspenseful shivers, recoiling fascination! as I had! That's right, she was also going to be brought close to being convinced that all games—fantasy-dramatization—had ceased; that the barrier between simulated and actual knife-utilization had been breached; that what had commenced harmlessly had evolved into a clear and present danger! She was also going to be afraid and believe—even if it be for but a moment, single convulsive surge!

And so I found myself biting my lips, stifling my laughter, erasing all trace of warmth from my face, assuming a mien of icy aloofness; found myself methodically pinning her to the mattress—lying on top of her, winding my legs about her legs, entrapping her arms with my elbows, grasping her hair, glaring into her eyes. For how long did we remain thus? For as long as was required for me to be convinced I'd blocked all channels of communication, transformed myself into a stranger; for me to be convinced I was indifferent to her feelings, surrounded by untraversable silence, absolutely alone even though our bodies were pressed together; for me to be convinced I'd soon succeed in frightening myself, recoiling from myself—even if it be for but a moment, single convulsive surge!

I remember disentangling my left hand from her hair, placing it over her mouth to prevent her from speaking; remember watching hints of bewilderment appear on her face, not allowing the slightest acknowledgement of such to creep into my gaze; remember waiting until twitches of discomfort announced themselves in her body and unease clouded the clarity of her eyes; remember retrieving the knife from the nightstand with my right hand, bringing the blade—dull side or sharp?—to her throat; remember beginning a slow, barely skin-grazing, cutting movement—whispering, "You're going to die, my dear, die..."

* * * * *

I was eager to be anywhere but on the bright busy street where I was, half-dashing down the crowded sidewalk in an effort to get away from the light and noise as quickly as possible—get away from something the light and noise was associated with. Was it something I'd done? something someone else had done? or something I was afraid I might do? God, because I was beginning to find myself—each and every night! caught up in doings which alarmed me, and the most alarming thing about them was that they were constantly suggesting further embellishments to me! Again and again, I was being placed on the "Not enough!" treadmill, forced to confront aspects of myself I was increasingly feeling ought to be left alone—there were far too many sleeping dogs within me that I was being tempted to awaken despite myself! and... Oh, all I know is I wanted to be off of that street, away from the distress it was producing in me; all I know is I wanted to hide somewhere, refuse to be conscious of myself...

A few minutes passed: I came upon and entered a narrow, feebly illuminated, alleyway; was soon leaning with my back to a brick wall, pressing both palms against it—thankful for the cold wetness of the masonry which was a soothing contrast to my condition of excitement, balm for the disquietude of my mind. I was gazing to the left, where the airborne droplets of a gathering fog were intercepting, refracting into hazy aureoles, the gold-orange light of five or so door lamps which were spaced at uneven intervals into the distance—into the distance where all outline, distinction between solidity and gaseousness, vanished. I was aware of wanting to sink into, become indistinguishable from, the chilly motionlessness of the wall; of wanting the utter insensibility of stone to seep into, harden like cement within, my veins and nerves...

And sure enough: following an indeterminate amount of time I was looking at nothing whatsoever, not even the empty air, and it seemed to me I could no longer feel the wall supporting me; that numbness was spreading from my back down to my toes and up into my neck and head; yes, that I was steadily losing the use of my senses, approaching the desired condition of insensibility, and would soon be untroubled by feverish thoughts, no longer in thrall to inner disturbances...

But it was only wishful thinking: suddenly a loud smacking of shoes on the pavement approached me and abruptly stopped; suddenly an insistent voice was hammering at my ears, piercing the armor of my torpor, badgering me into attentiveness, forcing me to focus my gaze. The intruder's face was directly in front of mine, and I wanted to hit it—just like I always want to knock a ringing phone to the floor, smash a flashlight that's been aimed in my eyes. I didn't want to have to grasp the meaning of words, follow the details of descriptions, understand the logic of trains of thought. I wanted to smack the impudence from his face, dull the glint of his arrogant stare, bathe his smirking mouth in blood; and felt the muscles of my arms tighten, felt my fingers curl into fists...

But, strange to tell: the moment I was ready to strike him, and firmly believed I would, I found my arm wouldn't move when I heard him say he'd come from "over there" while indicating, with a jerk of his head, the same area I'd recently fled. Ha! Was it a coincidence? or had he seen me there and followed me to my place of refuge for the purpose of unsettling me with his confidences? The questions flickered in my thoughts: I sought to cling to them—ponder them, reply to them—but found myself, despite myself, listening to him instead. Why was his voice so beguiling, such that it rapidly supplanted my thoughts and lured me into listening to it? All I can say is that it was as if his voice was echoing the pulsations of my nerves, keeping time to the beat of my heart:

"I've been over there before—too many times to count," he began, "and have never thought of it as being anything other than harmless titillation, an inconsequential means of teasing myself. But this time matters were different from the start—yes! when I first glimpsed the neon over four hours ago from a few blocks away and its multicolored brightness sent shock waves through my nerves, tightened the pit of my stomach, inundated me with more churning eagerness than I knew what to do with! No choice!

I had to quicken my pace—had to! and was soon in the midst of the neon's hissing colors, surrounded—on all sides! by flashing red and slashing green; by knives—swords! of blue-white which were thrusting, stabbing—dicing my thoughts, scrambling my sense of balance, confusing me as I've seldom been confused before!

"Yes, I was glancing this way, glancing that; now at the neon outlines of dancing girls; now at the signs which blared 'Sexstasy!,' 'Feline Funtime!,' 'Fantasy Mates!'; now at my own writhing, blurring, dissolving reflection on the liquid surfaces of the windows; and felt I was being infiltrated by an unnatural amount of expectation, fanned into an uneasy—searing! fever of anticipation—yes! goaded, dared—seduced, ensnared! into wanting things I didn't want to want, doing things I didn't want to do!

"I wanted to get out of there—run fast and far! but: where else could I go? what was I to do with all the burning yearning with which I'd become afflicted in the blink of an eye? I turned this way—turned that! in an effort to locate a direction to flee in, even while realizing the effort was futile on account of having already ceased to be my own master—been caught in the trap of unwanted hunger, imposed need! Ha! I spun around and around like a wildcat in a cage and, in each instance of pausing to obtain my bearings, found myself facing the entrance of an arcade, gazing—against my wishes! into the ghostly silver luminosity within, coming under its spell like a lonely moth in the night!

"I ceased bothering to pretend escape was possible and approached one of the arcades; was soon purchasing twenty dollars worth of tokens at the admissions booth, stumbling into the shimmering embrace of the interior, surrounded by more blinking—glaring! lights which were pulsating in my head, sparkling under my skin! Did I have any idea what I was searching for—what I wanted? Neon arrows were directing me this way, that; signs were commanding me to insert a token here, insert five tokens there! Insert! Insert!

"I stepped into a booth for no other reason than that it was the closest one. Upon the insertion of a token, a film commenced to play on a small screen: the camera was stealthily creeping towards an open window on the ground level of a large house, peeping-Tomish, and the camera was intended to be one and the same as whoever watched the film. Which is to say that I'd been cast in the role of Tom and was soon standing at the window, watching a girl who was sitting on the edge of a couch in a semi-transparent nightie; watching her slip the nightie over her head, caress her breasts, ease her hand into her black lace panties; watching her remove the panties, spread her legs, stimulate herself with eager fingers, shiveringly arch her back; watching her suddenly raise her eyes, gaze upon me with a look of bliss, invite me to join in! But I declined the girl's invitation, rebelled against the role in which I'd been cast—rebelled against the film! I wasn't going to permit myself to be swindled into making love to patterns of light on a screen, panting in time to the movements of a mirage!

"I exited the booth, was again instantly surrounded by a kalei-doscope of pulse-quickening—imagination-whipping! attractions; by all the life-sized pictures on the doors of the booths of girls pleading, pouting, smiling, teasing, triumphing—or showing fear, recoiling—or taking the initiative, advancing! while striking every conceivable pose in various stages of undress; by more blinking lights, flashing arrows!—'Come here!'s, 'Go there!'s—an ab-solutely maddening proliferation of promises of instantaneous gratification of impossible demands!

"I had no choice but to duck into another booth, obey the om-nipresent 'Insert! Insert!' The required two tokens disappeared into the illuminated ruby red slot and the shade rose from the win-dow before me: three girls—one redhead, two brunettes—were on the other side of the glass, undressing one another on a large circular bed in the middle of a circular room; yes, playfully tick-ling, slapping—ardently kissing, nipping! each other from their ankles to their earlobes while unbuttoning blouses, unzipping skirts, unfastening brassieres, sliding off panties and stockings, flinging them in every direction. Upon liberating themselves of every shred of clothing they leaped from the bed, commenced kicking the clothes about the floor, striking poses—wriggling,

shimmying, crawling, rolling about! How captivatingly the brightness of the lights raced up and down their limbs, caressed their
curves, pulsated in their hair!

"The redhead was suddenly at my window, undulating in slow
hula movements punctuated by abrupt thrusts of her pelvis, toss-
ings-back of her head; was alternately lifting her breasts towards
her chin and releasing them, allowing them to jigglingly bounce
back to their natural stance of pert uprightness: how my palms
itched to seize and squeeze them, how soothing their softness
would've been! She began caressing them, along with her shoulders and throat, with delicate, quivering, crimson-nailed fingers—
lightly scratched herself, left vague pink streaks of irritation on
her otherwise unblemished skin; and all the while putting on the
cutest little-girl pout, a most engaging look of innocence! She, indeed, knew all the tricks! My nerves were being toyed with, tied
into pleasingly uncomfortable knots, by a consummate professional! And then she abruptly about-faced, turned her back to
me—left me alone, in anxious suspense: was she through with
me? was she going to advance to someone else's window? Ha,
she flawlessly executed a back-bend and handstand, swiftly and
seamlessly passed from one stage to the next: she was facing me
upside down, with her feet against the wall above the glass and
head below, vibrating her legs while steadily spreading them!

"My chest froze, trapped my breath; my breath accumulated—
swelled! inside me, gripped the muscles of my back—every limb!
in a vise of vibrant tension! Ha, and it was then that the token machine started blipping, warning of an impending descent of the
shade! Damn! I fumbled for two tokens, dropped them on the
floor—the shade unfeelingly came down, blocked my view, separated me from my redheaded darling!

"When I'd sufficiently recovered myself (gone through a rapid
cycle of stunned annoyance, stabbing impatience, and willed co-
ordination) to gather the spilled tokens, slip them into the magic
slot... The shade lifted anew and the succulent redhead, miracle of
miracles, was still there, standing upright again and facing me;
yes, smiling an 'I knew it!' smile, openly displaying gratitude

even, bestowing a look of kindness upon me; and then an 'All right, lover, let's set the house ablaze!' glance of stated purpose; immediately succeeded by a thorough licking of the glass during which I was avidly watching every quick lap, flirtatious curl, extended slow up-lick of her tongue; watching her saliva accumulate on the glass—seize, bend, and blur the bright light! Then she trained her tongue upon herself, was licking her fingers, advancing to her wrists, following both arms (alternating between them) to her shoulders—lappety-lap!—finally biting each shoulder firmly enough to leave faint teeth imprints, and again displaying that lost little girl pout! The sequence periodically blurred and became clear according to the location of her saliva on the glass—saliva which was replenished by another licking, then pushed about when she swirled her fingers in it, writhed against the glass. She paused for a moment... Then, limber feline that she was, she raised a leg over her head until she was pointing at the ceiling with her toes—doing the splits standing up—and licked and bit its calf; first one leg, then the other—with her red hair streaming down each thigh in turn, catching the light, flinging orange iridescence which scampered about the surface of the saliva-dripping window like flames! Ha! How am I to communicate the full measure of all which was simultaneously occurring within and without me?

"I managed to prevent another shutting of the shade by instructing myself, 'Keep two tokens in your hand at all times; listen for the warning bleep; insert them quickly and accurately!' (The antiquated machine wouldn't allow me to insert all the tokens at once, accumulate time.) Even so, I felt I was rapidly being deprived of the ability to respond in the amount of time allotted to insert the tokens (about thirty seconds—thirty seconds that always seemed like two), what with the way the redheaded honey was now lingeringly kissing the glass, peppering it with carmine lip-imprints—smilingly applying fresh coats of lipstick to insure the newer imprints were as vivid as the first; often pursing her lips, suggestively sliding the tube of lipstick in and out between them; starting to press her breasts against the glass, slide them from side to side, paint their whiteness with the lipstick's red...

"No! No! No! Would you believe it? I ran out of tokens and the unpitying shade slammed down again! I was suddenly alone—staring at the shade's blank white, unable to believe the lissome redhead was no longer in front of me! I was also aware of a stabbing sensation of inner emptiness: I couldn't help but crave more addictive—blood-heating, soul-stirring, time-erasing! images!

"Within two minutes I had a fresh supply of tokens—twice as many as before—and was again strolling among the sizzling lights, blazing arrows: why was I failing to locate the booth I'd vacated, find the delectable redhead? Try as I might to backtrack to its location, it persisted in eluding me! What was I to do? It seemed to me that I was owed some consummation, and I was determined to collect! What sort of consummation? I had no clear idea: it was almost as if I was convinced another glimpse of the redhead would dissolve the glass which separated us, allow me to get my hands on her; or somehow be the equivalent of getting my hands on her!

"I entered a booth that I was almost certain was the correct one: the phone on the wall adjacent to the shaded window informed me I was mistaken. I turned to leave, resume my search for the elusive redhead, but... Ha, the amount of hunger I was under the influence of had already allowed me as much leeway as I was going to get! I hadn't found the redhead yet: time up! Another girl—any girl! would do! My hand dove into my pocket, seized several tokens, inserted them—five this time—into the familiar ruby red slot. The shade rose, revealed an unclothed beauty: she was seated in a padded leather armchair, with upraised legs spread and the soles of her feet placed squarely on the glass. Her eyes brightened as she gestured towards the phone on my side of the window; she was already holding a phone to her ear.

"I barely recall what was said and don't feel it matters: preferences were certainly discussed, instructions as to how to best indulge them were certainly issued; of course flirtatiousness fluttered. But if the specific words of our exchange escape my recol-

lection, the succession of sensory impressions—their overall tone
and effect—does not. I remember the sultry coos and purrs—
blithe teasing and laughter, rippling excitability and sighs—of her
voice steadily slipping under my skin, massaging my spine, sending sparkling warmth throughout me as I watched her free hand
caress each of her thighs in turn, advance to where they met, commence to stroke; remember I was seeking to cross the distance between us, dissolve the intrusive glass, with my voice; seeking to
attune myself to the shivers of her body—quivers of her fingers
as they parted the pink in her black fur, probed. Yes, for certain I
was seeking to emotionally and imaginatively trade places with
her fingers by listening to the fluctuations in cadence of her voice,
the electricity of which was massaging me from the inside out—
as if steadily exchanging places with the rhythm of my blood-
beat. The extent of the perceivable world was her voice, her
fingers, and the shimmers within me; the extent of all possible aspiration was to use my voice to inspire her fingers to stimulate
her further, thereby causing her voice to reverberate with greater
depths of sultriness—communicate stronger upwellings of both-
eredness. That's right, I was intent upon heightening her feelings,
following them every step of the way during their process of transformation, humming in unison with them. We were a team, propelling one another towards divine dissolution...

   "A team? Ha! How much of her share of the action was playacting—scripted behavior, rehearsed recitation? How much of this
phone routine was dependent upon the customer being as uncomfortably overwrought as I was? too knocked about by inner
fireworks to be capable of noting put-on expressions, assumed at-
titudes, artificial vocalization? I don't pose these questions because I'm interested in the answer; whatever the answer, I don't
care. I ask them (1) to further indicate the extent of my arousal by
stating the questions are impossible for me to answer, and (2) to
drive home the fact it didn't matter to what degree she was sincere
or fraudulent in her transports. After all, the glass was between us
and was going to remain there: however much I might succeed in
becoming charged with electric sensuality and transferring it to

my voice—succeed in tapping into her nerves, matching myself to her emotion-whirl—the glass would always block an exchange of the other components of desire: no physical contact, enthralling friction of skin on skin! Only extrapolations via sight and sound, frustrating attempts to approximate the whole experience with a fraction of it!

"Yes, I certainly turned over inside myself, was suspended in a state of charged weightlessness, a number of times; certainly felt waves of tingles come and go up and down my spine, spread over my back, engulf my limbs; certainly gasped, sighed, trembled with delight which hinted at that of easing myself onto a woman on a bed; but, at all times in the background of my feelings and perceptions and thoughts, there was the awareness that the glass—cold, inanimate, dead glass—was between us; that I was merely enacting a farce in front of myself, indulging in a sensory con; that, at best, the phone routine was foreplay which was priming me for authentic consummation—teasing which was increasing my need for authentic consummation; that, in the end, it would never be more than an irritatingly insufficient taste of what would be required to acquire calm.

"Did I run out of tokens or did the futility of phone-play finally become too apparent for me to be capable of continuing it? All I know for certain is I exited that booth feeling far more unfulfilled, desperate, and unstable than I was previous to entering it! What to do? Where to go? Ha! I could've fed token after token into slot after slot for days and days—watched girl after girl strike poses, perform—heard voice after voice become sultry, coo sweet rapture! and I wouldn't have come anywhere close to appeasing my hunger, achieving satiation; would've done nothing but fill my head with more fever-inducing pictures, increasingly entrap my senses in explosive waking dreams, further whip myself into a state of searing need!

"Yes, what I needed right then and there—sooner than soon! was to get my hands on what was on the other side of the glass! What I needed was to touch, feel—seize, squeeze! a woman of flesh and blood if I was to escape the treadmill I was on, cease

being at the mercy of all the tantalizing images which were promising everything, delivering nothing; cease overloading my senses,
unbalancing myself, coming precariously close to screaming at
the top of my lungs!

"Where to go? What to do? I commanded myself to forget the
booths, raced downstairs to the basement area in the hope of finding hustling entrepreneurs, but only encountered racks of maga-
zines: nothing! I returned to the ground floor, discovered a
stairway in an out-of-the-way corner, and didn't hesitate—was
soon at the top of the stairs, strolling down a long corridor, impatiently turning at the knobs of several locked doors. One of the
doors—with a sign on it which read 'Dress'—yielded: I stepped
inside a white room, shut the door behind me, was met by the startled features—alarmed eyes—of a girl who was watching me in
the mirror of the vanity before which she was seated with her back
to me: she looked as if she was ready to spring to her feet, wave
a can of hair spray in my face. I took a couple cautious steps forward: she turned to face me with an expression of defiant fear,
began hiss-insisting, 'I'll scream! I'll scream!'

"I'm not certain what I said: all I know is she not only lost her
fear at the sound of my words, but became ashamed of it; that she
was soon seeking to put me at ease, saying, 'I'm sorry, I... It's just
that there are a lot of creeps around here, and... Why don't we
start over? My name's...,' while taking my hands in hers, stroking
my palms with her fingers, glancing at me with hesitant hopeful-
ness, as if afraid I might choose not to remain. Ha! Necessity is,
after all, the mother of invention: it's my guess I put on a face of
upset innocence, made a show of being baffled and hurt, with the
aim of arousing her sympathy, animating her with maternal concern. Yes, I do vaguely recall informing myself that a convincing
dose of vulnerability was what was called for, and hastening to
administer it...

"Be that as it may: we were soon getting acquainted, coming
to an understanding. To summarize: she'd completed her shift,
and her time was her own; it being after three AM and a week-
night, there were fewer girls working and it was unlikely anyone

would need the room we were in when plenty of others were vacant; therefore, we'd probably be undisturbed and, in the event we were discovered, it was not necessarily against the rules. Such is what she told me.

"She'd already changed into her street clothes, and proceeded to remove them again; I followed suit. She then turned her back to me, began combing her hair while watching me in the vanity's mirror. I remained standing in the center of the room, was curling and uncurling my toes in the thick white fluffiness of the carpet while watching the bouncing waves and curls of her long gold hair swish to and fro across her back with every brush-stroke; watching her kind smile become teasing, lascivious, sly; watching her caress her throat with her free hand, lick her lips, toss the brush onto the shelf... She turned towards the right, straddled the bench, reclined onto her back, became a burst of movement: one moment was forcing her breasts upward by pressing her arms against the sides of her chest and the next moment clawing at the carpet with long carmine nails; then raising her feet to the bench, rubbing her calves and thighs together, extending one leg straight out into the air while folding the other back until its knee touched her chin—then alternating legs; and while twisting slowly this way, emphatically that; and with the bright light tracing the lines of her litheness, dancing upon her curves!

"Ha! Another exhibitionist routine was the last thing I needed! I stepped forward, slipped my arms under her shoulders and thighs, lifted her from the bench, and—God! the softness of her body, energy of her body!—the sheer miracle of her living and breathing muscles and skin!—the dizzying sensation of finally having a girl of flesh and blood in my arms! Yes, in light of the prolonged frustration of downstairs—my having dashed from one unseizable glass-enclosed beauty to another for over two hours! imagine the effect of her breasts swelling—like melons ripe to bursting! against my chest; effect of her hands grasping the back of my head, pulling my face to hers; effect of her lips pressing against—sucking at! mine!

"I lowered her to the carpet; was, I'm not exaggerating, gazing at her in a state of wonderment, half-disbelieving joy! I swear I was running my hands up and down her arms—about her chest, belly, legs! as if seeking to confirm I wasn't dreaming, make certain she was real!

"'Honey!' she laugh-gasped, and pulled my face to hers again (resumed what I'd interrupted with my apparent need to authenticate her materiality), slipped her tongue inside my mouth, wiggled it against the roof, sent tingles rippling down the back of my neck, while... Ha, I was so giddy with eagerness, impatience—enrapt by thoughts of doing this, that, everything with her—overcome with the urge to simultaneously begin a whirl of things which could only be done one at a time! that, for a few moments, I was unable to do anything at all! Blind impulse surged to life in my limbs: as if in an electrified waking trance—while seeming to be half-suspended outside of my body! I was wrapping my arms about her back and my legs about her legs, clasping her as tightly as I could, thrilling to the responsiveness of her muscles—thrilling to her softness, her breathing, her...! Soon I was imprisoned in my own turn—delightedly so! as her arms and legs locked me in an equally ardent vise; as she insistently undulated against me; as she...!

"I remember that sometime later I interrupted our kissing—again—to have a fresh look at her; remember the glow of excitement on her face was leaping out at me, blurring the air between us; remember the features of her face were trading places with one another—alternately running together and scampering apart—like bursts of light on agitated quicksilver as her voice rose and fell in slurred purrings, fluttering sighs; remember she exclaimed, 'Ooooo!'—took a sudden deep breath, coughed! and that my attention was drawn to the fact my fingers were entangled in coarse hair—that one of them was stroking slippery warmth... But I'm not certain at what point I was yanking her to her hands and knees, turning onto my back, sliding underneath her until my head was between her thighs; or when I was sucking on her neck while her fingers alternately squeezed and released between my legs; or when she was face down on the carpet and I was straddling her back while facing her feet, bringing pink splotches to her rear with a flurry of slaps; or when she was lightly scratching my chest while massaging my back with her breasts; or... Ha, all I know is that with each caress, kiss, embrace—grasp of a hand, wind of a leg, exhale of a breath! I could feel my sense-combustion increasing, spreading—like gust-fanned flames! up to my cheeks, down to my toes! It was as if electric juice was being pumped into the pores of my skin, accumulating in my veins and nerves; as if my body was becoming a field of energy—whirl of tingling mist! and she was dissolving out from under me!

"It was as if in a dream that I entered her, began to undulate my hips; that I watched her seize ahold of my upper arms with jerkily quivering fingers, noted their joints were white with the effort of their exertion; that I felt her legs wrap about me, tighten; yes, as if in a dream that I tore her hands from my arms—felt her nails rake across my skin like clinging claws—and pinned her wrists against the carpet, held them firmly. Ha! She was pitching, twitching—difficult to restrain, challenging me! She half-twisted to the side, lifted one of her shoulders a few inches from the floor: I lowered my corresponding shoulder onto it, flattened her. She twisted again, attempted to kick; then suddenly became rigid in every limb, absolutely still—inhaled sharply, moaned—surged inside herself! before vanishing from view—yes! as a final acceleration of my hips lifted me into an outpouring which was all too evanescent, over far too soon!

"I remember sliding off of her, lying chest-down on the floor with my left arm and leg slung across her and my face turned away; remember shutting my eyes, wanting nothing more than to become limp in every limb, dead to the world. An interval of semi-lassitude followed: I've no idea how long it lasted. What I do know is that the more I attempted to persuade myself I'd soon be overcome with exhaustion—lapse into sense-numbing drowsiness, merciful sleep—the more I realized prickly warmth was lingering inside me. And the more I realized that prickly warmth was lingering inside me, the more it accumulated, swelled into waves

of stinging sparkles. And the more forcefully the waves of stinging sparkles broke across my nerves, the more I was compelled to
realize renewed entanglement in desire's hot knots couldn't be far
away...

"God! I was sitting bolt upright beside her with no recollection of having placed myself thus—no comprehension of how
dangerous it was for me to be staring at her as I was! She was on
her back, gazing into the empty air with wide unseeing eyes while
aquiver—trembling, shaking! like an addict in need of another
dose of a waning drug; yes, was erratically twisting on the carpet
as if, at best, half-conscious of her actions while caressing herself—thighs, belly, breasts, throat! with jittery hands, turning her
glowing face from side to side, spilling her golden hair every
which way!

"I couldn't stop staring at her; couldn't prevent her smooth
sweat-glistened curves—light-kissed litheness! from sliding into
my eyes, slipping into my nerve-stream, engulfing me in churn-
ings of restiveness; from stockpiling—knotting up! in the pit of
my stomach, contracting—straining! my muscles, bringing on
bursts of panic! I was not only still afire inside, I was more so! Our
frolic, far from mitigating my condition of unrest, had only exac-
erbated it—intensified the prodding of my senses and tumult of
my emotions, bound me more firmly to desperation, backed me up
against the wall of devouring need!

"No, I couldn't run—couldn't hide! as I continued to stare
while she lay there so unwary, oblivious to all but her fever; lay
there so defenseless, at the mercy of whatever new impulses I
might come under the influence of! Damn! Why had she permitted herself to be alone with me? Why hadn't she remarked the
warning flags which were certainly being waved by my manner
when I'd first entered the room, detected I was far from stable,
not to be trusted?

"Please understand! I was taking her part, sympathetic to her
situation, fearing for her safety! I was seeking to avert my eyes
from her, forget she was there; to crawl to my clothes, dress, exit
the room, return to the streets! I wanted nothing more than to re-

move my state of disturbance from her presence, deal with it in the comparative safety of isolation! I was eager to spare her from any consequences attendant upon the resentment which, despite my most strenuous efforts to prevent such (the fact I more than dreaded being afflicted by such a sentiment), was steadily creeping into the forefront of my feelings, displacing my better instincts!

"No, I didn't want to blame her for having failed to sate my hunger, rescue me from the state of disturbance I was in; didn't want to blame her for having increased instead of appeased my desire, fanned my hunger until it was little different than pain; especially, I didn't want to hate her for lying on the floor in a state of oblivious lassitude (having ceased altogether to tremble, caress herself) when I was in the toils of a flagrantly opposite condition of body and mind!

"But how I wanted to feel and what I wanted to do had no influence whatsoever upon the decision which my overwrought senses was making of their own accord: the cast of my nerves—my inner tone—was rapidly veering towards out-and-out anger! After all, how dare she lie there in a state of contentment with her eyes shut (Had she dozed off?) when I was experiencing nothing of the kind; how dare she be satisfied with so little when I needed more, far more; especially, how dare she lead me on with the implication of being willing to keep pace with me only to stop before we were barely getting started—leave me stranded in inner claustrophobia, silent screams!

"And there were additional reasons for my anger: I hated her for being naive enough to trust me, stupid enough to get in over her head! More to the point: I hated her for being unaware of the danger she was in; for dropping her guard and sleeping (Yes, she *had* dozed off!) when I was in no condition to view matters rationally, restrict my behavior to socially acceptable boundaries; hated her for failing to flee the room!

"I was still struggling to tear my eyes away from her, rise to my feet, dress, race from the room: my body wouldn't obey me; the muscles of my neck refused to pivot my head to the side and direct my gaze elsewhere; my legs remained as immobile as if they were weighed down by concrete slabs! But I had to get out of there, had to! A new batch of nefarious thoughts—detrimental-to-her-safety suppositions! was separating itself from the background din in my head—threatening to crystallize into clarity, determine my actions! What thoughts? Listen: she was beautiful, shapely, desirable—dozing right in front of me, inches from my burning fingers! Certainly a few well-executed caresses would rouse her from her languor and reawaken her interest; certainly she'd be willing to commence a second round! So why wasn't I proceeding to awaken her? I wasn't doing so because I'd become convinced that resuming regular relations would do no more towards calming me than squirting a drop of water on a hot iron would lower the latter's temperature; that, in fact, I'd only continue to climb the sensory ladder of fire until—God! my reason was strained to the point of...

"'No! No! No!' I clearly heard myself shout. 'No!' My chest contracted as if seized by a strong hand, erupted in pain as if squeezed by that hand! My head—entire body! was vibrating! I... Oh, from out of nowhere (with, I'm absolutely certain in retrospect, no evidence whatsoever to support such a perception) it occurred to me that she wasn't actually asleep, only pretending to be; that ill-willed smugness—self-satisfied contempt! was plainly stamped upon her features; in short, that she was laughing at my plight, congratulating herself on having greatly contributed to it; yes, on having cold-bloodedly held out a false promise of deliverance from my state of pent-upness only to treacherously slam the door on satiation, deliver me over to acute physical and mental distress!

"Suddenly dark wings were flitting about the room, making whispery swishing sounds, hissing louder and louder; suddenly my vision was ablur, and her face disappeared behind a cloud of silver-gray mist... I was rising to my feet, seizing ahold of the nearby bench, lifting it from the floor; I was standing above her, raising the bench higher...

"Ha! A movement at my back startled and annoyed me: I turned towards it, found myself face to face with my reflection in the vanity's mirror, and was no longer able to restrain the anger which was shoving my reason aside, singeing my flesh—was instantly hammering at the mirror with the bench, filling the room with shattering thuds! Yes, I'd see my face here—there! in an undamaged portion of the mirror's silver—smash! I'd hit it straight on, watch—with savage satisfaction! it tumble down in splinters, be replaced by the blank white of the wall behind it! Smash! Smash! I was watching my reflection become scattered—lost! among the makeup on the vanity; was, once no portion of my reflection remained on the wall, slamming the end of the bench onto the vanity—splintering the mirror into smaller pieces, breaking bottles, crushing compacts, denting cans!

"My arms grew tired and I dropped the bench onto the floor— the room was shifting in and out of focus: one moment frozen in stark clarity, the next sliding about—spinning, dipping, rising! in shadowy blurs! Flicker-flash, flicker! I was dressing in stunned haste, hardly conscious of what I was doing—my clothes were as if leaping onto me of their own accord: pants pulled up—with belt left undone! shirt yanked on—inside out, unbuttoned! coat flung over it all—held shut with shaking hands! I was glancing this way—glancing that! taking in—all at once! the abandoned bench, damaged vanity, scattered glinting shards of silver while momentarily at a loss of what to do!

"I stood there—for ten seconds? thirty? a full minute?—while the room and its contents continued to flicker and whirl; and the walls were becoming brighter, increasingly crisscrossed—obscured! by blinding white light; they were collapsing towards one another, enfolding the room, leaping at—threatening to crush! me! I lunged towards the door —ha! just as quickly found myself pausing in alarm, cautiously peering into the hall, ascertaining if others were there... Strange: the walls of the room instantly lost their glare, receded, ceased hammering at me: such rapid switchovers of perception, oscillations of optical illusion! I was on the point of stepping into the hall; for some unaccountable reason, I turned to face the girl instead: she was seated with her back to one of the walls, wringing her hands in front of her face—God! staring at me with supplicating, disbelieving, horrified, accusing eyes! I couldn't hold her glance—couldn't endure her reproach!

"I sprang into the hall, located the stairs, raced through the arcade, was soon on the sidewalk outside—oh! again surrounded by noisy bustle, jarring neon; by colors—seething red, blazing blue, stabbing green! which were swooping down from all angles above, shooting up from all sides below, ricocheting off the windows and wet—sparkling, iridescent! surface of the recently rained upon pavement!

"No refuge, no escape! I was stumbling through the neon kaleidoscope while all too aware that I still had a thirst to quench, cravings to sate; that I still needed to be liberated from the drawn-bow tautness of my body, hot jabs of my insomnia-flayed nerves—liberated from my apprehension-fueling awareness of myself! I just wanted to forget *everything* about this night, get away from the brightness and clamor which was ceaselessly reminding me of how frightfully close I'd come to subjecting the girl to violent treatment she'd by no means deserved—ceaselessly parading her terrified face before me, forcing me to dwell upon the disturbing impulses which lurked within me!

"No, I couldn't get away from the neon-diced—noise-splintered! street soon enough, and was dashing—all but tripping over myself in my haste! towards... It wasn't long afterwards that I found myself in this soothing shadow and silence suffused alleyway, and had hopes of being alone, with no eyes—mirrors! to reflect myself back at me; hopes of calming myself, drifting into a state of passive dreaminess, dazed oblivion, and... God, it was then that I found you here, standing with your back to this wall, and began to speak of myself—dredge up the events of this night! without wanting to do so! That's right, without wanting to do so! And why did you—yes, *you*! have to be here? I haven't settled myself down at all, I've only succeeded in working myself up! And stop looking at me like that—stop it! I..."

He ceased speaking, was too overcome with anger to be capable of articulating anything besides a loud hiss, smothered yell—was shoving his enraged face oppressively close to mine! I shut my eyes to escape his stare, was pressing my back into the wall so hard I could feel it in my joints—was forming fists with my hands, preparing to pummel his face! Yes, I was ready—more than ready! to knock him to the pavement, kick him again and again! My arms were already in motion; I was on the point of rapid-stepping from in front of him, delivering the first blow from the right; I opened my eyes: *he wasn't there!*

Yes, I was alone: vigorously blinking my eyes, glancing up and down the alleyway, seeking to comprehend how he'd vanished as quickly and completely as an approached mirage. And then I became aware, for the first time, that my reflection was in the large window of a shop situated directly across from where I was standing; that, on account of the narrowness of the alleyway, the window—and therefore my reflection—was quite close to me; that the mist in the air was functioning as a magnifying glass, enlarging my reflection to greater than actual proportions; that a faint breeze was agitating the mist and the agitation of the mist was transferring itself to my reflection, making it almost seem to be alive!

Judge of the extent of my distress when I realized that there had never been anyone but myself standing in that alleyway; realized I'd distorted and misread the representations of my senses to such a degree I'd supposed my reflection to be a separate person standing in front of and addressing me! The evidence was inescapable! It was suddenly all too clear that the voice of the unsettling intruder had been none other than that of my memory describing my actions to myself; yes, that I'd been the one unbalanced by a busy street's glaring lights, grating noise; that I'd been the one under the influence of an agony of expectation, whipped into a frenzy by yearnings I hadn't been able to keep pace with, desperately dashing here—there! in a flaring fever which had refused to break; been the one delusionally racing out through the in-doors of accumulating desire, doing nothing but increase the hunger I'd been endeavoring to sate; in short, that I'd been the flayed soul who'd come precariously close to subjecting a kindly girl to violence—who'd fled to spare her further exposure to unsociable inclinations!

Consciousness neither willingly nor easily bears such revelations: I was grinding my back into the wall as hard as I could, endeavoring to bring about jabs of pain sharp enough to blind my awareness to all else. In vain! The realization that there had been no stranger speaking to me; that all the confidences I'd been privy to had been my own; that every action and sensation described in those confidences had been performed and experienced by me; that I'd been the one who'd been brought to the point of unleashing my unexpended energy in a highly unsavory manner: this information effortlessly trivialized the pain in my back, masked it as effectively as a powerful anesthesia!

Listen: I couldn't stop myself from remembering the girl as I'd last seen her; couldn't stop myself from watching her back away from me in fear, pin herself to the wall; couldn't stop seeing her hands flail in front of her face, eyes gaze disbelievingly and accusingly into mine; no, couldn't stop shuddering at the thought of how close she, who'd been charm incarnate—nothing but kind, considerate, obliging! had come to being at the receiving end of my bench-wielding outburst; at the thought of how close her body—beautiful, supple, white-as-milk, smooth-as-satin body! had come to being blackened with wounds, cringing in pain! Nor could I prevent myself from further twisting a knife in my unease with the following sequence of inner monologue:

"What if, when I was standing above the girl with the upraised bench (at that critical instant when the tumult within me was uncontrollably surging to the surface of sensation, engulfing me in the need to lash out at something, anything), my attention hadn't been caught by that movement of my reflection in the mirror at my back? What if, upon turning to investigate the source of that movement, the sight of my reflection in the mirror hadn't been sufficiently absorbing to supplant her as something to direct my rage upon? Because if one more instant had passed without the distraction of my reflection presenting itself, then she might very well have been the recipient of my rage, with the result that I'd presently be guilty of a heinous crime! Yes, one more instant— one! and, right now, I could very well be wrestling with a far more horrible memory than the one which already troubles me; could very well be watching—in my mind's eye—the bench strike her lissome curves; watching her sleek limbs explode into epileptic-fit-like flailings as strident screams sting my ears; watching the bench descend a second time, hit her face, cause choking gurgles to muffle her screams as dark red bubbles from her mouth, spatters her cheeks, stains the carpet! She attempts to raise herself to her elbows, escape! Too late: the bench strikes a third time—a fourth! Crack! Crack! My arms and shoulders shudder—twinge! with the reverse impact of the blows, but I still can't stop producing those blows! Crack! The flawless ivory of her skin yields to inflamed discoloration, swollen splotches; her fingers stiffly curl, cease to move; her eyes, formerly bright with yearning— darting silver sparks! are suddenly lusterless, still as stagnant water! I blankly gaze upon her inert body, am unwilling to comprehend what's occurred, desperately wondering what's become of the other girl—become of the sweet, graceful, vivacious girl! Because it's unthinkable for her to have been transformed into a lifeless object, unresponsive matter; incomprehensible that she'll never smile, toy with her hair, or flex her legs again! Nausea tightens my stomach, swells into my throat—inundates my mouth with bitter spittle, acrid foam! as my eyesight blurs and the room spins, and... God, but why am I flaying myself with a hypothetical recollection? What's the point of 'What if?' I didn't strike her, harm a hair on her head: following a restful sleep, she'll awaken as physically fit—athirst for caresses, sensual transports! as she's ever been—yes! and others will take her in their arms, scratch her sexual itches, erase my face and tonight's episode from her memory! So, that being the case: why am I cringing against this wall, wishing I could sink into it, turn to stone? Why am I detecting fear and accusation and guilt in my eyes as I stare at my reflection in the shop window opposite? Why am I asking myself questions which twist hot screws in my chest, send icy shivers through the muscles of my shoulders and back? Why...? Oh, but I could stand here for the remainder of the night and throughout the day until to-morrow night without making the slightest amount of headway in my efforts to calm myself, forget what I've done, cease seeing her frightened face, and... God, I'm so sick of my stare—sick of my reflection's stare! I..."

My right arm twitched towards the sidewalk before I instructed it to do so; my fingers wrapped themselves about a hard object; my body lunged forward as my arm rose in a swift blur: the object struck the shop window—tumbled my reflection to the pavement, obliterated it! Then I was running towards the left, away from where I'd entered the alleyway, while surrounded by banks of mist which fitfully shifted, alternately separated and merged, in the suffused amber of the door lamps. At the end of the alleyway an opening in the wall, wide enough for one person at a time to enter, allowed me to pass onto a dim stairway which wound downwards at a steep angle between buildings barely over a yard apart. I became so preoccupied with negotiating the steps in the bad light—feeling for their edges with the tips of my shoes, clinging to the railings on both sides of me—that the girl's frightened face momentarily departed from my mind's eye...

All too soon, however, the first feeble light of dawn began to trickle down to my level between the sides of the buildings—illuminate my path—and I no longer needed to devote overmuch attention to the task of descending the stairs; which is to say that, the moment my attention was liberated from the necessity of seeing to it I failed to lose my balance, I again found myself recollecting the girl's distraught face, watching her stare at me as if I was a rabid animal. Likewise did I resume monologuing inwardly, as in: "What about the next time I'm alone with a girl, needful of assuaging stabs of desire in her embrace? The next time a girl's stretched out before me, extending her arms in my direction, flowing outward from within herself in sweet, trustful, loving surrender? The next time I surrender in kind—caress every succulent inch of her body, lick and nip her from her neck to her toes, thrust myself inside her, obtain the thirsted-for moment of release—only to find that, instead of calming myself, I've only engulfed myself in greater unrest? The next time every kiss, embrace, outpouring of procreation does nothing but intensify, fan into increasingly unendurable flames, the hunger which is already burning me up? Yes, I ask: what about the next time my unexpended energy accumulates to such a degree my judgment's impaired and I begin to wrongfully blame a girl for my inability to escape that energy, rid myself of myself? The next time I, despite strenuous efforts to the contrary, begin to ascribe sinister intentions to innocent behavior, distort the facts until a well-intentioned girl of kind disposition is imagined to be a heartless schemer bent on my destruction? The next time I find myself being incited to harm a girl by the desperation-fueled thought it will be circumstance-dictated retaliation, justified self-defense? What about it? Because, try as I might, I can't shake the feeling that it's by the slimmest of margins that I avoided directing my outburst upon the girl earlier—escaped hammering bruises into her body, dimming the light in her eyes! Nor can I answer for a continued ability to catch myself—turn away! at the last moment! How can I guarantee that the rage-sparking energy-accumulation won't be greater on the next occasion I'm with a girl?—guarantee that it won't get the better of me, compel me to commit the crime I dread committing?"

The stairway emerged from between the buildings and I found myself surrounded by a grassy hillside. I climbed over the railing on my right, reclined onto my back on the grass, ran my fingers through the cool dewy blades, wiped their wetness on my cheeks and forehead in an attempt to induce a measure of calm, counter the flarings in my nerves, quiet the din of my fevered thoughts. I simply wished to stare at the dark gray of the clouds—be unaware, indifferent, insensible. In vain! Disturbing reflections continued to leap into the forefront of my awareness, command my undivided attention: "No, it's no longer safe for me to be alone with a woman! I'm no longer able to anticipate in what manner the sight of a woman's lithe, submissive, aroused body will affect me; anticipate what impulses I might come under the influence of, to what degree the friction of our caresses will reverberate—accumulate! within me, stir whirlpools of audaciousness to life; to what degree tender foreplay will evolve—erupt! into fantasies of domination and violence which are being too convincingly play-acted; to what degree the boundary between pretense and earnestness will begin to blur, such that I lose the ability to determine which side of the boundary I'm on—start to believe the outburst-fueling concoctions of my fancy are the beginning and end of the possible world! God, and there's no doubting I've conjured forth far too many unfamiliar shades of feeling in too brief an interval, gone overboard in setting the stage for experimentation, exploration; no doubting I've thrown myself off-balance—undermined my self-possession, embraced the unknown! to a greater extent than I'm at present emotionally equipped to handle! Ha, and I emphatically inform myself that women must be avoided for as long as I'm in this state; but, at the same time, every spark in my nerves—surge in my veins, throb in my muscles! cries out for their company, and... Oh, if I avoid women—keep my own company, remain alone—then how am I to preoccupy the unrest which unremittingly whips and stings me? What am I to do?"

I could remain still no longer, rose to my feet; was straddling the railing, about to climb over it and resume descending the steps, when my attention was arrested by the view that the hillside—higher than the eastward portion of the city stretched out before me—afforded; by the glow of the sun, its disk still hidden, where the buildings met the sky; by the large number of illuminated windows in the residential buildings, the appearance of morning people—readily distinguishable from night denizens—on the sidewalks; whereupon I realized that it was later in the morning than I'd thought it was, and heard myself silently hiss: "How swiftly the hours of night have rushed towards dawn, stranded me in daylight! Yes, already the day-world intrudes, unkindly brushes the cloak of night aside; already the bright windows of breakfasting nine-to-fivers warn me the streets will shortly be clamorous with hurry-scurry, no place for me to be! God! How time mocks me as the hourglass runs out of sand! I've failed to expend myself—unite with a hint of inner quietude! in the interval allotted and will now go into the day more unsettled than I was when granted a leave from it hours ago when the night was in its beckoning infancy, bursting with possibility and promise! So much for promises! So much for hope, even! I'm cast into the streets at dawn with no idea when or where or how I'm going to manage to calm this hyper-stimulated body of mine!"

Not long thereafter I was walking through a narrow street at the end of which, between the parting of the buildings, the sun's orb was cresting the horizon; with its red-orange dancing on the undersides of the clouds above—shimmering on the windows to my left and right, flaring on the puddles at my feet! as knife-edged excitability continued to tighten—electrify, flay! my muscles, surge through—mount in, engorge! my veins, prod—stab at, sting! my nerves! I remember hearing myself exclaim: "I'm unable to so much as pause on a corner—stand still for five seconds! right now, let alone confine myself to a hotel room, lie on a bed, fall asleep; but, at the same time, I need to sleep—need to subdue my overactive senses, cease conversing with—unnerving! myself! and... God! Something's got to give! I..."

Part Three:
The Sanity-Swallowing
Infinity of Insomnia

I've now reached the end of the first month or so of my program/adventure of self-transformation; that is, the end of the period during which I was exclusively engaged in the pursuit of women. Perhaps it will be recalled that I stated at the onset of my adventure that I was going to attempt to present a number of examples of my associations with women in the order in which they occurred. In glancing over the proceeding pages in which I've provided the examples, I confess to being unable to determine if I've been successful in my attempt at order of occurrence. In fact, all I can say with certainty regarding order of occurrence is that the last-cited example—the bench-wielding episode—is in its proper place; in other words, that it's the episode which describes the manner in which I became convinced of the necessity of avoiding women, finding an alternate means of preoccupying myself.

As to the events which followed: for a week or two—perhaps longer—I was exclusively absorbed in seeking to disregard the warning I'd received regarding the dangers of continued associations with women at the same time that I was being forced, from within myself, to comply with it. I certainly couldn't put the memory of myself standing above the girl while holding the bench out of mind, cease feeling panic churn in my breast whenever I pictured her fear-constricted face; but, with each passing day, I was becoming more impatient with and resentful of the memory's hold upon me, doing my best to reason it out of existence, persuade myself it represented nothing more substantial than a temporary—impossible-to-be-repeated—aberration. Yes, it would have been very nice to conclude that the memory of smashing the vanity's mirror and frightening the girl depicted something shamelessly exaggerated, all but fabricated, by my drama-infatuated imagination!—very nice to conclude it was little more than a recollected dream, fiction!—very nice to disentangle myself from the restrictions it had imposed, resume pursuing women as previously!

After all, I'd been doing nothing but think about and thirst for and chase after women for over a month, spend every waking hour either in their company or anticipating the moment when I'd be so engaged; nothing but thrill to glimpse after glimpse of their lissome curves, flushed faces, excited eyes; nothing but inhale whiff after whiff of their fragrant hair, shiver-inducing perfume, sweat-slicked skin; nothing but grasp palmful after palmful of their crackling hair, cushiony breasts, satiny thighs; but hear snatch after snatch of their sultry purrs, fluttering sighs, delighted cries; but taste of honeysuckle lips—rose petal pink, surrender's nectar! and... Oh, I'd become so absorbed in pursuing (being captivated by, seeking to captivate) one randomly encountered woman after another that, as improbable—outright impossible—as such seems to me at this moment (as I write these words of retrospection), all thoughts of my spellbinding beauty had been driven from my awareness and all trace of her face had been erased from my mind's eye!

Ha! As I believe I made abundantly clear pages ago, my bewitching beauty was the one solely responsible for my having embarked upon my adventure—conceived of and commenced a rigorous program of self-discovery and -transformation—in the first place: having her slip from recollection, undergoing an interval of forgetfulness of her existence, was the last thing I'd expected to occur! I'm unable to recall at what point after embarking upon my adventure that her image had become unfocused, then dissolved altogether; at what point thoughts of her had ceased to monopolize my attention—ceased to exist. And as to whether I was ever under the impression that she'd submerged herself in my subconscious and was continuing to orchestrate my actions without my knowledge; as to whether I ever suspected I was little more than a puppet on strings which she was secretly operating; in other words, as to whether I ever thought of her obliquely, indirectly sensed her presence in the shadows... But why am I bothering with "as to whether" when I've no clear idea as to whether I did or not? And, as far as that goes, I'm certainly allowing myself to veer away from what I wish to say! All I can do is ask for the reader to make allowances, have patience; to understand that, during the transitional period which I'm seeking to describe here, several opposing impulses were competing for dominance within me and it's not an easy matter to detail the manner in which the said impulses clashed, merged, and resulted in a new variety of orientation.

So I'll again attempt to describe this transitional period: it's a given that I'd been ceaselessly hungering for, getting together with, women for the better part of a month—conducting emotional experiments in their company. It's also a given that I'd gone overboard in these emotional experiments—overboard in encouraging my hunger to smash through familiar boundaries, stray outside of the mitigating influence of reason—overboard in stoking my newfound appetite for fantasy- and obsession-enactment; yes, a given that I'd become possessed by an intensity of desire too volatile to risk sharing with others and, on account of such, been forced to abandon women as a means of preoccupying my-self. And, lastly, it's a given that I was unable to turn away from women overnight, forget they existed in the blink of an eye—no matter how compelling the reason to avoid them was; no matter how many times I found myself wincing at the recollection of my-self standing above the girl while lifting the bench higher, shud-dering at the lineaments of terror upon her face; no matter how many times I was overcome with distrust and fear of myself due to an all too clear perception of the way in which my senses, emo-tions, and thoughts were starting to become dangerously unsta-ble—overwhelm, disorient, enslave my better judgment—each time I sought to lose myself in another's arms. That's right, I was-n't able to forgo women—seemingly my sole source of distrac-tion, means of sticking to my program of self-transforma-tion—without a psychic wrestling match, close to maddening on-slaught of self-dividedness.

Listen: I'd sight a cute, slender, graceful, frolicsome woman on the sidewalk and begin running my eyes up and down her legs, undressing her in my imagination, while struggling to look away; begin following her while doing my best to turn in the opposite di-rection. In vain would I bite my lips, slap my cheeks, pinch my ribs in an effort to remind myself it was no longer safe to whet my appetite with lingering looks, even think of making her acquain-tance. In vain would I seek to snap out of the spell her face would be casting upon me—escape the magnetic pull of her swishing bouncing hair, laughing dancing curves, teasing inviting stride. I wouldn't be able to stop myself from following her into a café—stop myself from watching her fidget in her seat, cross and un-cross her legs, arch her back, toy with her hair; stop myself from feeling her inner electricity flow into and cross the space of air between us—ignite my nerves, sparkle in my veins, tense my muscles; stop myself from strolling towards her while envision-ing my fingers in the cascades of her hair, envisioning my lips pressed to hers, envisioning the brightening of her eyes during love-games: I'd almost already be hearing the stirring music of her coos, sighs and moans! But then the thought that I might be

capable of harming her would break into—scatter! my fanciful
hopes, freeze my feet to the floor—throb in my temples, jab
knives in my chest! Yes, imagine it: I'd be walking towards her,
unreservedly thrilling to the sheer beauty of everything about her,
wanting her more and more, and then—in an instant! terrified beyond measure, seeing mental pictures of bruised skin, splattered
blood, dead eyes! Only then would I be able to do what I'd wanted
to do since first glimpsing her: reverse direction, dash from her
presence.

Nor was the above-described sequence an infrequent occurrence: I couldn't begin to count the number of times I fled from
situations which were conducive to receptive facial expressions,
lingering eye-contact, inviting gesticulations—to surges of inner
recognition, captivation—unspoken agreements, sighs in unison,
gasps of delight; couldn't begin to count the number of times I
found myself strongly attracted to a woman—lingering in her
vicinity, preparing to approach her—only to flee on account of
various unpleasant things I thought I might—and didn't want to!
be brought to do to her; the number of times I fled even though I
was already aflush with longing, taut with anticipation; even
though I wanted nothing more than to unite with her hunger—expend myself, obtain some sleep!

And, also, what of the many instances of being alone in a hotel
room, with no temptation immediately before me, and informing
myself (again, without being able to stop) how easy it would be
to be strolling about at sunset, feeling expansive and free (comparatively speaking, that is) on account of the approach of night;
how easy it would be to stumble upon a dance club and lose sight
of the fact that it was unsafe for me to enter it and proceed to do
so—soon find myself standing near the dance floor, casting ap-
praisive glances among the revelers, searching for a vivacious
beauty; how easy it would be to spy such a beauty and commence
to admire her sly smile, sultry laugh-inflected voice, sleek legs;
yes, how easy it would be to drop my guard, persuade myself all
intimacy-trepidation was an illusion—that there was no reason
why I shouldn't make her acquaintance. And then I'd see it unfold

in my imagination: see myself approach the girl, smile, speak to her; see her flirtatiously run her fingers through her hair, lick her lips, thrust out her chest; see her soon drop the act, become earnest, train sweetness-brimming eyes upon me—eyes which would, as it were, wrap themselves around me, bring a warm flush to my cheeks, sizzle under the surface of my skin; yes, before long, would see us emerge from the club, advance down the sidewalk arm in arm... Perhaps we occasionally pause under a street lamp, delightedly examine each other's face in the light—exchange kisses, caresses, leg wrap-arounds; certainly we don't take too long to hail a cab, direct the driver to her place of residence; nor do we waste time once we're inside her apartment—we quickly remove our clothes, climb onto the bed, tighten our muscles in an ardent embrace. Listen: I'd be envisioning this encounter with such clarity that I'd begin to come under the influence of emotions identical to those which would be brought about by the actual experience; that's right, would be sighing, tingling, inward-thrilling in time to every movement of my fancied girl's lips, limbs, torso while alone in that hotel room! I wouldn't be able to stop watching the lithe grace of her body in the bright light while hearing the sheets rustle—hearing her coo, purr, cry out; no, wouldn't be able to stop the sequence from running its full course even though I'd begin to be afraid of the direction in which it was headed! And I hasten to remind the reader that I was merely imagining the encounter; that I was alone, without a single flesh and blood woman in sight! God, but how vivid—all-absorbing, immediate! it would be when I'd imagine myself becoming far too stimulated in far too short an interval—infused to bursting with intensity of desire, stung from the inside out... I suddenly need more than the woman's able to offer, am as if backed into a corner, screaming for an exit!—suddenly feel my fingernails dig into—cut! her skin! Then I'm watching her blood's red intermingle with her skin's white—hearing shrieks ricochet off the walls, feeling her arms and knees strike my belly, face!—watching my hands jerk towards her throat—hearing gurgling hisses, a sputtering wail!—feeling terror erupt in my chest, en-

velop me in searing flames! Unendurable! I wouldn't merely be
terrified in fancy, I'd be so in actuality! I'd be thrashing on the
hotel room bed—violently shaking my head! with a constricted
throat, throbbing temples, painfully hammering heart! I'd be unable not to leap to my feet, dash from the room, exit the hotel as
if fleeing a real enemy! I'd soon be pacing the streets in an effort
to erase the violence-pictures from my mind's eye, stop dread
from continuing to surge; in an effort to beat the excitement from
my body, transform the ability to sleep from a distant hope into an
actual situation: thus do unpleasant fancies become flesh, stir to
life in—bedevil! the living!

Yes, such imagination-enactments were a frequent occurrence:
no sooner would I remove myself from the presence of actual
women than hypothetical women would take their place and I'd
find myself experiencing the same emotional excesses, contemplating the same dangers, in the grip of the same fear! I couldn't
stop recollection-reliving the obsession-fueled practices which
had, at various points during the preceding month, succeeded in
repelling either my partner or myself or both of us: all the suffocation simulations, mock chokings, playacted slashings—murder
fantasies, death teases! which had convincingly seemed to approach actuality, resulted in authentic terror, and ultimately
birthed the episode with the bench: the horrible suggestion of myself being capable of harming an attractive, inoffensive, sweet-
dispositioned girl! That's right, over and over again I'd find
myself musing on how easy it is to be attracted to a trim profile,
abundant cascades of hair, pair of frolicsome eyes; how easy it is
to be compelled to convert glances into approaches—approaches
into playful flirt-ups—playful flirt-ups into lighthearted touching—lighthearted touching into strolls towards private places—
strolls towards private places into embraces-in-earnest—embraces-in-earnest into resurgent obsession—resurgent obsession
into impulses to commit violent acts! God! Over and over again
I'd swiftly arrive at the point at which my musings would be interrupted by unmanageable bursts of panic, and... Listen: if I'm re-

peating myself to such a degree now—as I write this—it's because I was ceaselessly repeating myself *then*!

My situation was that all the attention, desire, and energy that I'd been directing towards women was entrapped inside me, building up to such an extent I could hear it humming in my temples, feel it throbbing in my veins. And more: this entrapped energy was beginning to accelerate my senses, distort my perceptions, invest my imagination with an almost otherworldly vividness. I was, on account of the inability to acquire more than two or so hours of sleep at a time, steadily being propelled into a frenzied somnambulistic dreamworld where sensory impressions were hyper-intensified, carried far away from their original stimulus; as for instance, a casual glimpse of a dull gray patch of asphalt—with the patch of asphalt instantly acquiring a shimmering silver surface, twitching like agitated mercury, somehow sending icy hot flickers up and down my spine. And, so... Suffice to say it began to occur to me that a new interest—means of engaging my attention, preoccupying myself—was replacing the old. As they say: "When one door shuts, another opens." I'd been exiled from the caresses of women? relegated to a state of perceptual inflammation which was altering my emotions, dictating my thoughts, determining my actions? All right, then! This state of perceptual inflammation was, in itself, a means of preoccupying my attention—a new world to explore. From now on, instead of seeking to sleep—rope in my excitement with slumber—I'd do my best to prolong sleeplessness, propel myself into engrossing states of dreamy disorientation. In short, insomnia replaced women as the object of my yearnings—became my new means by which to conduct sensory and emotional experiments, map unfamiliar frames of mind, taste of the unknown.

When was it that I first became conscious of this new means of charting unaccustomed emotional territory, extending the boundaries of experience? I recall it distinctly: I was in the streets one morning when dawn's first light was evident above the building tops, at the hour when the street lamps have turned off but the full glare of day hasn't arrived yet. Previously, I would've been annoyed and alarmed at the approach of daylight; in this instance, though, I was noting the manner in which traces of darkness were lingering in sheltered corners and alleyways, clinging to the undersides of awnings, slithering among the litter in the gutters; was struck by the notion that these lingering shadows of nighttime were complimented by lingering nighttime emotions within myself—a continued sense of urgency, thrill, and wonder. Instead of arming myself against the arrival of daylight—pulling myself inward, erecting a psychic wall of detachment—I found myself rejoicing that insomnia had, as it were, enveloped me in a protective veil of bedazzlement. Yes, that's the morning when I first became aware that my half-conscious intimations of the previous week had crystallized into actuality—aware that insomnia was a means by which to perpetuate the depths of nighttime experience during daytime, safely inhabit a world of accelerated emotion even though I be surrounded by busybody superficiality. A breakthrough, indeed: how convenient to be able to pursue nighttime activities—familiarize myself with the unidentified impulses within me, travel the lengths of new avenues of desire—even though I be amidst those preoccupied with daytime routines. How convenient to be able to make use of the full twenty-four hours of a day, pursue obsession regardless of whether the sun was up. Mostly, what a relief to be able to challenge myself—surprise, shock, alter my personality—without being dependent upon encounters with women, having to fear placing them in danger.

To summarize: I'd been, for over a fortnight, divided between flinging myself at women and resisting the urge to do so; divided between dwelling upon them in thought and doing everything I could to avoid being conscious of them; but then the conflict between chasing and not chasing women had receded into the distance, ceased to exist, because I'd become absorbed in pursuing sensory and emotional intensity via insomnia.

Ha, and it wasn't long after becoming aware of my alteration of orientation that I began to loathe, as one does a mortal enemy, the faintest suggestion of the sensory sluggishness—mental dullness—general feeling of *ordinariness*—which afflicts one following a lengthy undisturbed sleep; that I began to find waking hours intolerable unless they were heightened by insomnia's way of wrapping a cape of fire about me from the inside out, transforming my body into a shimmering nerve-conflagration. Yes, indeed, insomnia was my new best friend—my savior—and we were getting acquainted! Insomnia was my radiant fresh-faced bride, and we were honeymooning! As for how long the honeymoon lasted... I'm not certain for how long I relished, reveled in, thrilled to the revelations of sleeplessness as if sleeplessness was my wild new lover; for how long willful sleep-deprivation was a playful, buoyant, invigorating roller coaster ride. All I can say is that, while this magical interval lasted, I was assuredly to be counted among the most content of men.

But all honeymoons—despite the initial loving enthusiasm of the participants—generally come to an end. In my case, my infatuation with insomnia evolved into a desperate love/hate entanglement that first became noticeable two or three days previous to the morning on which I glimpsed a dog in the rush hour crowd and began following him because I urgently needed to be distracted from myself, absorbed in the contemplation of anything that had nothing to do with the state of excessive excitement I was in. Yes, by the time that morning of following the dog arrived, the tone of my relationship with insomnia had changed: instead of being a place of refuge and safety, insomnia had become a means of endeavoring to threaten all sense of refuge and safety; during the week or so leading up to that morning I'd been doing my utmost, by means of insomnia, to determine what my physical and mental limits were. How enthralling it had been at first! I'd been stomping through the streets as if with an upraised fist, defying every smug face, pitying those imprisoned in daily routines— those whose manner of living I felt formed a barrier between them and the higher echelons of intensity. I'd been uninhibitedly savoring insomnia's calling cards: the fountain-bursts of tingles which would shoot up my spine, spread across my back in warm humming waves, momentarily engulf me in electric sighs that were like fainting without fainting, dreaming I was awake even though I was already awake; yes, the steadily mounting—seemingly inextinguishable—euphoria that would appear to acquire an existence of its own independent of my body, begin to suggest the idea it might be possible to surrender to it to such a degree I'd take leave of my flesh. I'd paused to examine my reflection in store windows, make visual assessments of my condition, a number of times: my face had been aglow with my state of stimulation, and I'd barely noticed its features; my strongest impression had been that my visage was losing its boundaries, vaporizing, passing into—becoming one and the same as—the charged brightness which surrounded me; I'd been stirred to bursting by thoughts of blazing like an undying star, being metamorphosed into the substance of the Gods. It was on account of such thoughts that my efforts to remain awake for as long as possible had been resumed with a vengeance, in a state of delirious anticipation I could barely keep abreast of.

Yes, during the days which immediately preceded and resulted in that morning when I began following the dog: I'd been bound and determined to induce a fury of delirium—soar to a height of frenzy—I'd never known before; that, but a week or so previously, I'd have balked at the thought of pursuing, considered dangerous—not to mention impossible—to reach. I'd been doing nothing short of seeking to increase the territory of my sanity, force myself to be capable of withstanding psychic extremes which were in all probability coming precariously close to being outright madness. And success had, indeed, seemed to crown my efforts: day and night had ceased to differ from one another, such that I no longer noted either dusk or dawn; the brief catnaps which, due to the unavoidable imposition of physical necessity, occasionally punctuated my wakefulness had begun to seem little different than intervals of open-eyed entrancement; my surroundings—no matter where I was or what I was doing—had begun to resemble images reflected on rippling water, a restlessly shifting—ever waxing and waning—mirage; I had virtually lost the ability to communicate with my fellow human beings due to the ever-widening gulf between my inner state of affairs and theirs. But perhaps I'd succeeded only too well: stabbing unrest infiltrated me so thoroughly that it began to strike me as being oppressive instead of liberating; increasingly, I felt as if I was being lured into a trap instead of indulging in emotional innovation—backed into corners instead of smashing through the restrictions of personality to places of free-flow. I was beginning to have second thoughts about the course I'd embarked upon, regret I'd happened upon insomnia as a means of engaging my attention, experimenting with and testing myself.

And on the morning of which I've been speaking, as the streets were beginning to clatter and screech with rush hour's first urgent stirrings: suddenly I was afraid of the amount of sensory stimulation within me instead of relishing it—aware that insomnia had turned on me! Yes, what had once been a state of soaring on wings of euphoria was now claustrophobic panic, actual physical distress! Listen: it was as if my nerves were electrical wires from which the insulation was being stripped until nothing remained to shield my flesh from their stinging scorch; as if these exposed wires of my nerves were brushing up against each other, crackling and flaring into a fierce blaze; as if this blaze was rushing towards the center of my chest, gathering itself into a fist-sized sphere of impatient energy; as if this sphere of energy was continuing to accumulate strength and density, wind itself tighter and tighter, with the aim of—I was certain of it! eventually shooting through me—annihilating consciousness! in an eruption of pain! Yes, insomnia, formerly a friend and savior, was now an enemy! The sphere of hostile energy was humming—buzzing, twitching! immediately below my breastbone, rapidly nearing the point at which it would engulf me in a violent seizure!

I remember shaking my head as my thoughts scattered into discontented colors, enraged light—became clashing edges of red and purple and green, squiggles of knife-blade silver, pulsations of sunlight-on-water glares; remember a loud "Crish! Crash!" as of glass being smashed! Glass? I was standing on the sidewalk, facing a building: the jagged remains of a broken window were clinging to the edges of an empty frame which was shifting in and out of focus in front of me, splintered glass was sparkling at my feet; a hot, throbbing, faintly numb sensation in my right hand drew my attention to it: my knuckles were bleeding. Then a man was angrily addressing me, seeking to seize me by the shoulders... Had I...? Ha! The truth suddenly flashed through—momentarily dispersed! my electrified daze: I had, indeed, smashed that window! I'd put my fist right through it—ha ha ha! And now that I comprehended what the civic-minded meddler was upset about, I wasn't going to stick around! I turned my back to him, defiantly raised my bleeding fist over my head, walked away with firm and purposeful step—was aware of relishing the astonished looks on the faces of those who'd paused to observe the spectacle, laughing at the alacrity with which they scooted aside to permit me to pass!

But no sooner did I turn the corner at the end of the block, place the smashing-of-the-window incident out of sight, than I realized I'd momentarily been distracted from the existence of the buzzing sphere of ill-intentioned energy inside me—obtained a respite from the fear it was inspiring—on account of that smashed window, and... God, I was alone with the angry sphere of energy again, fully—dangerously! conscious of the threat it posed, informing myself: "If I'm to mitigate the intensity of the disturbance inside me—escape the seizure it's building towards! I'll need to cease being directly aware of it again, provide myself with another mental cushion of distraction! I won't be able to maintain a semblance of emotional equilibrium unless I do so, and *quickly*!" And that's when I glimpsed the dog in the rush hour crowd—why I began following him...

And it wasn't easy for the dog, a medium-sized terrier, to weave his way through that crowd, dart between the scurrying legs which were constantly changing direction—he was coming precariously close to having his belly bruised by the pointed toes of shoes, paws crushed by heavy heels; frequently having to steer clear of the irregular to-and-fro of briefcases and purses, swirling folds of lengthy dresses and baggy pants. Nor was it easy for me to follow his smaller—far more agile, deft—body, keep pace with his four legs on my two. Now and then he'd disappear in the blur of hurried bodies, agitated clothing; whereupon renewed panic—at the thought of being robbed of my latest lifeline of distraction—would seize me, force me to hasten my step, shove my way through tight clusters of animated chatter—jostle, be jostled—in an effort to locate him. I'd be on the point of giving up the search, seeking a new anything to fasten my attention onto, when I'd find him sniffing the air, putting his nose to the pavement, lingering as if at pains to decipher a scent-riddle...

Yes, luckily for me the dog was busy keeping in touch with, remaining faithful to, his shadow-world of odors: the invisible vapor in the atmosphere—beyond the grasp of human senses, but as vivid to him as black on white—which was permeated with canine threats and trysts, territorial rights and romance. What use, after all, did he have for the world of the rush-hour throngs? To the degree that I was still capable of formulating thoughts concerning matters besides my unenviable frame of mind, I had the distinct impression that, to him, the pedestrians were nothing but a bunch of puppets, pointlessly animated toys; that, to him, they were merely mist, patterns of motion—fretful flittings of sunlight, a hallucination. He was only concerned with making the rounds of the communal lampposts, fire hydrants, and newspaper dispensers; with sniffing at each, reflecting a moment, leaving his reply, and proceeding to the next.

The dog failed to pause at the curb of an intersection, stepped into the street with an insufficient amount of caution. A delivery truck was unable to swerve at such short notice and the dog was instantly tumbling about underneath it, doing a frenetic loose-limbed dance. The truck passed over him, flicked his body at the grille of a low-slung car, where it became entangled in the metallic ribs. The car immediately jerked to the curb and stopped. The driver emerged, visibly annoyed, to knock the dead dog loose—tumble him into the gutter—with a rolled-up newspaper. "Stupid mongrel!" the driver muttered before getting back inside his car, speeding away...

I was standing at the curb; my thoughts, due to their having been deprived of their latest diversion, wasted little time in flaying me anew. Once again, I couldn't help but be uneasily aware of the barely containable amount of energy within me, inform myself I'd stupidly overstepped the line of my sensory limitations; that the act of whipping myself into an insomnia-fueled frenzy had been tantamount to nurturing a demon in my breast—a demon which had unexpectedly acquired a will and purpose of its own, become deaf to all injunctions to moderation, and was threatening to destroy me! And as if my rapidly rising panic was content to leave it at that! As if the thought of being abruptly deprived of sentience, transformed into a comatose thing, by a violent inner eruption didn't immediately follow, along with yet another vivid mental picture-sequence of how the fearful event would occur! First, there would be an uncommon amount of warmth in my fingers and toes; within instants, the warmth would accumulate until it was itching heat—heat which would creep towards, rapidly inundate the muscles of, my arms and legs; within a few more instants, the heat would intensify until it was a searing sensation strong enough to numb my limbs, lead me to believe they no longer belonged to me; I'd be unable to move—a helpless observer of my imminent demise! as the searing sensation would proceed to rush towards the center of my chest, gather itself into a fierce blaze; within seconds, the blaze in my chest would shoot up my neck, engulf the contents of my skull in a jolt of electricity: I wouldn't have time to scream; night would enclose me; I'd never awaken!

Such is the sequence—imagination-fit! which instantly crystallized in my mind's eye—further eroded my already fractional awareness of my surroundings, filled my head with a noise as of swarming bees, forced me to flinch at the nothingness of the air! God! I was vigorously shaking my head without caring—or possessed of the ability to care! if I made a spectacle of myself—was seeking to push the disturbing sequence out of consciousness, erase it! I only wanted to plunge into the crowd again, find another dog to follow, anything capable of diverting my attention from what lurked within me!

I was on the point of crossing the intersection, searching for salvational distraction in the next block; instead, for some reason, I about-faced and glanced down the length of sidewalk I'd already traveled. My gaze came to rest at the base of the lamppost where the dog had deposited his last communication—I could distinctly see his message, an amber puddle glimmering in the sunlight: the dog's last words, his posterity. And had the crowd no respect? His message was thoughtlessly being trodden upon by dozens of anonymous strangers, taken to other destinations, diluted to nothing! Ha! A voice was suddenly audible above the general din in my head, saying over and over, "...ashes to ashes, dust to dust, ashes to ashes, dust to..."—ha ha ha! I couldn't help laughing— I *had to* laugh in order to keep my mind off of, sway it from fixating upon, the state I was in! Because my ears were still humming, buzzing! Surges of dizziness, as palpable as gusts of wind, were shooting up my neck into my forehead and swirling there! I was earnestly afraid of fainting—falling! and was already visualizing myself (I couldn't stop myself from doing so!) lying inert on the pavement as a circle of bodies formed about me, drank in the spectacle—feasted on my misery! with parasitic eyes! And the pressure in my forehead was increasing, my temples were twitching! Was my skull contracting? God! I would, indeed, soon be lying on the sidewalk; would, indeed, soon be surrounded by human vultures; would, indeed, soon be a source of diversion for others while taking leave of this life!

I recall jerkily lunging towards a nearby newspaper dispenser, placing both palms squarely on top of it, leaning on them heavily; recall that, although it was a bright summer morning, veils of dark gray obscured my vision. The crowd continued to swish in all directions about me. I was expecting at any moment to be overcome by the state I was in but was nevertheless fighting to impose distance between myself and that state, drive a wedge of alertness between myself and disorientation, remain conscious. Perhaps I was shaking my head again, perhaps not; if so, I arrested this activity for long enough to, as it were, sneak a glance outside of my inner tumult, look at my surroundings straight on. It was when I did so that my attention was caught by a woman emerging from a cafe—not merely caught, but held! Ha! None too soon! Because if the said woman hadn't appeared at that critical instant and drawn my awareness away from myself—away from my inner disturbance-fueling fear! then who knows if I would've escaped succumbing to the blackout I dreaded?

Be that as it may: the moment I was aware of having noticed the woman I willed myself to remain focused upon her and began following her with my eyes. She'd exited the cafe at a point midway between myself and the dog's last communication and was strolling straight towards the latter, where it was trickling from the lamppost towards the center of the sidewalk. I noted the fact well and, as soon as my feet started to join my eyes in following her, caught myself wondering, "What if she were to, purely by chance, step into—absorb into the porosity of her soft-soled shoes—an important and much sought after portion of the dead dog's last communication, and be observed by another dog while doing so? What if this other dog, upon visiting the communication and perceiving it to be an infuriatingly indecipherable hint of its original message—far too diluted to be of any use—were to begin following her with the object of obtaining enough additional information to restore the communication's clarity, decode it? Yes, what if this dog—a large, black, strong dog with eyes of fire, an uncannily human cunning—were to begin following her? What if this black dog was a devoted denizen of the night, and disliked the day? What if, after he'd finished investigating the dead dog's last communication, he'd fully intended to return to his den and sleep until sunset? What if he was, because of the woman's unwitting interference, torn from his night-world like an infant from a nourishing breast—forced to follow her home? forced to, first, locate her place of residence and, thereafter, plan how to best lay siege to it? What if?"

Ha! The fantasy-speculations that insomnia-flayed mental faculties will resort to in their desperation to provide themselves with a framework and remain functional, forestall collapsing into form-lessness! I'd already lost the woman in the crowd, was walking in a mechanical manner with no idea or care of where I was headed; indeed, while nearly oblivious of the fact I was moving. Only one thought was uppermost in my mind: to rid myself of the specter of the stalking dog, replace it with another means of distraction! Useless thought! It wasn't as if I could afford, for a moment, to re-linquish a diversion from my condition once I'd latched onto it; wasn't as if I possessed the amount of emotional leeway which would allow me to be capable of choosing what variety of diver-sion suited me best!

So yes, despite myself: in my mind's eye I saw the dog shadow the woman for the whole of the morning, wait outside stores while she shopped, discover her place of residence when she returned home shortly after noon; saw him return to his den to pass the remainder of the day tossing and turning in an insuffi-cient approximation of sleep; saw him reemerge from his den at dusk to forage until past midnight (this summary of the dog's pre-liminary doings flashing through my head in seconds), and... Oh, saw the dog, at an hour when the greater part of the rush hour reg-ulars were fast asleep, on the sidewalk in front of the woman's place of residence: he's glancing at the windows of her building, seeking to ascertain if he's being observed at the same time that he's unable to fully care; after all, thoughts of exercising prudence and caution are rapidly being swept aside by the necessity of ob-taining the solution to the riddle of the communication that she's inadvertently pilfered. Yes, the dog knows the solution's in her apartment—that it's either still clinging to her shoes or been stomped into the carpet—so he nuzzles her building's entry door open without further hesitation, walks to the stairwell, ascends to her floor. Soon he's facing the door of her apartment, scraping it with a paw—asking to be admitted, demanding to be indulged. But no flicked-on light dispels the strip of darkness at the door's base; there's no indication of movement within...

And in my imagination I saw it far more vividly than I wished to, as in a crystal ball: how the dog would rear up on his hind legs, paw her door more insistently, fill the air with rasping sounds; how, at length, he'd succeed in waking the woman and she'd approach the door cautiously; how she'd peer through the peephole, call out, "Who is it?" and, upon neither seeing anyone nor receiving a reply, back away in fear. Yes, the dog can feel her standing a few feet away on her side of the door, scanning it with a worried look, hoping—against a rapidly rising tide of doubt—it's but one of her friends indulging in an ill-considered prank; and it doesn't take him long to become annoyed at the manner in which she, by means of her fear, is erecting a barrier between him and the crucial communication. Originally he'd borne the woman no ill will, considered her interference accidental and blameless; but now that she's chosen to expect the worst, insult him by supposing him intent upon harming her...

God! I could see it as clearly as if it was an actual event unfolding before my eyes: the dog wraps his jaws about the doorknob, grips it tightly with his teeth, commences to pull and grind in order to weaken the lock; then he releases, backs away, throws his full weight against the door: once, twice, three times. The door remains shut, however—a circumstance which only infuriates him further. He seizes the doorknob again, violently twists it back and forth while yanking downwards, and his persistence is rewarded—not only does he tear the doorknob off, he splinters the mechanism of the lock's bolt: a simple push is sufficient to swing the door inward, permit entry. And it's likely the dog would leave the woman unmolested—refrain from so much as darting her a hostile glance—if she were willing to comprehend why he's there, give him an opportunity to go about his business, search the carpet for the dead dog's last message, get a noseful of the scent in which it's contained; but she persists in assigning ignoble intentions to his actions, further bars his way with a rapid succession of high pitched screams. Yes, the dog hates her for her inability to understand; for her screams, frantic gesticulations, haphazard dash to the far side of the room; for the way she's behaving as if he's

Cerberus risen from Hades to carry her across the river Styx, lay her at Pluto's feet...

As I've indicated, I by no means wanted to follow this imagination-enactment any further—watch it speed towards a distressing conclusion! The choice, however, wasn't mine: the black dog's shaking, growling, gnashing his teeth—enraged enough for the force of it to throb in his temples, claw at his chest, paralyze his breath. He's momentarily forgotten why he's come to the woman's apartment, is only intent on eliminating her unkind opposition to his being there; and so quickly closes the distance between them, backs her into a corner. She hasn't a second in which to say a prayer as he springs at her throat, pulls her to the floor, tightens his jaws, abruptly twists his head: a crunching sound, as of bones being splintered, accompanies the move. Her body shudders from the neck down; her spasmodically kicking legs knock over a table and lamp, smash the light bulb, dust the corner with sparks. The dog tightens his hold upon her throat, violently shakes his head from side to side: he's fed up with the woman's pointless struggles, has lost all patience with the manner in which her body continues to jerk and twitch. He wants her to be motionless and silent sooner than soon...

God! The scattering silver of the woman's eyes, as the dog continues to crush her throat with his jaws, is becoming brighter—wilder; but then the light in her eyes abruptly fades as if severed from its source, switched off—steadily sinks into twin holes of darkness, finally disappears altogether: where has she gone? The sudden absence of vitality, cessation of life, appears to intrigue the dog: one moment bone-straining struggle, vein-bursting gasps; the next moment indifferent inanimation, sensationless death! No more muscular exertion, electrified nerves, expressiveness of face! Simply: *nothing!* The dog begins walking in slow circles about the body, observing and sniffing at every particular of its motionlessness as if unconvinced it won't manage to leap to its feet, resume screaming...

"No! No! No!" I heard myself emit in a smothered yell while shaking my head, desperately seeking to direct my gaze outside of

the distressing pictures in my mind's eye, discern my actual surroundings: I found myself in a trash bin cluttered alley, hemmed
in by windowless walls, surrounded by glaring sunlight. I continued shaking my head in further efforts to flush out the nightmare,
cease dwelling upon the stalking dog, consciously place myself in
my surroundings... Alas, I succeeded only too well: no sooner did
I manage to make myself realize that the black dog was a concoction of my imagination—distance myself from the fear his doings were inspiring—than my far more immediate fear of being
struck down by a violent inner convulsion (the one which had
birthed the dog to begin with) returned to flay me! No mercy! A
flickering shard of glass at my feet was thrusting piercing amber
light at my eyes, commencing to rapidly pulsate—suggest com-
bustion, explosions, annihilation! I dashed from the alley, resumed
searching for a means by which to divert my attention from myself...

* * * * *

Yes, my infatuation with insomnia had clearly gotten out of
hand: throughout that day which began with me shoving my fist
through a window and following the medium-sized dog and
glimpsing the woman and watching (in my imagination) the large
black dog slay her in her apartment—throughout that day, I say,
and those which followed hard upon it (I, for the life of me, have
no idea how many)... It was as if I was being relentlessly hunted
from the inside out—routed from every possible place of psychic
concealment, driven from my inner hibernation dens! not merely
by randomly encountered people and objects, but by every perceptible portion of myself—the sparks in my nerves, twitches on
the surface of my skin! Ha! Did the extremities of emotion that I
was being assailed by actually belong to me? Who was experiencing them?

Yes, my pursuit of insomnia-altered perceptions had leaped
clear of the boundaries of the manageable and I was (for God only
knows how many days) being repeatedly backed into sanity-
threatening situations which would suddenly vanish—allow me

the barest amount of the mental respite I needed to continue to comprehend the concept of reason—at the very moment when I firmly believed my awareness was on the point of permanent collapse. That's right, no sooner would my predatory delusions succeed in persuading me they were the beginning and end of the apprehensible world than they'd dissolve, return to the shadowy realms from which they'd sprung; no sooner would I have every reason to believe I was about to pass rationality's point of no return than I'd be given a new lease on sanity! I was rapidly exchanging one brush with madness for another...

* * * * *

I'd make bold to descend stairs to the underground transit in an effort to escape the brightness and bustle—slashing light, shrieking noise—of the day; ha, would be staggering as if in the most advanced stage of inebriation which still permitted of walking, grasping the handrails like lifelines: the stairway before me would immediately become a revolving tunnel, dizzily spin. I'd become distrustful of my feet, be afraid to take another step, stand frozen amidst waves of nausea—fight to maintain my balance— while pondering my next move. And the longer I'd stand there the more susceptible I'd become to my imagination's cruelty: I'd envision myself falling forwards, repeatedly striking my head on the edges of the steps as I tumbled down them like a limp doll; then would see my body lying at the base of the stairs—see myself clutching my head with quivering hands, unseeingly rolling my eyes—while aware of an aching pulsation in my ears, about my temples: a steadily stronger and louder throb-throb of pain. Yes, I'd both see and feel it: how a great number of the commuters would forget about their destinations, put their haste on hold, for long enough to form a circle of feasting eyes about me; how I'd want to sink into the concrete—melt, dissolve, disappear! so as to escape the stares, hulking bodies!—the unfriendly forms bending over me, looming between my eyes and the lights on the ceiling! I'd feel them twitching with excitement—titillation, thrill! while crowding closer and closer, smothering me with the proximity of their aroused parasitism, bringing me to the point of a scream with the palpability of their thirst for tragedy and death! That's right, I'd see it while standing immobile—dizzy, nauseous! at the top of the stairs; see myself lying seriously injured—in shock! at the base of the stairs; feel myself becoming close to oblivious of my pounding head on account of a far more vivid and unpleasant awareness of *them*: the starved scavengers shamelessly feeding on, intoxicating themselves with, my misery!—quickening their sluggish pulses with each gloating glance, sucking glare! I'd be pressing my palms tight against my eyes in order to blot out the sight of them, submerge everything in darkness, while silently shrieking, "Vultures! Vampires! What do you want with me? How can you just stand there, and... God, please! Just go away! Leave me be!" continuing, "Oh, there has to be an exit from this unendurable nightmare! Has to be a region of insensibility inside me that I can run to!—a place the nightmare can't penetrate, summon me back to awareness from! Has to be!"

Yes, I'd be seeing, feeling, hearing all of it with stomach-wrenching vividness while still standing at the top of the stairs—clasping the handrail for dear life! and... At some point my actual (as opposed to imagined) situation would begin to get the better of me: I'd start to lose ground in the real struggle to maintain my balance at the top of those stairs, find it increasingly difficult to keep my dizziness at bay; start to sway—totter! as if standing on a disintegrating cliff edge giving way to open air, an unavoidable plunge! But then, at the point when I'd authentically despair of resisting the vertigo; when I'd be firmly convinced I'd shortly be feeling my head strike the stairs in actuality—already be flinching against anticipated bursts of pain: that's when I'd notice that the stairway's overhead lights were cluttering the air with bright shattered glass patterns which resembled spider webs and (Ha ha, will I be believed?) suddenly focus upon this one detail to the exclusion of all else. That's right, I'd instantly forget to be dizzy—actually cease to be so—while listening to myself inquire, "The tenants of the webs—the spiders: where are they?" Ha! No sooner thought than done! I'd glance ceilingwards, carefully examine the crisscrossing strands of light, detect they were quivering, experience stabs of dread on account of believing the quiverings to be telltale signs of the spiders—spiders still invisible on account of being within the glare of the lights. But they wouldn't be invisible for long! They'd soon be crawling down those strands of light, emerging from the glare, with the aim of attacking me! And I'd see the spiders as clearly as, moments previously, I'd seen myself tumbling down the stairs: see them descending by the dozens, alighting upon my face, shoulders, arms! Spiders! Ugly bloated abdomens, sinister arched legs, unblinking bloodthirsty eyes! And the horrible stillness which clings to them, hovers about all their movements: a spine-freezing distillation of unadulterated hate! Yes, the sensation—soul-numbing terror! of a spider's eight icily deliberative needle like legs on one's skin! Soon they'd be wrapping my face in their ghastly silk! Soon my cheeks would be blotched, swelling, oozing from their bites! Soon their venom would be turning my vitals into black glue, fetid slime!

God! I'd locate my feet again, all right, and use them! I'd dash up those steps, return to the open air, walk fast and far without looking back! I never failed to believe I'd barely escaped those stairways alive...

* * * * *

But how can I hope to come close to communicating the enthralling heights and frightful depths of "No sleep!"? Insomnia's a seizure of the emotions—possession of inclination! which is stronger than love, hatred, terror, pride, joy; more addictive than opium, alcohol, the curves—volatile arousal! of a beautiful woman's body! Insomnia's the irresistible urge to tempt the Gorgon's stare, rehearse annihilation! And if one fails to approach insomnia with a respectful amount of caution; if one rashly fuels insomnia until it acquires a life of its own which is separate from and rebellious towards one's rational will, intent upon permanently eroding it...

* * * * *

I'd be sitting in a cafe, attempting to calm myself (or at least mimic the outward appearance of being calm), when I'd begin to notice the particulars of the layout—arrangement of tables, presence of decorative objects, location of exits—which dictated where people were able to walk. It never made any difference what these particulars were: they existed for the sole purpose of unnerving me, bringing on surges of panic, putting me to flight. Nor did these movement-dictating particulars of layout need to be within the café: features outside, visible through the windows, could likewise be used by my cursed imagination to unnerve me: there was no refuge from this inner predator that I'd recklessly awakened!

For instance, at one of these cafes I was seated close to the front window, such that my left shoulder was brushing against it. The window faced the bright white parallel lines of a busy crosswalk on the avenue outside; in other words, streams of people were periodically, as the traffic light permitted, walking both away from and straight towards me. From the corner of my eye I'd notice the people who were walking towards me; I'd see them on the other side of the street, as they were beginning to cross it; I'd perceive them as animated blurs, energetic concentrations of haze, which were becoming larger and larger—increasingly sharp of outline, resolved of purpose—the closer they came to me until they'd seem to be looming up against the window, towering above me—bigger than life, blatantly menacing! God! They'd continue walking forwards and crash through the glass—fall onto me! at any moment! They'd be shrieking—out of their senses, violent! with the agony of their broken-glass-inflicted wounds, and—in their fury! would kick, pummel, claw at random—perhaps seize me by the throat, pound my head against the floor! But then, at the last moment (just when it would seem impossible for them to not crash through the window, be upon me), they'd abruptly turn either left or right and continue down the sidewalk, vanish from sight!

Ha! It was all a trick, malicious false-alarm game! Yes, these unconscionable souls were indulging in a charade at my expense—one calculated to freeze me with apprehension, bring me to the point of bracing for a vicious attack; calculated to get me to recoil from mirages, flinch at the empty air, summon energy for nothing; calculated to fill me to bursting with—leave me alone with! a gnawing grating accumulation of intensity as they turned away, laughed! And this charade of theirs was succeeding only too well, systematically robbing me of what little inner stability I still possessed! And they were continuing to approach the window, one batch after another; continuing to tease, prompt, bait me; continuing to stimulate, hammer at, frazzle my reflexes with their nefarious game!

But, people? No, they weren't people at all! They were automated mannequins, robots! They were metallic bodies with blank faces, powerful swinging arms, stamping feet! They were pieces of heavy machinery which were being guided by remote control—pointed straight at me! by unseen enemies of mine in a building on the other side of the street! Yes, any moment now those at the controls would judge that the period of bluffing—thoroughly unsettling me, working me up to the point of needing to scream! was over; and then they'd see to it that those robots crashed through the window for real! *Smash!* The air would be thick with splintered glass whirling—darting, stinging! like infuriated bees! I'd be on the floor with one of the robots on top of me! It's unfeeling arms and legs would be pounding the life out of me, reducing my body to an oozing heap of mutilated flesh!

"No!" I silently yelled while leaping from my seat, knocking over a chair on my way out the door: I couldn't have been more alarmed than if the beams of light from the overhead lamps were scalpels peeling away the uppermost layers of my skin! Nor did being in the open air bring me any ease of mind! An inner tone of ominousness—as of a postponed, but still inevitable, seizure—continued to afflict me; so that the feel of the breeze against my flushed skin was irritating friction, a steady electric crackle as of hair standing on end; so that the slightest shift in brightness—flicker-flash of light! was a splash of burning liquid in my eyes; so that the unceasing drone of the city was a pounding throb-

throb—shrieking din! in my ears; so that all movement was a maddening barrage of jerking angles, zigzagging lines, spinning perspectives! No, the nerve-fireworks wouldn't abate: the assault of needle stabs, blinding glares, grating noise—endless crish! clatter! clack! if anything, was becoming more unrelenting, more insistent! And so: retreat, retreat! I'd not lose consciousness, but would flee from it—withdraw from the surface of awareness (the unendurable sense-frenzy which the perceptible world had become) and arrive at an abode of stillness, sheltered eddy of silence, in my depths. That's right, I'd suddenly vanish from in front of my senses, slip outside of memory, for unspecified intervals (seconds? minutes? the duration of how many strides down the sidewalk?) and then just as suddenly reappear, be assailed anew by the hysterical eruptivity of my surroundings. And then I'd vanish again, reappear again, over and over; so that the cityscape was present one moment, absent the next; so that one moment I was hyper-aware, the next a blank to myself. And, as usual, I've no idea for how long I thus walked the streets...

*   *   *   *   *

Yes, it's when one's been driven to the far side of frenzy—become hyper-impressionable, painfully sensitive, electrifyingly alert—that one's most susceptible to lapses of awareness, prone to temporarily taking leave of one's perceptions: this is because one *must* have a means of relieving the tension, attaining a respite. The mechanism by which one passes from a barely endurable degree of alertness into a state of unrecollected oblivion is purely on the order of an automatic response, blind impulse of self-preservation: one isn't able to choose to do so; one, quite simply, *must* do so, and it happens of its own accord. And one can do no more than begin to hint at the full spectrum of the possible sensational and emotive variations within oneself; no more than begin to vaguely delineate the inner travel routes of one's mood-shifts, impulses, and obsessions...

*   *   *   *   *

I was, in an instance that I recall only too well, forced by the flow of traffic to come to a stop at the curb of an intersection. Instantly, I was irritated at the fact that my feet weren't moving; that the scenery about me wasn't shifting; that the shop fronts, lampposts, newspaper dispensers, and kiosks were stationary; that my view of the sky was locked in place! It wasn't merely that I found being compelled to stand still and wait annoying, it was that I was afraid of doing so! Because the fact is that the deceptively passive act of waiting is sometimes a threat on one's life! Why? For the simple reason that waiting is inactivity, and therefore an opportunity to think! opportunity for one's imagination to run riot! opportunity for dangerous impulses to appear from out of nowhere—nourish themselves on next to nothing! and frighten one into leaping from the frying pan into the fire! Because the moment I became idle and was no longer absorbed in the energy-dissipating activity of walking—the attention-dissipating activity of keeping track of ever-changing surroundings: that's the moment when the deadly impulse to fixate—my all too familiar nemesis! again took possession of me! Listen: my eyes were irresistibly drawn to the traffic light which was suspended above the intersection; yes, I began to focus upon the bright green disk which was allowing vehicles to continue to bar my way, silently repeat, "...green, green, green..." to myself. And it didn't take long for the green disk to become the sole focal point of my awareness, such that all else in my field of vision acquired the quality of a mist enshrouded dream; didn't take long for unease to seize my body from the inside out, paralyze my muscles with tension!

God! I couldn't so much as avert my eyes, glance to the side or at the sidewalk, let alone pivot my head or about face, attempt to flee! I was helpless to prevent myself from continuing to come under the influence of the spell—stare at the insidiously whispering glaring green of the disk, hear the oppressive incantation of "...green, green, green..."! Why was my will refusing to obey me? Why was I disengaged from my instinct for self-preservation—unable to mentally demand its assistance, emotionally seize ahold of it? Ha! I was separated from my will by an inner barrier of intensity! The churning unrest within me (which, I repeat, had been deprived of the moderating influence of physical activity by my having come to a standstill) had, itself, chosen to fixate upon the green disk and I had no say in the matter! If, perchance, this act of fixating was detrimental to my well-being, such was immaterial: the separate entity of energy within me had its own agenda from which consideration for my welfare was excluded!

And the green disk was becoming brighter, whispering louder; the passing—swirling! seconds of unease-accelerated time were hissing like angry breezes trapped in corners, racing up and down high walls, whirling litter into piercing clatters, yelps! Another moment or two swished by—another surge or two of panic crested in my chest—another... God, the green of the disk was advancing towards—thrusting itself at! me, swallowing the sky and the streets and the motion of the vehicles and the chatter of the passersby—engulfing the periphery of my vision and all points within it, as good as blazing inside my head! And I was still staring at it! Yes, my gaze had been turned inward: I was fixated upon—to the exclusion of all else! a sphere of glaring green which seemed to be located between and slightly above my eyes, an inch or so behind them! I was gazing upon it with such single-minded intentness it was as if I exchanging places with it, becoming one and the same! And more: the sphere of green was collapsing upon itself—shrinking! and still holding fast to my attention! I was blind to all but a fiery green dot—receding pin point! of light within me, being drawn into an ever tightening vortex of hyper-concentration! My ensnared awareness was collapsing upon itself, on the point of... Listen: it was as if I'd become a whirlpool which was being drawn into its own funnel, in danger of erupting as a result of being crammed into a space too small to contain it! Soon... Oh, I couldn't help but envision myself being engulfed in a white hot flash of blinding white!

Yes, the thought of perishing in a violent inner implosion had returned to haunt me and I was unable to prevent it from rapidly acquiring the urgency of an immediate danger, bringing on ungovernable bursts of fear! What would I not do, against my better judgment, to escape such an attack? Ha! Did the luxury of "better judgment" exist? There was only terror-stoked impulse, like that of leaping from a cliff to escape a brush fire's flames! Listen: I swear the yellow dividing line in the center of the street suddenly pierced and dispersed the green in my head, became as vivid as if it were a strip of gold; swear it was yanking at me like a strong sucking wind! That's right, a pronounced urge to fling myself in front of the speeding vehicles abruptly broke the spell of the blazing dot in my head, and I was seeing—all but feeling! the result of such an act in advance: thigh bones shattered by a bumper, body mangled by the base of an engine, head crushed by a tire!

"No! For God's sake, no!" I was shaking my head, slapping my cheeks; was... I jerked myself away from the insidiously beckoning dividing line, began racing down the sidewalk! No sooner was I running than the sidewalk began to tilt!—its build-ing-bordered side was rising, higher and higher! Ha! I'd slide off the sidewalk—into the street of speeding traffic! and be slaugh-tered all the same! Yes, the curb was the edge of a cliff, gaping abyss—as the rock falls! and I was on the point of an irreversible plummet, certain death! I was going over the edge—over! I...

"Enough! Enough!" I ducked into a large supermarket, where I thought I'd be safe: wrong, all wrong! The brightness of the overhead lights was shimmering about me—as good as shouting, shrieking! Gleaming silver asterisks were dancing on the linoleum—leaping, whirling! Rivulets of mercury—disturbed, er-ratic, squiggly! were flicking like snake's tongues in my eyes! *I went blind!* I kid you not: I was suddenly stumbling about in one of the food aisles, fumblingly grasping for shelves, stacks of boxes—any tangible object, means of seeing via touch! But noth-ing I touched was recognizable; touch itself was unrecognizable—my hands couldn't detect anything outside them on account of the tingling within them! I was doubly blind, adrift in an inner whirl of nerves! As a consequence, my panic redoubled—all but oblit-erated thinking, nearly smothered all sense of space and time...

Listen: it was during those moments of blindness, both eye-sight- and touch-wise, and of rising panic, such that I could barely manage to believe I still inhabited my skin... It seemed to me—in a rapid-fire inner picture-sequence—that I sank to my knees and was raking at the floor with my nails as my body shook, pitched to and fro; that I then fell onto my side, writhed onto my back, flopped about like a fish on dry land; that I was attempting to yell but only managing a stifled gurgle, smothered half-choke; and, further, that grating—derisive, hateful! hyena-like laughter was suddenly audible above, below, all about me; and that the ap-pearance of the laughter coincided with a jolt of physically painful fear—caused my muscles to sharply contract, entrapped my breath in my throat! And still the laughter persisted—became louder, more contemptuous in tone! At the same time, the atmos-phere became oppressively humid—nearly as dense as water and almost as difficult to breathe, such that thoughts of imminent suf-focation sprang into my head! "Escape! Escape!" came a piercing hiss of a whisper from somewhere; upon hearing the whisper, I was blinking my eyes as furiously as I could—seeking to remind them of their existence, goad them into piercing the blinding sil-ver! And, following what seemed like minutes (which were in all probability seconds) of blinking, the blinding silver did, indeed, begin to subside; yes, the magnitude of the illumination of the overhead lights was lessening, approaching normalcy—again out-lining the objects about me, ceasing to drown them in glares...

No sooner did I emerge from what I can only consider some sort of seizure—no sooner did the laughter lapse into silence, was I able to discern my surroundings—than a new circumstance con-trived to disturb me: I found myself standing near the cash regis-ters, at a fair distance from the aisle where I'd taken leave of myself, and... How panic surged as a result of realizing I'd crossed from one side of the supermarket to the other while struck blind in eyesight, hearing, and touch! I neither had any idea what had transpired during that interval of blindness nor any way of know-ing how long it had lasted! Had I really and truly been down on the floor? It seemed far from likely, given that I'd opened my eyes to find myself standing squarely on my two feet without anyone so much as darting me a quizzical glance (for the store, a further surprise to me, was quite crowded), but... Listen: the thought that I was capable of strolling several dozen yards—apparently without bumping into objects or appearing questionable to others—not only while deprived of all conscious apprehension of my surroundings, but while consumed by excessive inner disturbance—hearing hallucinated laughter, in thrall to a frightful whirl of mental pictures! was far from being a comforting one! Why? Because it implied that I could do *anything* while thus beleaguered and blinded by turmoil, and have no idea what I'd done or not done once the turmoil departed!

God! I fled from the store in a vain attempt to escape from *them*: those moments of blindness and questionable memory which immediately began to pursue me in the form of a triumphantly mocking voice, attacking me thus: "Yes, yes! We, the lost moments, saw it all! And we, the lost moments, bear witness against you! against your right to dwell upon the face of the earth in the guise of a rational being! against your right to sleep peacefully at night, unmolested by the proddings of conscience! Because, yes! You *were* down on your hands and knees in an aisle of that store like a four-legged animal, clawing at the linoleum as if possessed, shivering like one racked by stabbing chills! You *were* thereafter on your back, thrashing about like a dog struck by a car, making gurgling sounds! And the laughter? That was a gathering of spectators laughing at you! Yes, every employee and customer in the store: they were laughing at you up to the point when they saw you regaining your feet while blinking your eyes—at which point, they immediately fell silent and resumed their business as if nothing untoward had occurred! And so, yes! Once you'd recovered your senses after having returned to your feet, you had no means of confirming either that you'd been down on the floor or that others had crowded close and watched! That's right, you're utterly ignorant as to what happened! But we, the lost moments, know everything! And we, the lost moments, sentence you! We sentence you to unending sleeplessness, blood-curdling waking dreams in the solitude of night! We sentence you to unalleviated disorientation, self-doubt and -loathing, and thirstings for death!"

"No! No! No!" I screamed in reply: in reply to what? Accusations being leveled against me by a voice in my head? an auditory hallucination? God! I was frightened in earnest, as only one bedeviled by a maliciously taunting inner voice can be! Because, try as I might to reason the damning voice of the lost moments out of existence, chalk it up to the usual handiwork of an overactive imagination, I continued to hear its incessant, "Yes, yes! We, the lost moments, saw...! We, the lost moments, sentence...!" I redoubled my pace—was dash-walking the streets again, abruptly turning every which way in as haphazard a fashion as possible— in an effort to... What? Outrun the voice, hide from the voice? Ha! I simply wished to exhaust and distract myself to the extent that I'd no longer be able to listen to the voice, even though it might still be there...

And yes, I realize the situation begs the following questions: what was so special about the moments of temporary blindness I'd undergone in the supermarket? What distinguished them from the other instances in which I'd momentarily disappeared from before my senses, been incapable of recollecting what had transpired during the disappearance? Why had they alone acquired a voice, commenced to pursue and unsettle me? I've an idea: perhaps the moments of absence that I'd endured in the supermarket were representative of all the lapses of consciousness I'd undergone during my recent exertions? representative of all the activities I'd pursued while under the influence of such lapses of consciousness? representative of all the uneasy self-questioning I'd indulged in after emerging from such lapses of consciousness? Yes, perhaps the case was that all of the lost moments of the past two or so months were speaking to me via this voice, and that this voice had merely been triggered—in the manner of one more drop causing the cup to overflow—by the moments of waking blackout I'd experienced in the supermarket: certainly it was so.

To return: I continued to walk fast for I've no idea how long or far before finally realizing that the voice of the lost moments had subsided, and I was beginning to hear my own voice in its place, as in: "If only I could decelerate—reverse! this anti-sleep metamorphosis I'm undergoing; if only... I mean, what I need to do is somehow distance myself from the tumult within me—attain to an emotional vantage point outside of it, obtain the ability to contrast it with other shades of feeling and frames of mind!—yes, somehow locate myself—determine where I am! in the greater scheme of all possible feeling! Because I no longer know what I'm doing, how I can continue to continue... God! This nonstop somnambulistic frenzy that's acquired a momentum of its own independent of my will, such that it's threatening to wholly engulf me! I admit it: I've taken on more than I can handle, overstepped the boundaries of the bearable! I've naively—presumptuously, hubristically! fanned sparks into flames which have become a roaring conflagration that's determined to continue to blaze and devour until nothing remains! Yes, I've foolishly teased a sleeping beast into awakening—doubly foolishly opened the door of his pen, goaded him into chasing me! and now I'm backed into a corner, cursing my rashness, regretting the day I spied him dozing on the other side of that fence! And it's too late to undo the insult, make amends, pacify the beast: he's poised for the final pounce, I can already all but feel his fangs in my throat! Oh, if only I could awaken from *everything*: from this entire unending waking dream which can no longer be traced to a beginning; which, as far as my despairing reason can determine, seems to be nothing less than a self-perpetuating wave of delirium that will continue to exist for its own sake long after it's tumbled me under itself, drowned me!"

My thoughts were interrupted—splintered into senseless noise—by a sensation as of being wound tight in a cape of stinging sparkles from the inside out. I began out-and-out running with no ability to wonder either if I'd win the race or what it was that I was racing against...

Sometime later I found myself—I've no recollection of entering it—in a vast lobby, or waiting area. Was I in a train station? a municipal building? a hotel? Not that it matters. What does matter is that a comely girl was seated directly across from me, not three yards away, and that we were already attractionally in tension with one another—becoming emotionally aligned, sympathetically demonstrative—and that I was uneasy on account of it, seeking to glance askance, halt the proceedings, forget she was there. But, my God! She was so healthy, fresh, forthright, cheerful! She had such charm hovering about her eyes, and a beautiful smile! And, moreover, how long had it been since I'd permitted myself to notice such a girl, much less relish the sight? How long had it been since I'd been capable of gazing outside of my inner state of affairs at the face of another, discerning the features thereupon? And, as far as that goes, I was quite frankly amazed—in equal proportion to my uneasiness—that I was managing to linger upon and arouse the beauty of the girl in that lobby; do so while not merely still in thrall to insomnia-flayed senses but while seemingly at the height of my thralldom! How explain such a thing? How was it possible for me to suddenly find myself, as it were, in an oasis of sensory normalcy; whereby I was not only able to clearly read the feelings upon an attractive girl's face but commence a hint-session with her? How was it possible for me to be perceiving and sustaining the build-up of interest between us while, at the same time, never being allowed to stop believing I was in now-constant danger of being permanently overwhelmed by inner strain?

But it hardly matters how it was possible for me to be gazing at and steadily bringing a look of trustful anticipation into the girl's face while seemingly far too aflail inside to make such an activity possible: what does matter is that my uneasiness concerning this activity soon began to gain the upper hand, shove aside any pleasing sentiments I was experiencing. But I still couldn't stop undressing and caressing the girl with my eyes; stop flicking my eyes towards her feet, sliding them up her calves and thighs, dwelling upon the flat firmness of her stomach, pert cream of her breasts, satin smoothness of her throat; stop admiring the slender symmetry of her arms, tumbling darkness of her hair, clear oval of her face, smiling dartings of her increasingly bold eyes!

And why did she have to be wearing that dress? An aquamarine one-piece with indigo polka dots, clinging to and highlighting her delectable curves; sleeveless, low at the neckline, high at the hemline: little different than if she'd wound a gossamer veil about herself as snugly as she could! The steady rise and fall of her chest in breath-rhythm, every quiver of her torso, the twitches of her muscles under her skin were plainly—unnervingly! visible, steadily bringing on pulsations of dizziness-inducing excitement, inner coiled-upness which was like claustrophobia threatening to explode!

No, I couldn't remain there—I had to break the attraction-inundation spell, put a stop to the mutual magnetism, flee! Her eyes were shimmering with awakening insistence: I could feel their electric look setting off wave after wave of charged friction inside me, infiltrating my depths, awakening God only knows what unpredictable impulses! Yes, I had to put a stop to it, get out of there! I could feel my fingers commencing to relinquish their grip of the edge of my seat, uncurl; I was convinced the muscles of my legs were tensing, preparing themselves for the weight of my body; convinced I'd soon be rising from my seat, standing; I'm almost positive I was beginning to tear my eyes away from the troubling glow of hers. But, before I could follow through on these intended maneuvers, she (as if sensing my imminent escape) suddenly scooted to the edge of her seat, grasped her knees with her hands, and smiled at me as her eyes brightened, widened—God! immobilized me with terror, brought about an instance of delusion as unexpected as it was unimaginable! Because I swear (and sincerely wonder if I'll be believed) that at the instant when she brought all of her blithe, kind, generous self into that smile and made a gift of it to me (while her body language was overflowing with trustful benignity) that it occurred to me—from out of nowhere, with no supporting evidence whatsoever! that her eyes were those of a *hag*! Yes, the remainder of her face and the whole of her body indisputably revealed her to be a young, healthy, fresh-complexioned girl; but...

God! How was it possible for me to come under the influence of such a fancy? possible for me to be instantly frozen to the chair with dread, convinced that the business of the girl's eyes being those of a hag was the truth? A more persuasive example couldn't possibly be advanced in support of the contention that my imagination had taken up arms against me, was twisting every potentially beneficial and undoubtedly beautiful thing into its opposite, sucking at my vitality like the most relentless of parasites, bound and determined on my destruction! Listen: I couldn't stop informing myself that the girl's satiny skin, luxuriant hair, and lovely smile were nothing but a masquerade; that she was an ancient crone who'd assumed the form of a girl in the full flowering of her radiant charm—clothed herself in fluid curves, ingenuous grace, expressions of kindness—for the purpose of ensnaring the unwary, smothering the living in a deadly embrace of death and decay; that the impersonation was undetectable except for the eyes, undisguised eyes!

And what of the girl's eyes? Was there anything about them which warranted the conviction that they were those of a hag? Of course not! Certainly they were as clear, guileless, and awash with sweetness as ever; but I was blind to such loveliness; or, rather, my cursed imagination was thrusting its duplicitous self between me and the truth! Because in place of the girl's eyes (which, mind you, I didn't want to look at and was struggling to tear my eyes away from) was a pair of lusterless, stagnant, festering sores of dead darkness! Yes, those twin terrible holes: cancerous corrosion was glowing with a sickly hue in them; grasping hate was writhing in the depths of them; an unslakable thirst for the health and vitality of others was leaping forth from them! God! I couldn't help but construct, from the evidence of the eyes, the lineaments of the hag's actual appearance beneath the deceptive cloak of her youthful mask: she was—oh, horrible! a wheezing, drooling, twisted-boned, crookbacked, malevolently grinning thing with flesh like the fungus-ravaged bark of a rotting oak! Yes, that's what the delectable costume of young beauty concealed; that's what belonged to the eyes; that's why terror was tightening its fist in the center of my chest, squeezing the breath out of me, causing me to gasp for my life!

Oh, why was I unable to leap to my feet—run! even though every fiber of my being was straining to do so? What was the source of this nefarious fixation-impulse's strength? How was it able to override the muscle-straining directives of raw reflex? Ha! Ask a deer transfixed by headlights the same question! Because I was, indeed, a transfixed deer!

How escape? The deadness of the hag eyes was exerting a palpable gravitational pull on my nerves, infecting them with an unfamiliar sensation of sluggishness. What was happening? And then it occurred to me that the hag had commenced feeding; that she'd tapped into my nerves, pulled them into her rapacious magnetic field, and was rapidly draining them of their spark and verve; that soon they'd be dead wires with no trace of electricity remaining! God! I was attempting—as a last resort! to contract my throat, summon my voice, make some sort of sound—even if but a whisper! Anything to exercise my will in some capacity, bring about a contrary movement of my attention; anything to disentangle my eyes from the hag eyes, break the hold of the nerve-grip, escape the devouring fixation's clutches! But I attempted in vain!

Yes, the infectious black deadness in the eyes which (I've got to say it again so as to seek to keep my facts straight) belonged to someone I'd encountered, inadvertently linked glances with, in some waiting area somewhere shortly after I'd been taunted by a voice in my head! My imagination was certainly outdoing itself—scaling new heights of infamy! in its efforts to propel me towards mental collapse! And then—oh, no! the blackness of the hag eyes became an advancing mouth—huge yawning vortex of a mouth! and I thought I heard a voice intone: "Please God, I beg of you! No more!"

No, there's nothing easygoing and conciliatory about an insomnia-ignited imagination; systematic sleep-deprivation isn't a lighthearted game to play, superficial recreational thrills; isn't for the emotionally pusillanimous, faint of heart, weak of will! One can boast of having taken journey after journey to the furthest boundaries of sanity and back, insist one's unsurpassed at sensory and psychic exploration, suppose one's in command of the situation and able to resume normal life whenever one wishes; but such conceit overlooks the fact that, with each successive journey, one's personality is further exposed to and infiltrated by a tone of insistence—purposefulness of impulse, concentration of obsession—with a life and mind of its own over which one's will holds increasingly smaller amounts of influence. And then, before one knows it, this tone of insistence is forcing one to devote every waking hour to indulging it, maintaining the fiery euphoria of sleeplessness-inundated senses; yes, before one knows it, night spins into day and day into night until the days and nights and weekends and weekdays blur into nonstop dreaminess, excitation, overload! Ha! Time ceases to be measured in hours, minutes, seconds; in their place are crests of elation, troughs of fear—mood-swirl, imagination-spin! Yes, duration is measured by the twirlings of one's waking-dream kaleidoscope; sensory fire-storms mark off the difference between yesterday and today, an hour ago and now; with the result that, following weeks of insomnia-saturation, one loses the ability to cross-reference one's inner world to one's outer surroundings, place oneself in a time-sequence, understand why one's feeling the way one is. Disorientation, panic, and terror succeed in displacing wonderment, delight, and euphoria: one arrives at a dangerously unstable condition of mental and physical overinvolvement and is no longer able to determine what brought it about—a fact which multiplies one's vulnerability and distress, further enmeshes one in explosive formlessness, flings one two steps backwards into fear with each attempt to step out of it. One's no longer able to trace one's predicament back to its origin: no longer able to understand that one's condition of instability has been brought about by a deliberate cultivation of sleeplessness; that the deliberate cultivation of sleeplessness originated with the desire to experience new sensations; that the desire to experience new sensations was born of a specific incident which disrupted the established routine of one's life, and hinted at other things. That's right, one's forgotten where one came from; one's lost sight of, been cut off from, the original source of one's obsession; and is therefore in danger of being stranded in one's present condition of overload, entrapped in a frenzy with no rhyme or reason to it. And time's precious: with each passing moment the frenzy gains ground, further distances one from the likelihood of emerging from it; with each passing moment madness comes closer to being a fact instead of merely a fear! What one *must* do is contrive to climb outside of the frenzy, reimpose the distinction between it and other modes of feeling: only by so doing will one make it possible for one's memory to return, rescue one from the impending breakdown of rationality...

In my case, the manner in which my memory resurfaced and yanked me clear of the ever-gathering frenzy, and attendant sanity-straining delusions, is as follows: at the moment when the girl's eyes—that is, the hag eyes! became an advancing black mouth I was engulfed in a distinctly stronger burst of terror which was separate from the uniform state of terror that I was already in—yes, engulfed in a burst of terror which was strong enough to, as it were, tear me away from—break the immediate hold of—the stimulus responsible for it. Listen: suddenly it was as if I was watching someone else stare at the advancing black mouth instead of staring at it myself; suddenly it was as if there was a bubble expanding in my head and as if I—my sensory net, consciousness—was located on the perimeter of it; yes, as if this bubble soon expanded to the extent that its dimensions greatly exceeded those of my body, with the result that I was suspended in the air above my body, looking down at myself... Then I was watching my body abruptly stand, erratically stumble-dash from the waiting area as if being shoved by invisible hands; watching... Oh, vision vanished: I was again on automatic pilot, propelling myself while deprived of conscious apprehension of my surroundings...

To continue detailing the manner in which my memory returned: at some point—following I neither know how long of an interval nor how much distance traveled—I became aware of being able to sense the heaving of my breath in my chest, the impact of my feet striking the pavement, the swiftness of my stride; yes, became aware of returning to my body, reassuming the boundary of flesh, reattuning myself to the flow of blood and sparkle of nerves; especially, became aware that I was looking through my eyes again: I was gazing upon a clearly delineated street scene—sunlight dappled tree lined sidewalk, cheerful breeze-flapped awnings, colorful fruit heaped on stands outside stores. Ha, no sooner did I find myself in these benign surroundings—so opposite in tone from the sight I'd fled—than I was infuriated that I'd been subjected to the amount of terror the black mouth eyes had inspired; than I was amazed that I'd been subjected to such terror, vowing it wouldn't happen again; than I was demanding, "Why this terror? How this terror? Who...?" And it was then—at the moment of inquiring, "Who...?"—that the locked door of my memory finally swung open; that I began to comprehend—reassemble the sequence of—how I'd been brought to a dangerously unstable state.

I can't claim that this business of remembering was a deliberate imposition of will on my part: it was far more on the order of a fortuitous panic reaction, a mental reflex; it was almost by accident that I intoned, "Who...?," happened upon the one word— magic incantation—which would cause the salvational time-sequence of the past several months to stream forth. Who, indeed! Riveting composure, charged serenity—an idea was metamorphosing into a picture: raven black hair, a flawless complexion— the picture was coming into sharper focus: disarmingly enigmatic face, dark wellspring eyes—yes! a smile which was at once a sarcastic jibe and tender caress, glance which was a stomach-twisting—breath-stealing! stab of euphoric dread, fearful bliss! In short, my bewitching beauty!

The impact of recognizing who it was in my memory's picture tore me from direct awareness of my surroundings again. Joy, instead of duress, blinded me to the direction in which I was strolling; tears of liberation wet my eyes, distorted my vision, made the blocks swirl by like indistinct patterns on a moving collage; absorption in inner tingles of triumph rendered me incapable of keeping track of time. All I know is that I was in a park, on my hands and knees on grass, when my eyesight again returned to me: my bewitching beauty! Yes! She who I'd first glimpsed in that cafe so many experiences—personality alterations! ago; an uncountable amount of emotional roller coaster rides—revelatory mood-shifts, inner depth-charges! ago: it seemed like years ago! I'd lived an untold amount of lives since then, acquired and discarded enough selves to seemingly suffice for a dozen lifetimes! Yes! It was on account of my spellbinding beauty—and nothing else! that I'd flung myself towards the unknown, striven to surpass my most uninhibited dreams; that I'd been fooled into believing there were no limits as to how far I could stoke my hunger for self-transformation; that I'd permitted myself to become precariously immersed in sensory acceleration!

Yes, I was memory-flipping through—making a rapid mental summary of—the weeks of hallucination-engendering unrest I'd endured, and everything made sense again: in recalling my bedeviling beauty to mind I'd recalled the rationale for my behavior, reobtained the ability to understand the motives governing my actions—dispersed the formlessness surrounding my feelings, rescued myself from irreversible immersion in the sensory frenzy which had engulfed me. How fortunate I was to have remembered her! Not a moment too soon...

I seated myself on the lawn—was running my fingers through, refreshing my sense of touch via, the coolness of the soft blades of grass, soothing my harried eyes and overwrought nerves with the sight of the bounties of nature before me: the ivy which all but smothered the lampposts, flower beds which bordered the walkways, pines which gracefully swayed against the backdrop of a cloudless afternoon sky. How beautiful the park was, and how wonderful it was that I was able to perceive and enjoy such beauty! God, was I (to repeat myself) grateful that I'd managed to recollect my spellbinding beauty! How comforting to know that the extraordinary state of excitement I'd been in had had a purpose; that my unaccustomed activities could be traced to a cause; that I was a rational being after all!

I took a deep breath and reclined onto my back—extended my arms and legs, flexed my shoulders, twisted my torso from side to side, wrung out my body with a thorough stretch. The tension departed from my muscles, delicious languor began to course through me in gentle waves. I shut my eyes against the brightness of the sun, began to recollect the circumstances of my first encounter with my raven-tressed beauty—how, purely by chance, I'd strolled up an inconspicuous side street and seen her in the window of a cafe. In remembering this first meeting, I felt all over again how I'd become weak in my knees, momentarily lost my balance, staggered—been robbed of my ability to willfully direct myself; yes, how a sliver of steel in the immediate vicinity of an electromagnet wouldn't be more helpless to prevent itself from being instantly affixed to the magnet's surface than I'd been to stop myself from being yanked in the direction of the cafe, grabbing at its door, half-dashing inside. My mental and emotional memories were equally clear—I both saw and felt the sequence unfolding as if it was occurring at that moment, as I lay on the grass: how, once inside the cafe, I'd been at an utter loss as to what to do with myself, unable to about-face and flee at the same instant I was seized with panic—rapidly accelerating fear! due to not being able to hide from she who was turning me inside out—summoning my innermost recesses to the surface! simply by being in the room!

But no sooner were the recollected details of our first encounter flashing before my mind's eye than I became impatient with them; after all, there was no need to dwell upon every particular: as, for instance, how I'd been terrified of falling to the floor before miraculously mustering enough self-control to advance to the bar, order a cup of tea; and how I'd then happened to raise my eyes from the counter, meet her glance in the mirror behind the bar. No, no need to dwell either upon the electric—searing! moments during which our eyes had merged in the mirror or upon the barely endurable minutes which had followed when, after somehow managing to remain on my feet for long enough to sit at the nearest table, I'd stared straight at the tabletop—sought to empty my head of awareness! while knowing her eyes were upon me, feeling them delve into my secret places! No, no need to dredge up every last detail: the bottom line was that I'd, during that first encounter, experienced a violent psychic seizure—spasm of inner rearrangement—which had offered itself as the proof that there existed sides of myself I knew nothing about. And as I'd struggled with all of my will to maintain some semblance of equilibrium while under the influence of the seizure, I'd begun to further understand that I was becoming acquainted with, being forcibly introduced to, these unknown sides of myself. Yes, I'd felt my accustomed world slipping from my grasp; felt my life-plan being altered to suit someone else, that someone else being an embodiment of the unfamiliar impulses which had begun to stir within me. That's right, I'd been unveiled to myself; my hidden depths had been flung open to the light of day; the secret urgings which lurked within me had fought their way into my foremost thoughts. I'd been abruptly pointed in the direction of a new life of heightened emotion—intensified experience—which had terrified and attracted me in equal measure, confused as much as it had enlightened me. Yes, that's what had occurred during that first encounter, the effect my spellbinding beauty had had on me: I remembered it so vividly that a surge of stunned awe swept through me as I continued to lie on my back, attempt to relax!

I remained on the lawn with my eyes closed as my memory continued to reveal its contents, provide me with the explanation of my behavior; as it continued to populate my mind's eye with pictures, preoccupy my nervous system with responses to those pictures—oh, began to inundate my nerves with prickly tingles, dispel the languor which had had precious little time to reacquaint me with what it is to experience sighs of relief! I recollected how, in the days immediately following that first encounter, I'd been uncommonly restless—incapable of spending a waking hour sitting still, much less at work—on account of the fact that my bewitching beauty's visage had ceaselessly blazed in my fevered head; fact that her innate inaccessibility had haunted me day and night; fact that she'd unabatedly maintained me at the highest pitch of endurable excitement! How long had this condition of arousal lasted? Ha! I passed over with impatience—dismissed as something I couldn't quite believe—the fact that, in those days immediately following the encounter in the cafe, I'd had no idea who she was or where she lived and had therefore been without the means of seeing her again and sustaining the state I was in. Yes, I but briefly dwelled upon—as something of no conse- quence—the fact that the spell had, indeed, worn off; that she had, indeed, faded from focus and ceased to dwell within me; that I had, indeed, succumbed to indifference and boredom and been forced to abandon belief in the promise she'd held out to me...

I opened my eyes—was compelled to glance towards the warmest portion of the sky, stare straight at the sun; at the same time, I dug my fingers into the grass, tore at its roots with my nails, tensed the muscles of my arms and legs, made my body rigid. I shut my eyes again, momentarily entrapped the sun's brightness within my eyelids, and began to recall the details of my second encounter with my spellbinding beauty: how, when sitting in my car at a red light, I'd become aware of being uneasy for an unidentifiable reason; how I'd soon realized I was being closely scrutinized by the eyes of another, and had turned to meet and challenge the gaze; how I'd then found myself to be looking straight into the eyes of she whose mere presence was a frighten- ing illumination of the hidden aspects of myself. God! The shock of recognition—revelatory eruption! which had as good as set the interior of the car ablaze, so that I was instantly as if sitting on an electric seat—seeing, feeling, hearing nothing but hot hissing blinding white! And a minute or so thereafter: no sooner had the first wave of the shock passed and allowed me to regain, to a small degree, the use of my senses than I'd seen the car in which she was riding advance and come to a stop in the middle of the next block—seen her exit the car, stroll to a residential building, turn a key in its door, vanish within! And no, I hadn't been capable of fully realizing the consequences of this discovery at the moment of making it; but by the following day... Oh, there'd been no es- caping the fact I'd discovered my bewitching beauty's place of residence; fact I now had the means of seeing her again, and therefore would—for a certainty, whether I wished to or not—see her again...

I was instantly sitting bolt upright; all trace of the lassitude which had all too briefly inundated and soothed my body, provided a sorely needed counterpoint to the tension which had been threatening to overwhelm me, was gone. My vision was beginning to blur; I was losing the ability to appreciate, calm myself via the sight of, the lush greenery and cheerful flower beds which surrounded me... "And so," I was telling myself, "the moment I discovered my spellbinding beauty's dwelling-place—possessed the means of seeing her again, realized seeing her again was as inescapable as the body I inhabit—all which had been hinted at during our first encounter became an actual situation, bewildering reality! Ha! The cafe episode? It had been nothing but a practice run, hint of authentic fixation; nothing but the fledgling stirrings of an obsession which had lacked the means of perpetuating itself—a brief eruption from and rapid return to an easily manageable state of dormancy. But the instant she acquired an address, became an unavoidable event in my future, instead of merely being an apparition which had briefly appeared only to vanish without a trace: that was the instant that I'd been abducted from my accustomed manner of life in earnest, irrevocably severed from the ability to cling to a vestige of familiar routine; that I'd been invaded to the roots of my consciousness, displaced in every nerve, by a fully developed obsession which had acknowledged the existence of nothing besides itself; yes, that I'd been transported into an all-absorbing struggle to maintain some small semblance of self-possession in the face of an apparently limitless onslaught of intensity which was as captivating as it was fearful!"

An uncomfortable accumulation of restlessness compelled me to rise from the lawn, commence pacing about the park—up and down its brick walkways, around and around its circular flower beds—while continuing to recollect: "Yes, my accustomed manner of life and all that linked me to it—friendships, occupation, habits, inclinations—had ceased to exist from the moment my beguiling beauty reappeared, revealed her place of residence; nothing had existed but the present—the present became an unending inner convulsion fueled by her alone! Yes, her portrait had taken up residence in my mind's eye instantaneously—invaded my dreams, erased my memory! She'd altered the very physiology of my body—regulated the tension of my muscles, flow of my blood, charge of my nerves! She'd splintered, shuffled, merged my moods—whirled me into an unfamiliar emotional kaleidoscope, brought about patterns of feeling I'd never known before!"

I continued to pace, was but vaguely aware of and no longer being soothed in any degree by the verdancy about me. Ha! Obviously a different person had been lying on the lawn a few minutes ago, and had had chimerical thoughts—laughably misinformed hopes! of calming down, being granted an extended leave of absence from inner unrest! Oh, as if such unrest as was afflicting me could be cast off—stripped from my nerves, erased from my feelings! in an instant, simply because I wished it so! "But," I was shaking my head, "to have been ensnared—depth-stirred! to that extent so quickly; to have been robbed of my emotional directional sense—uprooted from inner substantiality! as if I was an awkward schoolboy in love for the first time! God! It wasn't as if I'd never been affected by, courted, and won over a beautiful woman; wasn't as if I wasn't accustomed to random fling-frolics galore! Ha! Previous to crossing paths with my bewitching beauty, I'd been of the opinion that there were no further surprises in store for me in the female department; that women were no longer capable of stirring me without my consent; that equilibrium-loss in the name of love was something only the inexperienced, or plain stupid and weak, were prone to; but then she'd turned everything upside down in an instant, flung me headlong into the maelstrom of the very sort of all-enslaving love I'd always chalked up to mythology! Yes, she'd transformed fantasy into actuality, swirled the temporal into limitlessness, flung the gates of emotional possibility wider than the spaces between the stars in the sky! Suddenly, no manner of behavior had been walled about by caution! Suddenly, nothing had been taboo!"

The park had virtually vanished from my awareness—was little more than a background of patterns which swished about me, blurred and ran together like dyes in water, too rapidly to be recognizable as I continued to pace. "God," I persisted in reflecting, "for myself to have been that susceptible—unknowingly vulnerable, ripe for a psychic assault! Ha! Some subconscious, and highly influential, part of me must have wanted it to happen, thirsted for it; yes, this part of me must have been waiting for an unfathomable beauty to appear, sever me from the life I'd grown accustomed to! I ask: had my life become too easy, lapsed into being characterized more by evasiveness than affirmation? Had I been arrogantly seeking to oversimplify matters?—steadily shutting myself off from authentic experience, enmeshing myself in an emotionally censored vacuum of an existence? Had unfounded self-assurance and conceit crept into my life-routine, befouled it with falsity, created a barrier between myself and inner growth? Yes, as a matter of fact (now that I stare straight at it in retrospect), I probably did have my life down a trifle too pat; probably did go too far in my efforts to deprive it of surprises; probably did tighten the bit on my feelings to the extent an inner revolt was inevitable! It was simple: cultivate a persona of competent dependability at the workplace, present an exterior of unquestioning devotion to the interests of the company, while secretly regarding the office with cynical contempt; yes, dupe my associates into believing I was all work and no play to better conceal the fact I respected very little connected with my place of employment. Ha ha, and then make the interminable playacting bearable—wash away the dividedness within me—with the kindly smiles, amusing patter, and ardent embraces of obliging women; that's right, alleviate the soul-numbing boredom of my occupation by squeezing as many brief intimacies as possible into the evenings and weekends. No, not love: whirlwind pick-ups, one night infatuations, easily relinquished fancies. Yes, it had been too easy: accumulate investment income, relieve the tedium in any cute slender's arms. So yes, it's all but certain that I'd been thirsting for a change—yearning for a shock, lasting arousal. But—God! for that shock to have been as disorienting and explosive as it was! For myself to have been torn from all I was familiar with in an eye-blink, seized by the roots of my consciousness, propelled into the frenzy of rationality-usurping—memory-warping! sensory excitation that I'm still in! Yes, frenzy that I'm still in! Ha! Who was I kidding? Did I really believe I'd extricated myself from it, returned to manageable emotions? It persists at as high a fever pitch as ever at this moment!"

I came to a standstill without comprehending why; then realized my glance had been caught by a wet patch on the walkway; that the silvery glare of the sunlight upon the wet patch was darting at my eyes, threatening to further unsettle me! I jerked my head away, resumed pacing with a vengeance; the glare, however, lingered in my eyes—superimposed itself upon my surroundings, erased them! "Right now," I continued, "as I turn here, dart there—pace in circles! I'm... God, I'll never again be the person I was before watching my psyche-displacing beauty emerge from that car, show me where she lived! No, will never be able to retrace my innumerable personality alterations back to my former life, reobtain the casual cynicism of the innocent days! And what does it matter that, but a short while ago, I managed to tear my eyes away from those black mouth eyes, break the hold of that one waking nightmare, escape from that one accumulation of reason-endangering stress? Ha! As if freeing myself from the stranglehold of one instance of self-destructive fixation is tantamount to disengaging myself from the condition of inner tumult which serves as the breeding ground for such experiences; as if recollecting she who's responsible for my having become enmeshed in inner tumult is the same as ceasing to be enmeshed in inner tumult! And the fact that I, once again, comprehend that my seizure-inducing beauty is the reason why I was propelled into the unmitigated disorientation of these past weeks by no means dispels the uncertainty which gnaws at my peace of mind the moment I begin to wonder what actually occurred during the periods when I was the most excitement-prone; by no means sheds light on the missing intervals—blind spots! which maliciously bait and taunt—laugh in the face of! my memory! My sorry situation is that the more I seek to probe these instances of memory erasure in order to settle myself down, the more I'm prodded into unsettledness on account of failing to do so; that the more I seek to encircle this state I'm in with reason, vanquish it with understanding, the more I'm drawn into it! God! I who once, in the pre-upheaval days, was the epitome of tact and discretion; who was unsurpassed at the art of charming women out of their clothes, minimizing the interval between first words in public and first caresses in private, now find myself... Oh, I hesitate to say it—balk at permitting myself to be aware of it! but the fact of the matter is that, if I were to venture to approach a woman at this moment with the object of spending the night with her, then that night would never materialize because my hair-trigger imagination—this state I'm in! would immediately thrust itself between us, sabotage my attempts to make my desire apparent! That's right, distrustful thoughts—wild suspicions, bursts of paranoia! would appear from out of nowhere, be concocted from nothing, and further draw me into the overwrought condition I'm already in—flay me alive with panic, plunge everything into blind fear! Dare I say it, admit it? It's only too true: the only means by which I'd be able to make contact with a woman at this moment, do away with the barrier between us, would be force—the imagination-counteracting straightforwardness of violence! But—God! I'm not a brawler! I'm not a rapist! I'm not a killer! No! No! No!"

There was a reflecting pool in the park, of which I'd been aware from the moment of commencing to pace, that I'd been taking care to avoid. Why had I avoided it? Because the surface of its water was an accumulation-point for the omnipresent brightness of that day and such a sight possessed the means of robbing me of my newly reobtained ability to organize my thoughts. Yes, I'd remained at a safe distance from the reflecting pool, not allowed it to become more than a faint sparkle, ineffectual hint of a threat, on the periphery of my vision. But now that disturbing thoughts had chosen, without my consent, to claim my attention; now that I was being forced to realize that my memory—my prematurely-supposed-to-be-completely-recovered memory! was littered with

highly questionable blind spots, as well as reflect upon my condition of tumult-generated isolation; yes, now that I couldn't help
but inform myself of the distressing implications of the state of
unending unsettledness I was in—help but understand others
might be unsafe in my presence... God, fear swept through me—
caused my head to reel, eyesight to dim, legs to shake! to such a
degree that I was placed in immediate need of a place to sit, and...
Oh, where did my misgivings concerning the reflecting pool go
when I needed them the most? I'll tell you where they went: the
fear shoved them into the background, deprived me of their guid-
ance! I needed to sit, and so... Suffice to say I found myself seated
on one of the benches which flanked the reflecting pool, regardless of the fact it was the last thing I'd wanted to do! Nor did it
take long for me to succumb to the reflecting pool's spell: its
shimmering water was rippling inside my eyes in instants, scrambling my thoughts! I did my best to preserve order in my thinking,
probe the troubling gaps in my memory in a rational manner—
determine what had occurred during the intervals of blindness
which punctuated the past several weeks—but the fear was rising
within me; the disruptive water was feeding the fear...

But I do remember wondering: "Have I transgressed? tres-
passed upon the domain of the forbidden? aroused the wrath of
spirits which won't cease hounding me until I've been dispos-
sessed of the ability to conjure forth coherent thoughts, comprehend the meaning of words? Have I? And will I ever know,
beyond a doubt, if I've transgressed or not? In other words, what
does transgression consist of? What's the full meaning of this state
of disturbance I'm in? What are the implications of being in a
frame of mind which one has good reason to believe could be conducive to the perpetration of unspeakable acts? And even if one
successfully refrains from the perpetration of such acts: is the fact
that one's in a condition of mind and emotion which is a possible
breeding ground for such acts, in itself, a criminal act? is allowing oneself to succumb to a sensory frenzy such as I'm in an instance of moral irresponsibility grave enough to constitute a
criminal act? Which is to say: isn't one duty-bound to avoid,

rather than encourage, states of inner imbalance which could place others in danger, even if one's able to refrain from dispensing harm? Or are these speculations nothing but more self-flagellation courtesy of my ever-active imagination? Ha! Even the certainty of knowing myself to be a sinner deserving of punishment is denied me! I've been deprived of penitent paths to follow, authorities to heed, guidelines to abide by! What I'd not give to be openly sentenced to a program of severe atonement, have my punishment and the reason for it clearly spelled out! But, then again, why this dwelling upon transgression and expiation? Why am I so willing to assume I'm deserving of punishment, almost eager to accuse myself? God! The not knowing what I did or didn't do, what I'm doing or failing to do, who I am or who I'm not! This ceaseless self-repetition, spinning in circles which do nothing but proliferate the vagueness and fear!"

I'd risen from the bench and was standing at the edge of the reflecting pool. I don't recall rising from the bench, have no idea how I'd come to be precariously perched on the golden hued tiling which bordered the pool, such that the toes of my shoes extended out over the rhythmically lapping—insidiously whispering! water; nor do I know how I was managing to maintain my balance while being all but blinded by the scintillant silver witchery of that water, desperately endeavoring to cling to comprehensible thought—proceed with my self-interrogation! as in: "What have I done, I crave to know? The possibilities are innumerable: anything or nothing untoward could have transpired in the full view of—involved! others during these past few excitation-inundated weeks! In theory—for all I know—the said time-frame could have sped by in innocent self-absorption, been nothing more than a self-contained state of sensory and imaginative arousal which has neither been apparent to others nor emerged into the realm of action—never been apparent to anyone but myself. Yes, perhaps the truth is that, throughout my ordeal, I've been an inoffensive dreamer: far too preoccupied with my condition of inner bedazzlement—in thrall to the nonstop fireworks of my nerves, parade of phantasmagoria in my fancy—to pose a threat to anyone but

myself? But why, then—given the implication of self-harm, danger of loss of my sanity—this condition of imagination-absorption
in the first place? Has it been brought on by activities which will
not bear the scrutiny of objective consciousness?—dare not reveal themselves to the light of reason? Yes, I ask: has the purpose
of this state of perceptual overload—electrified somnambulism—
imagination-absorption (whatever one chooses to label it)—been
to serve as a veil, shield me from the knowledge of having committed socially unacceptable acts? acts which, were I to become
cognizant of them in the face of indisputable evidence, would immediately plunge me into mental collapse? God! It could be true:
anything—savage assaults, out-and-out rape, murder itself! could
have been forced into the background by unrelieved sense-accel-
eration, imagination-immersion; enshrouded in intervals of wak-
ing-blackout, memory-gap! Yes, kinkiness could have become
cruelty—sex could have become violence—rough stuff could
have become homicide! Oh, has that been the case? Have I become absorbed in an insomnia-fueled frenzy not on account of—
as I've presented it to myself—a wish to explore seldom-traveled
extremes of sensation, but on account of needing to erect a barrier
between my conscience and myself? I swear I don't know!"

I continued standing at the edge of the pool, staring at the
water on the surface of which my reflection shivered—shook!
among the blazing patches of sunlight which now advanced, now
receded; on the surface of which my reflection alternately vanished and reappeared in swirls of clashing glares—flickers of
dread! as I sought to remain afloat in my thoughts, prevent them
from being scrambled—obliterated! by the steadily stronger currents of unsettledness inside me; yes, as I persisted in my efforts
to account for the doubts devouring my peace of mind! "Oh," I recall insisting, "the state I've been in—all but unendurable level of
tension I haven't ceased to be under the influence of for God only
knows how long! *is* highly suspect: how likely is it that I was able
to remain self-contained at all times? What's the probability of
having always succeeded in concealing my condition from the in-
quisitive glances—probing stares! of others? having always re-

mained inaccessible to those who might be inclined to seek to stir me up, force an eruption? Yes, in an unguarded moment—despite myself: did my inner state of affairs perhaps creep into—flash from! my eyes? perhaps animate—lend a tone of commanding audacity to! my gestures? perhaps envelop me in a captivating— irresistible! aura of freedom from all constraint? In other words, did the state I'm in ever cast a spell upon the attention of another, and refuse to let go? ever take possession of the will of another, and propel us both—she and I! into a place of stunned disequi- librium, flailing fear? into the shrieking claustrophobia—abrupt personality-displacement! of a traumatic encounter, sacrificial rit- ual, tribute to death? Yes, I ask: is there a dreadful behavior-se- quence lurking somewhere in my memory? God, I sincerely don't know!"

The water of the pool was becoming extraordinarily—sav- agely! bright, leaping straight at me, thrusting flaring—explosive! silver into the depths of my eyes! It wouldn't stop intruding on— undermining! my self-possession; wouldn't stop knifing to bits— dicing! my attempts to be detached and objective as regards my predicament—attempts to arrive at a bearable explanation of my doings, conclusion I could live with! Nor could I stop staring at the water, tear myself away, flee! The water had, indeed, cast a spell on me: I was being lured—against my will! by its hypnotic whirl and blur into posing question after futile question! Yes, I was delving and re-delving into my recent history and encounter- ing nothing but questions which were raising more questions; which, at best, were resolving themselves into infuriatingly in- complete hints—inconclusive suspicions, nondeclarative sugges- tions of stabs of conscience! that were only presenting me with increasingly difficult puzzles of self-dividedness to solve! No es- cape! I was being vanquished by sensory distortion on every front—rapidly being swept into a state similar to the one I'd been in while staring at the black mouth eyes!—yes, losing the ability to understand what reliable perceptions are, comprehend myself as being an individual in possession of my own encasement of flesh and blood!—losing the ability to cross-reference my very existence to the greater whole of space and time! All apprehensible realms were swirling into churning formlessness, unbounded fear! I... God, again I was desperately asking, "Why—how? have I come to be here? Where—what? is 'here'? Who...?"

PART FOUR:
GHOSTS, FURIES, & BLACKOUT

D earest reader, I've no idea for how long I continued
to stand at the edge of the reflecting pool, stare into its
bewildering water, whirl about in futile attempts to
explain myself to myself; nor am I able to indicate—beyond what
I already have—what those attempts were: the more I seek to pin
down that interval of facing the pool the more it swirls into blinding silver—erupts into tingles in my nerve-stream—at *this* moment! It's as if that interval's threatening to leap off these pages
as I write these pages—spill into the present, erase the distinction
between what I experienced then and what I'm experiencing now!

But I *am* able to clearly recall that I eventually stumbled backwards, as if in a loss of balance, from the edge of the reflecting
pool. Whether it was due to the sudden absence of direct apprehension of the shimmering water (on account of stepping back) or
the momentary distraction of being mindful of my footing or another cause, the panic-surge within me subsided just enough to
allow me to be capable of vaguely discerning my surroundings,

willfully directing my steps. I didn't squander this small window of opportunity—wasted no time in taking advantage of this improvement, however slight, in my perceptual faculties to direct my body to about-face and propel me away from the pool!

I recall a dizzy stroll on legs I could barely feel among greenery which erratically dipped and rose as if glimpsed from a Ferris wheel moving in fits and starts; yes, recall treetops doing blurred cartwheels against the blue sky, lawns tilting into waves of emerald haze, flowerbeds zigzagging red, orange, purple, white as the ground at my feet changed from tile to brick to spongy green. And then branches and leaves shielded me from the sun: I was reclining on my back in the shade of a tree, gazing sideways at grass blades, running my fingers through them...

Not long ago (an hour? two?) I'd stumbled onto grass somewhere else in the park (perhaps close-by, but not below the sun-obstructing branches of a tree) and succeeded in calming myself—a calm all too fleeting, obliterated by the time I was staring into the unkind silver of the reflecting pool. But now the memory of that calm was revived by the sight of the grass; and, following quickly on the heels of memory, came calm itself. It was as if the grass was a visual code-command, hypnotist's implanted signal, stimulus to pre-conditioned feelings: the soothing lushness of its blades! Ha! Thank God for parks; for luxuriant lawns, shade dispensing trees; for places where one can safely fling oneself onto one's back, relax tense muscles, quiet harried nerves, forget the city exists!

Yes, I was relaxing in greenery: the twittering of birds fluttered in my ears, echoed like a serenity-dispensing mantra in my head; the shade of the leaf-cloaked branches above, as well as the steady touch of a gentle breeze, cooled me. I made no effort to think; no conscious struggle for clearheadedness was apparent: it simply happened. Yes, at some point I was gazing across the lawn at a swaying bed of snapdragons and became aware that the unpleasant reflecting pool interval had, seemingly of its own accord, evaporated like a bad dream. Soon I was saying to myself, "Be content with the fact you've managed to swim against insomnia's frenzy-gathering current to the extent you're able to place yourself in the sequence of your recent tumult-distorted past, articulate the cause of this unprecedented onslaught of emotional extremes: this clarity in the midst of accumulated disorientation is a gift! Accept the gift with grace—offer thanks for the further lease on sanity which the gift grants you—and discontinue the vain and dangerous attempt to determine what transpired during those intervals of excessive duress which now appear as memory-gaps: take your hope of having behaved acceptably on faith, dispense with dwelling upon the uncertainties which grow stronger the more you endeavor to probe and disarm them! Yes, gather the memories which are confirmable, certain, solid as the ground at your back—embrace factuality, shake yourself free of mist-enshrouded trepidation! And, now, stand up! Place one foot in front of the other, start walking, return home!"

Ha! Who was it that was speaking, myself or a guardian angel? This mention of home, so surprising! Home? I did, indeed, have a home: a street-side two bedroom in an up-and-coming neighborhood. How long had I been away from it? Twelve weeks? Fourteen? More? And it struck and amazed me anew, the degree to which the chance encounter of a woman in a cafe and subsequent—equally coincidental—discovery of her place of residence had uprooted me from my life, transformed me into another person, made me a stranger to myself! I hadn't set foot in my apartment for at least three months, even though I'd been in the same city the entire time! I'd gone from one one-night-stand's apartment to another—one hotel room to another—one doorstep to another; gone from one emotional experiment to another—one surge of daring to another—one onslaught of frenzy to another—one glimpse of mental collapse to another!

Of returning home I remember next to nothing: I was, despite the fortuitous second interval of clarity in the park and last-ditch rallying of will, under the influence of sleep-deprivation so pronounced that my sustained perceptions of my surroundings were little better than if I'd been blind drunk. I'm able to recall entering the lobby of my building, asking a doorman I didn't know for

a set of my keys, watching him retrieve them from the cabinet behind the desk. Then I'm in the kitchen of my apartment: I open the
refrigerator, seem to be surprised it's empty, and turn towards the
sink. The water's brown for a minute or two; when it clears, I
drink greedily. Then I'm in my bedroom: no sooner do I lie on
my bed, than I'm fast asleep. Only after I awaken can I be said to
be fully aware of my surroundings and situation.

*   *   *   *   *

I awakened to find sunlight upon my face. At first, I thought
I'd only managed to doze for an hour or so, was annoyed with
myself for having neglected to draw the shades and make sleep
more feasible with darkness. Seconds later, however, the quietude
of my nerves—absence of chill-punctuated hot flushes, presence
of what I can only term inner-equanimity-bordering-on-
sluggishness—convinced me that I'd slept far longer; that, indeed,
it was possible I was gazing upon a new day. I glanced at the
clock: eleven forty-two. I searched my memory: I'd arrived home
in the afternoon. Well, then, it was confirmed: it was the following day and I'd slept for over twenty hours. When was the last
time I'd done that, if ever?
   But I didn't have the leisure to dwell upon how long I'd slept:
the claws of hunger in my belly wouldn't permit it. I reached for
the phone while opening a drawer of the nightstand, locating a
credit card and take-out menu; ha, was suddenly struck by the fact
of having a former life to which such things as credit cards belonged: a former life? Well, despite the gnawings of hunger (my
impatience to dial the number on the menu, place an order), I
found myself rolling onto my back and drawing a deep breath
while contrasting my nomadic dream-life of the past few months
with the concrete fact of this, my very own apartment! How
strange to be in possession of a valuable piece of real estate—
which attested to a fully documented existence—when I'd spent
my recent past wandering about town like a transient, under the
influence of impulses which had often precluded comprehending
what property is! Ha! I'd doubtless passed within blocks of my

apartment a number of times and, not once, had it occurred to me to pass the night, or day, in it! For all I knew, I'd stared straight at my building several times without recognizing it!

I reached for the phone a second time, dialed the restaurant, ordered two entrees; then phoned the nearest supermarket, ordered several bags of groceries. Upon the completion of these tasks, I couldn't help but return to the state of enjoyable amazement—amazement at the simple fact of going through this ordering ritual again, after...? Well, three or so months isn't a lengthy period of time; but I wasn't close to being the same person I was at the commencement of that period of time: I was outside of these once routine gestures, regarding them as something novel, exotic, miraculous. It wasn't only that I could barely believe I'd managed to return to them: what struck me more forcefully was that these gestures had once been mine to such a degree—so habitual, automatic—I'd taken them for granted, been close to unaware of them.

It occurred to me that, while awaiting the food, I could take a shower and put on a change of clothes. Again, the thought resurrected memories: what had I done for clothes during my dream-adventure? And then I recalled strolling the streets with a satchel slung across my shoulder; recalled clothes purchased with cash obtained from bank machines (I'd had my ATM card); recalled... Ha, what had become of the satchel? In which hotel room or apartment had it been forgotten? or perhaps I'd tossed it into a dumpster? Clothes bought, worn until soiled, replaced with new purchases! Yes, living out of a satchel had become too cumbersome: the sum total of my possessions had been the clothes on my back and contents of my wallet!

I undressed and was soon within the shower, exulting in the splash of warm water upon my parched skin. The soap and shampoo were where I'd left them, on the stainless steel shelf below the shower head. As I reached for them I was again struck by the familiarity of the gesture—a gesture belonging to a period in my life when I'd been a gainfully employed professional, valued in my department and compensated accordingly. And then I recollected the manner in which I'd resigned my position. Two weeks notice was the accepted, courteous, expected course of action but I hadn't done that: a call from a public phone fifteen minutes before I was due at work was how I'd resigned. I hadn't cared what impression might be created; hadn't cared about saddling the department with a short notice departure; hadn't cared about the project I'd been working on. "I can't come to work again," I'd said, before cutting the surprised, half-disbelieving, department head short with, "I'm not explaining—I've got to go." I'd hung up at the moment when an exhalation of annoyance had reached my ears, before that exhalation had had time to attach itself to words. I hadn't gone to empty my desk, turn in my security card, shake hands good-bye; hadn't done anything besides make that call, nor thought about my resignation from the firm for an instant after hanging up, not once during the interval of living away from my apartment; hadn't thought about it until stepping into the shower shortly past noon three or so months later, on the day of which I'm writing...

Bright sunlight was streaming through the bathroom window, striking the glass enclosure of the shower, flaring up and down the white tiling, sparkling in the splash and mist of the water, creating—along with the warmth of the water—a unified impression of cheerfulness and well-being. I hadn't had a shower like this in a long time: it seemed to me that all activities of this nature, those involving the maintenance of health and hygiene, of the past three or so months had been conducted in dim light and shadows; haste had characterized them, nothing had been savored; they'd simply been necessary tasks that I'd performed indifferently, mechanically, efficiently. But now, although summer was waning and hints of fall weather were already detectable, it seemed to me that springtime was bursting its buds and surging within me: how invigorating to stretch in warm running water, feel one's muscles absorb the joyful heat, relax! How delightful the scent of the soap, sensation of cleanliness! And I continued to muse about the manner in which I'd tossed away the former routine of my life without a thought...

Without a thought? Ha! I'd fled from the trappings of my life as if they were flaming rafters threatening to collapse atop me! I'd neither been foresightful nor considerate; I hadn't demonstrated a hint of the sort of behavior expected of me (by others and myself alike) because I'd been far too preoccupied with seeking to stay abreast of the inner eruption which had overcome me without warning! Indeed, that I'd managed to make the phone call announcing my resignation from employment had been surprising! Yes, the details were returning to recollection with increasing clarity...

The blare of the intercom reminded me I'd placed orders for food and seemingly forgotten them, despite my hunger. I stepped from the shower, went to instruct the doorman to tell the delivery man to deposit the order at my door; likewise, I told him, a second delivery man due momentarily should be told the same; it would be nice, I added, if he could give each a tip on my behalf (I stipulated the amount): I was presently occupied and would reimburse him. That done, I returned to the bathroom, turned off the water I'd left running, grabbed a towel, and advanced to my room. While drying myself I slid open a door of my closet and beheld the rows of coats and shirts on hangers, stacks of pants on shelves, dozens of belts and scarves dangling from hooks, heaps of shoes on the floor: such abundance! Again, I fell to contrasting my nomadic existence of the past few months with the sight of stability before me. So many clothes for so many different occasions: suits for closings, tasteful casual for ordinary workdays, leather and black for nightclubbing, jeans and t-shirts for play in the park; top coats, rain coats, leather jackets, down jackets, fleece vests, cashmere sweaters; a drawer full of sunglasses—gray, aquamarine, dark brown, all shapes; beach wear, workout wear, formal wear, lounge wear. What clothes had sufficed during the past three or so months of impermanence? Whatever non-gaudy shirts and pants had been the first to fit during impatient buying sessions. As for socks, they were easily obtained at curbside tables, no fitting required. Likewise with jackets: I'd bought a couple on the sidewalk when the temperature dropped, tossed them onto doorsteps when the warmth returned. Umbrellas had only been held onto for the duration of a rain. I strolled to the bed, examined the clothes I'd worn home: black cotton pants and a black and white striped cotton shirt (always worn untucked), both fairly odor-free. Yes, I'd often laundered my clothes by showering in them; between that and purchasing new ones, I'd maintained an acceptable level of cleanliness... Ha, suddenly I was laughing at the manner in which I was detailing my recent fashion options to myself, waving a hand in dismissal. "What's the point?" I inquired aloud.

None too subtly reminded by my stomach it was in need of nourishment, I dressed, advanced to the front door, opened it to find the food orders lined up against the wall in a number of bags. I made two quick trips to the kitchen with the bags, was soon emptying them onto the table and into the refrigerator. Upon discovering the fillet of sole entree, however, I ceased busying with the bags, commenced devouring the succulent fish and steamed vegetables. Few sensations can compare with that of tasty nutritious food entering an empty stomach: the uncomfortable cravings of the latter vanish within moments, are replaced by soothing inner caresses, vitality's comforting glow. Yes, while swallowing healthful bite after bite I could feel the fuel combusting within me, being converted into pulsations of substantiality, restoring equilibrium to my starved body. As if by magic the container was shortly empty and, before I'd finished chewing the last of it, I was busy with a salad; and thereafter scooping out a cantaloupe, the orange meat of which glistened with the hallucinatory vividness of a mirage; then a bowl of full fat yogurt: all of these morsels were accompanied by glassful after glassful of fresh squeezed grapefruit juice, each gulp of which soaked my mouth in refreshing bursts of tartness, as if the vitamins were being absorbed by and invigorating my tongue and gums. Upon completing my meal, I glanced at the remaining bags of food: it was as if mere seconds had passed since I'd first set them on the floor.

Having nothing more to do which entailed of urgency, I finished emptying the food bags, disposed of the used take-out containers, and brewed a cup of green tea. Upon accomplishment of the latter task, I betook myself to the living room, reclined on the couch, sipped the tea while gazing at the ceiling. It struck me that, since arriving home, the only thing I'd done in a manner that was similar to that of the past few months was consume the above-described meal. I recalled periods of making do with barely a bite—a hastily consumed banana here, health bar there—punctuated by ravenous gorgings: deli victuals spread out on newspaper on hotel room floors—herring, octopus salad, rye bread, brie, celery stalks, apples, grapes: all vibrantly aglow in blue-white fluorescence, perceived as some sort of miracle!—yes, recalled swallowing in semi-desperation, as if half-believing a few more moments of delay would result in prolonged shaking fits, illness brought on by malnourishment; recalled raging thirst in the dead of night, quarts of orange juice emptied in a single toss-back of my head... So many meals purchased in a glancing-over-my-shoulder manner, taken to hotel room hideaways; or to park benches and doorsteps...

Yes, eating in restaurants had become impossible: the chatter and clatter would roar in my ears with the force of a high waterfall; the bright lights and bustle would assault my eyes and nerves; the situation of being immobile, deprived of energy-distributing movement, would accumulate inside me to the point of being a silent scream. My imagination would persuade me the other patrons were staring at me, smirking and laughing, making malicious comments at my expense. It was as if a self-accusatory expression was stamped upon my face; as if my gestures hinted at suspicious surreptitious occupations; as if my tone of presence emanated infuriating reverberations; yes, as if others were overcome with revulsion—winced in recoil and gnashed their teeth—at the sight of me. Oh, was it true? Had I really been sleep-deprived, overwrought, and isolated enough to be subjected to such paranoid representations, credit their veracity?

I noticed my hand was trembling enough to produce agitation on the surface of the tea in the cup it held, cause the light reflected thereupon to zigzag back and forth. I quickly averted my gaze from the liquid, set the cup on the coffee table. I was staring straight ahead, with muscles slightly tense. The air of the room was beginning to acquire a blurred quality: the far wall and those to my right and left were bending, rippling like tapestries in a gentle breeze, alternately appearing convex and concave. I opened my eyes wide, shut them, opened them again—shook my head, slapped each cheek—in an effort to clear my vision, put the perceptual distortions to flight. The sharp stationary outlines of the room returned, but only momentarily: soon the air was refracting and smearing the light again; soon the walls were quivering and twisting again. I rose to my feet, began pacing in an effort to be aware of the physicality of my body, restore groundedness to my perceptions: the distortions persisted.

I strolled to my room, flung myself on my bed, sought to recover the sensation of well-rested content I'd experienced upon awakening: it refused to reappear. I rose from the bed, approached the closet, began reexamining its contents in the hope of bringing back the therapeutic realization I'd once lived a life that was solidly rooted in fully documentable professionalism, accepted societal values: again, the sentiment refused to reappear. Instead, I found myself sinking to the floor, propping my back against the wall, as unease continued to rise within me; as my perceptions of the simple dimensions of the room—of my hand which I was holding close to my face! became increasingly skitter-scattered with troubling warpings of light; as... Oh, God! I should've known! The visage of my bewitching beauty—she who'd torn me from the stability I'd spent years acquiring! was suddenly crystal clear in my mind's eye, gripping me from head to toe in a vise of tension, forcing me back to my feet!

Instantly, I was pacing rapidly from room to room of my apartment, up and down the halls! I opened windows to soothe myself with fresh moving air, allow contrary breezes to waft through the rooms; I stuck my head out the windows to bathe my eyes in far-flung perspectives, receding scenery—counter the sensation of being hemmed in, forced to apprehend what I didn't wish to apprehend! I returned to the kitchen, retrieved the second entree from the refrigerator, started eating with the aim of experiencing more full-stomach contentedness, inducing slowness in my nerves, reining in the accelerating flailings of my thoughts! All was to no avail: the more I sought to erase the features of my spellbinding beauty's face from awareness the sharper those features became; and the sharper those features became the greater were the starts in my nerves, the bursts of fear in my breast, and my gaspings for breath!

I dashed to the main hall, glanced towards the front door, and didn't hesitate—was soon strolling down the hallway of my building, taking the steps instead of the elevator, descending them two at a time! Yes, certainly a walk outside in the windy sunlight would dispel the gathering claustrophobia and panic! Certainly I'd be able to lose my beguiling beauty's image in the innumerable spectacles the city afforded—lose her image in the jumble of storefronts, window displays, signs; in the flow of traffic, receding distances of the avenues, expanses of sky! Ha! I'd simply mosey from store to store, buy some lightbulbs, add to the soap and shampoo supply, acquire some new music! That's right, I'd busy myself with mundane errands, and *forget!*

But no sooner was I outside than the sunlight shafting through the street dust, striking the metal and glass of buildings; than the hum and honk of traffic, bustle of pedestrians, chatter and shouts; than the crosswalks, newsstands, and awnings—advertising, litter, landings, doorways! brought memories of the past several months back more vividly, caused my spellbinding beauty's picture to flare more insistently, engulf me in stronger waves of excitation! Ha! My apartment, be it remembered, was a place I hadn't visited during the past few months. The city itself was saturated with innumerable recollections of the variety of panic I was endeavoring to escape—recollections I was increasingly unable to distance myself from on that ill-informed foray outdoors. And then it occurred to me that perhaps I hadn't managed to distance myself from my ordeal of the past few months in any manner whatsoever apart from vain wishful thinking. After all, only yesterday I'd been...

But, no! I wasn't going to allow myself to be pulled into the memory-current of my recent past, swept back into inner disorientation and tumult! I was going to shove all threatening memories away, fight! I was going to return to my apartment, phone work-acquaintances, become employed again! I was going to get the opera schedule, comb through my address book, contact old flames; was going to attend openings, go to parties, dance; was going to busy myself with making money, spending it freely, amusing myself! Yes, I was going to obliterate the past three or so months of sanity-skewing aberration, return to my former life!

Had I been dizzy with happiness in my former life? The question misses the point! All that matters is that I'd been *safe*! I'm sure I'd enjoyed life as much as the next man! Some nights out begin with a steady accumulation of anticipation: it's not what will happen but what might happen which stirs the blood, sets one's pulse to racing. Yes, I'd still, I was sure of it, be capable of thrilling to the prospect of a night out with a cute slender. First, there's the warm fuzziness of one's nerves at the office, tantalizing half-pictures in one's imagination of what's possibly in store. Second, there's the journey to the rendezvous spot with joy softly rising in one's breast; and then that initial glimpse of her face in the distance, bright eyes leaping in delightful reciprocation of the light in one's own. What follows? Perhaps playful flirt and tease over dinner, spark-transmission via trembly hand-touches, up-welling from inside locked looks of sweet regard? Perhaps arm-in-arm strolls, park bench kiss-fests, cuddly cab rides? Oh, the magnetic insistence of tensed muscles, dizzying silence of breathless pauses, sparkling pulsations of ignited chemistry! And then, perchance, dancing? By all means! Eye-caress, waist-grasp, body-rub! Hands in hair, legs intertwined, tongue in mouth to the disco throb and shimmy beat! Dip and twist until all inner recesses of reserve uncoil, surge to the surface, whirl away! And, once abed? Ha, engulfed by her hunger-widened eyes, embracing and licking and nipping liquid electric curves, writhing in charged wonderment, tumbling inside out in shimmering release!

Yes, my former life had consisted of such nights punctuated by work: a comfortable balance between restraint and abandon had seemingly been maintained without effort; I'd been as happy, it seemed to me, as is possible in this life. I wanted it back! While retracing my steps to my apartment I was vowing that such a life would be mine again; vowing to commence recovery of it immediately; vowing not to lose hold of the hard-fought-for victory, restoration to clarity, I'd gained—not to be propelled back into the waking nightmare of insomnia-flayed senses, imagination-manipulated sanity!

While thus recollecting my former ability to seize ahold of intervals of worthwhile living in the midst of nine-to-five habitude and resolving to reobtain that ability, I managed to distract myself from the unease which had driven me from my apartment. I congratulated myself: it seemed to me that this threat of a relapse had served a purpose; that it had shown me to be very careful to avoid complacency as regards the turmoil I'd emerged from—to never neglect to maintain a wary respect for it, accord it the ability to reensnare me; that it had not only provided me with a great deal of motivation to see to it the turmoil never overtook me again, but had forced me to adopt a viable plan for keeping it at bay. "Waste no time!" I commanded myself. "Return home, begin making calls, sign on with a new firm!—yes, immerse yourself in work responsibility, then reward yourself with some piquant flings! That's right, use the trappings of the old life to separate yourself from the churning shadows of the present, deprive them of strength: eventually they'll dissipate like fog on a sunny morning, leave you be! Damn! Too soon isn't soon enough!"

The moment I entered my apartment I went to the bedroom, extracted my address book from the top drawer of the nightstand, and began searching among the lower drawers for lists of people at sundry firms I'd dealt with. As my profession is understaffed and headhunters are constantly seeking to pilfer from other places (several of whom had approached me during the course of my career), I didn't doubt a few phone calls would result in a number of promising leads and that I'd soon be reemployed.

Having located the relevant personnel lists, I sat in the middle of the bed, spread them about me, and began searching for recognizable names; several minutes later, I'd circled at least a dozen. I reached for the phone and dialed one of the numbers, that of a department head at a firm where, on account of its large size, there were frequent vacancies. Upon the woman's answering, I said the usual in such cases: that I didn't know if she'd remember me, but we'd both been associated with such and such a project in a co-counsel situation about a year ago; that I'd taken a leave of absence from professional life, and wished to return; that I had a great deal of experience, could begin immediately, and wished to interview for present or future openings. But I'll leave off describing the exchange: the bottom line is that when I hung up, I had an interview appointment in two days—an interview which, given her enthusiasm, I considered as good as an outright offer.

I could barely believe it: a simple phone call, a few tactful words of introduction and explanation, and an interview and almost certain employment had been arranged! Yes, the old professionalism had resurfaced on cue; the protocol phrases and inflections of voice—phone etiquette, job-related lingo—had seemed to issue from my mouth of their own accord, with next to no active participation on my part. It was almost as if someone else had made the call, spoken to the woman; as if I'd been sitting idly by, observing the proceedings from an uninvolved distance. Less than ten minutes of detached recitation on the phone, and—presto! I was in possession of a lifeline: now I had a definite, confirmable, solid, real means in the present of pulling myself together, extricating myself from oppressive memories, obliterating the specter of the past few turmoil inundated months; in short, now I had a means of reobtaining a safe manner of life!

Yes, I'd had a scare: I'd been driven from my apartment by sensory disorientation, gathering claustrophobia, recollections which had conjured forth the influence of all too recent destructive stimuli; had raced outside only to be whipped back to my apartment by scenery rife with stronger reminders of the same destructive stimuli. But I'd vigorously protested—countered by locating papers which belonged to my pre-upheaval life, making use of them to secure myself a future. How relieved I was! I advanced to the closet, did an informed search of its contents, selected an interview-appropriate suit, arranged it on the back of a chair with shirt, tie, socks, underwear (placing the shoes on the floor); then backed away and surveyed the ensemble with satisfaction. "Yes," I told myself, "should the light commence to bend and blur in a troubling manner again; should nervous excitation, blind restiveness, traces of dread hammer at my thoughts again... Well, I'll simply glance at these clothes on this chair, apprehend their meaning, anticipate security in occupation, and disperse the demons!"

I raised a fist towards the ceiling, twirled about a few times, said aloud, "*Veni! Vidi! Vici!*" and then, as I was hungry again, went to the kitchen. Once there, I chopped up two avocados and a tomato and ate them while draining a quart of orange juice. Thereafter, I returned to my room, gathered the papers which were still on my bed, tossed them on the floor, flung myself on the mattress, and fell asleep...

My next recollection is of becoming aware of a sensation of paralysis, as if every muscle in my body was being seized from within and held in place by dozens of strong hands: was I fully awake? or suspended between grogginess and dreams, erratically oscillating from one to the other? or fully asleep while having dreams lifelike enough to create the impression of wakefulness? I know not which. What I do know is that I was explaining to myself, in a level-toned trance-like voice (with the tone of removal from the action of a narrator in a film), that the paralysis was only to be expected; that it was the logical outcome of the state of excitement in which I'd collapsed on the bed; that it was unfinished business, thwarted obsession, strangled impulse; that it was the truth shouting louder than lies, my actual emotional condition declaring it wasn't going to be displaced by an assumed one. Awake or asleep? or fitfully flitting between the two? I recall opening my eyes (whether in a dream or in actuality I, again, know not) to find night had fallen and that in place of sunlight streaming through the windows of my bedroom was street lamp amber. The amber was undulating on the floor, lapping up against my bed, climbing the walls, spreading over the ceiling; it resembled fallen autumn leaves whirling in a breeze, was flickering and flaring into deep oranges, bright reds—acquiring jagged edges, hissing! And then my body abruptly clenched inward on itself amidst an inundation of hot hard heat, as if my muscles were cramping: awake or asleep? Suddenly I was definitely—confirmably! wide awake, surrounded by the garish dancing hues of actual street lamp streamlets of light; aware of being wet with sweat, unable to move for one moment—two—three! of body and will immobilizing terror!

"No!" I heard myself yell aloud: the throat-movement which made the enunciation of the "No!" possible instantly spread throughout me, released my body from the nerve-grip in which it was being held: in seconds I was sitting bolt upright, switching on the overhead light, glancing about—wondering what to do, where to run! Run? How run from disturbances within oneself? How run from senses which are surrounding one with approaching walls, descending ceilings, rising floors, blurring outlines? from senses which are greedily gathering and fiercely exaggerating all available light, encircling the field of one's vision with blinding white, forcing one to gaze inward at troubling pictures? How run from images which come into crystal clear focus in one's mind's eye?—as, for instance, the image of my spellbinding fury's face? God! It was she, all right: larger than life in my head again, hissingly whispering, "You will not forget! You will not forget!"

"Why won't you leave me alone?" I shouted, pleaded. "All I want to do, I don't feel it's too much to ask, is..." I broke off, was searching my thoughts for a recollection, a response. "Yes, that's it," I resumed, "stare at those clothes on that chair, something beneficial's supposed to happen, trigger relief! Ha, now I remember! The phone call, reindoctrination into professional life, restoration of inner equilibrium, shelter from bedeviling extremes! Well, it was a fine interval of self-deception while it lasted! It slaps me in the face now, I avow myself beaten! Stupid charade! Nothing more than a gesture comparable to the soft twirling of a breeze-teased leaf on the surface of a river while powerful currents continue to churn in the river's depths! What does playacting on the surface of experience—putting on professional airs, engaging in repetitive robotic activities—have to do with erasing the influence of the past few months, obliterating the change that's been wrought in me by them? It's not likely inner trauma's going to be countered by hollow rituals of routine!"

I leaped from the mattress, dashed to the living room, was soon pacing back and forth on the Persian rug in its center, haranguing myself thus: "Well, there's no denying I've managed to return to my apartment, reenact gestures that were once second nature to me, remind myself of the life of safety I once led; no denying that this accomplishment, in itself, represents a small victory! Yes, comfort can certainly be derived from the fact I managed to hark back to my former life to the extent that I was able to determine who to call to ensure likely employment—not to mention actually make the call, accomplish its purpose! Never mind that I won't be keeping my interview appointment: what can't be taken from me is that I succeeded in arranging it! What can't be taken from me is that there are still concrete points of contact between myself and my past life, people who are willing to allow me to return to it! No, that's not to be disregarded! That's something capable of bringing about a fleeting interval of ease of mind! And who knows? I don't feel it's unreasonable to regard my return here and intact memory of what once was as a premonition of a possible future; unreasonable to refuse to rule out the possibility of someday again leading a fundamentally carefree life, and being content with and thankful for it; unreasonable to suppose my present troubles are a variety of purgatory necessary to be endured for a chance of overcoming self-dividedness—attaining to an inner union of opposites, lasting equanimity! in this life; or..."

I trailed off despite the fact that I wished to continue indulging in supportive reflections, tossing myself small bones of comfort. Why did I trail off? Because my surroundings were no longer allowing me to toss myself such bones of comfort: the red, black, orange, and purple patterns of the rug at my feet were tugging at one another, erratically shifting at their edges, thrusting their contrasts at my eyes, tearing into my nerves; and the air between my eyes and the rug was thick agitated glass—magnifying the effect of the clashing colors! God! The walls were aswirl again, ceiling was descending again—all solid objects were becoming vaporous again! I was areel in renewed panic, being forced to account for the said panic, confront what was hounding me!

I darted into the kitchen, returned to the living room, strolled the length of the main hall and back, several times—around and around the couch, on the Persian once more! Pace! Pace! Pace! Ha! As if I could, by indulging in physical activity distraction—no matter how frenetic! prevent the face of my upheaval-inducing beauty from blazing brighter in my mind's eye, shoving thoughts not having to do with her aside, forcing me to address myself thus: "God, there's no denying my beguiling beauty has as firm a hold on me as ever: I see it far more clearly than I want to, am forced to admit it! Yes, now I realize she's been with me all day, hovering in the background of my every glance and gesture! Ha! All my pathetic attempts to refamiliarize myself with my former life, reobtain employment, slip into the framework of professional life again—erect a barrier of busyness between her and myself, defuse unease with the trappings of comfort! The mere props of comfort do not ease of mind make, and... Oh, I ask—I demand: why—how?—does she have this unbreakable hold on me? Why am I being yanked at deep inside myself by a type of gravity which acts on the nerves and emotions, twists thoughts into dreaded pathways, replaces self-direction with compulsion, bends my will in directions it doesn't want to go? Because I *am* being pulled: her place of residence shouts out its address, bids me hither! God! I don't want to go there, but know I will! I'm afraid to go there, but know I will! Why am I afraid to go there? Why does my spine turn to ice the second the streets which mark its location cross my thoughts? For Christ's sake, she's only a woman! I've never felt like this before; I've never cringed before a woman before; I've... But that's precisely it: she's more than woman; she's imagination-congregation, a walking and breathing screen onto which all manner of wild mysterious awe-inspiring phenomena have been projected! Ha! Is it nothing but an instance of my fancy running amok, playing games with me? Is that it? I proceed to her building, either wait outside until she shows or go to her door; I gaze upon her and, in so doing, perceive it's all only imagination—and, in so perceiving, dispel the bedevilment, confirm my apprehensions are mirages, tenuous as mist in dry air? Is that it? But then why such enervating dread? Why the fear which tightens my muscles, flays my nerves, scrambles my senses, devours ease of mind? No, the fear isn't going to go 'poof!' into thin air! The fear's too substantial for that! The fear has its own life—it's own density of existence! God! All I know for certain is that the fear's bound up with her, and won't be gone without her participation! Whether it be passive participation, as in being seen by me; or active participation, as in responding to an approach by me, speaking to me; or..."

I returned to the bedroom for a fresh pair of durable shoes. "No, I don't want to do what I have to do!" I resumed while seated on the bed, placing the shoes on my feet. "Don't want to entangle myself in her again, reexpose myself to unsafe stimuli, be aflail like before! Because who's to say that, the moment I glimpse her anew, I won't be propelled into another month or two or three of dreamy hysteria? again be stalked and taunted by vague nondeclarative shadow-thoughts, prodded towards pronounced mental instability, forced to combat one self-destructive urge after another? But who am I kidding? It's not as if the first interval of upheaval has ended! How could I be vain and naive enough to assume it has? Simply because I happened to turn up here, am presently in the apartment which I owe to an evenness of disposition I no longer possess! And why did I come here, anyway? What's the point of lulling myself into a few hours of false security, fraudulent self-congratulation, unfounded sighs of relief? What was I asserting minutes ago? What was that nonsense about having won a small battle, being able to derive comfort from the ability to puppet behavior I once felt wholeheartedly? No, there's no victory here, only the dangerous false-assumption of it! Only the peril of supposing myself cured or semi-cured or somewhat calmed when such couldn't be further from the truth! Only the peril of being swindled out of my caution, preparedness, nerve! Only the peril of pseudo security while storms gather! Yes, I've got to wake up to the facts of the matter! This business of informing myself that distraction—getting a job, immersing myself in frivolous play outside of the job—is required to keep my self-possession out of the firing line of my compulsion-engendering charmer's influence, as if that selfsame influence isn't still as ubiquitous and impossible to escape as it's ever been!—as if it isn't still as strong as was months ago, in the days after my discovery of her place of residence!—as if she's not presently surging in my bloodstream, flaring in my nerves, claiming sole possession of my thoughts, making it crystal clear she's an unavoidable encounter en route to the remainder of my life!"

I sprang from the bed with the intention of fortifying myself with more food before venturing outside; but, by the time I reached the threshold of my bedroom, I'd forgotten why I'd jumped up: I began pacing again, in tight circles. "Yes," I recommenced addressing myself, "my inescapable rendezvous—my tumult-breeding beauty: the wavy pitch black hair which cascades about the pale oval of her visage aglow with inaccessible equanimity; the inward-turned smile which hovers about her soft ruby lips, flushes among the flawless contours of her cheeks, hints at remote realms of icy rapture! But her eyes monopolize the picture, draw my attention away from the remainder of her face: twin diamonds in bottomless wells of darkness, at once suffused with surging excitement and aloof composure! What shimmering friction erupts in my nerves, races up and down my spine, engulfs me from my fingertips to my toes as a consequence of meeting their gaze! No, I'll never know a moment's repose as long as those eyes inhabit my imagination, present me with their gleaming impenetrability, whisper, 'There are mysteries you know nothing of! There exists a vibrant, vital, volatile shadow-world of cataract-

swift life of which you've barely managed to taste—that mocks
every moment you idle in your shallow comfort-zone of counter-
feit experience! And we possess the secret of that life; we live and
breathe the unsullied unbridledness of emotion of ancient times,
are bacchanalian frenzy incarnate! Yes, we pulsate in unison with
the vastness of the night sky while you bewilderedly stare at that
sky, blindly stumble amidst earthbound pettiness, helplessly grasp
and claw! And, above all: you not only cannot conceal anything
from us, we know innumerable things about you of which you're
ignorant! We read your thoughts with ease, both the ones of which
you're aware and the ones of which you're not!' God! How are her
eyes able to get under my skin and stab at my nerves—taunt me!
thus? Of course there are many things of which I know nothing
and will remain ignorant! Of course our lives are little more than
fleeting dreams which represent but a minute fraction of the
wealth of experience existence contains! Of course our lives take
place alongside of mysteries which will forever elude us! Have I
ever despaired on account of such insurmountables? I haven't! So
why does the elusiveness of her eyes trouble me so? Ha! There are
altars before which one may prostrate oneself in humble admis-
sion of one's limitations, pray to be granted the ability to become
receptive to intimations of worlds incomprehensible to the understanding; but one should be permitted to decide when to approach the altar! My altar unendingly forces itself upon me, whirls
me into sensations I'm hard pressed to keep pace with, brings on
inner screams such as would delight my most unsympathetic enemies; my altar often seems little different than a rapacious fury,
avenging angel, enraged Goddess! And, damn! She's, after all,
only a fellow human being! She hasn't asked to be an altar, would
very likely be astonished were she to be informed of the effect
she has on me, and... Oh, curse this infuriatingly resilient obsession with projecting inner yearnings, suspicions, fears onto her!
And why onto her and no other? Why is my very soul-life intertwined with, knocked about and battered by, her? I've no history
of such! Me, the insouciant and cynical man about town? Me, the
unsentimental connoisseur of one night sex-fests?—laughing at

those determined on long-term commitment, pitying the miserably married?—indifferent to tomorrow, contemptuous of the past?—always delighting in the thought that each succeeding moment replaces and erases the one preceding it and therefore exists independently, owes the bygone one nothing?—delighting in the thought that the present is the only moment which belongs to us— only point at which we can sense the sunlight upon our skin, thrill to the beauty of a girl's face, surrender to an impulse, make a decision! in the unending march of time?—that those who preoccupy themselves with what's over and done or speculate concerning what's yet to be are ignoring the hereness in front of them, devoting their lives to what doesn't exist? Me? I was once that immediacy-worshipping, ties-that-bind-detesting, man! No longer! And curse the moment I turned that corner, glimpsed her in the window of that cafe; curse me for entering the cafe, being unable to flee; curse her for infiltrating my life, shanghaiing my will! I... Ha, again the self-repetition which only highlights the futility of attempting to think myself free of my situation, rein in the emotion-whirl with rationality, dredge bottomless depths with instruments that float on the surface! All I know is that I cannot remain here, in my apartment; that all efforts to recover my carefree life are wasted efforts as long as my bewitching beauty exerts an influence; that I must go to her place of residence, see her again; that I've no idea what the outcome will be, whether I'll acquire evenness of disposition or be flung into the maw of my imagination anew—be compelled to confront greater obstacles to my sanity! Will this equilibrium-assassinating association ever play itself out, release me? Will I ever cease spinning in futile thought-circles, tempting madness, murdering myself bit by bit...? God, enough! *Enough!*"

I found myself wincingly whipping my eyes about my bedroom, seeking to determine if an ill-intentioned something was present. Yes, the something was there!—in the scintillant shafts of light on the walls, advancing walls!—in the electric density of the air, suffocating air! My bedroom not only no longer belonged to me, it had turned against me! Had I ever lived in this apartment?

Useless question! I was already exiting the room, dashing to the front door and turning its knob, stepping into the building's hallway, approaching the elevator...

Once inside the elevator, conscious of it descending, I became aware of staring at my reflection on its polished stainless steel door: the brightness of the overhead lamp rushed at my image—splintered my facial features into jagged silver, slammed into my eyes! I could neither move nor yell nor think...

I've no recollection of exiting my building, having any idea where I was going or wished to go. All I remember—in isolated snippets—is the manner in which I was negotiating the streets: it was as if I'd been struck blind but that I somehow always knew when I'd reached the end of a block; when a curb was a stride away and required an adjustment of foot placement; when being struck by a car was a possibility and it was necessary to determine if one was near. It was as if conscious thought had detached itself from eyesight; as if eyesight was still there but had become as subconscious and automatic as the flow of my blood...

* * * * *

My next solid recollection is of standing with my back to a high stone wall: no street lamps were visible, darkness as of a remote country road surrounded me. Where was I? I found myself able to consciously climb inside my eyes again, was shortly peering intently into the night, seeking to discern outlines. By degrees the darkness lost its thick velvety quality, peeled layers away from itself, permitted me to detect row upon row of upright gray-white slabs among shrubs and flowerbeds, an occasional tall evergreen. Yes, that was the reason for the absence of street lamps, fact the city-roar was a distant-seeming hum: I was in a cemetery bounded on all sides by the wall I was leaning against and the wall was dampening the city's noise and illumination. But how, I wondered, had I come to be there? I glanced towards the left, detected a large stone sculpture of a seated figure adjacent to the wall, began to recall having seen a van parked next to the wall when I was still on its city-side; recall having climbed atop the van and, from there, onto the foot wide top of the wall; recall having crawled on hands and knees until reaching the sculpture, descending onto its shoulders and, subsequently, into its lap and onto the ground. Then I'd simply leaned against the wall and waited—waited, doubtless, for my condition of subconscious self-propulsion to pass, return me to waking awareness...

"How," I wondered, "is it possible to climb atop a van and thence onto a wall, and then crawl a distance along the foot-wide top of that wall, and then descend the tricky dew-slicked stone contours of a statue until reaching the ground—do it seemingly without being directly aware of it? And yet, I'm here! Safe and sound, leaning against this wall on its cemetery-side! Safe and sound? Ha! The quiet—the stillness—the dimness—are exerting a soothing influence, sure enough: on account of these things I awaken blinking like one following an exhausting debauch-frolic, glance about in wonder, welcome my senses back to equilibrium-encompassed perceptions. But safe and sound for how long? The stimulus I'm under the influence of, cause of my periodic retreats into states of suspended awareness during which coordinated physical volition's somehow permitted: by releasing its grip upon me the said stimulus also reveals and clarifies itself to waking thought once more! And who knows when such clarity will again become unbearable, force me to obscure it via yet another retreat from the surface of sensation? Who knows when I'll again be compelled to undergo paralysis of consciousness, be somnambulistically preoccupying myself with God only knows what? Yes, what an unkind joke! The cause of these attacks returns to my understanding due to the fact that the latest attack has passed—fact that this cool dark quiet place revives me: she whose beauty is as sharp as a slap in the face, sting of a whip; and, at the same time, as elusive as a reflection on a swift stream's surface, the cries of gulls in a high wind! She whose energetic placidity of manner is an instant disturbance in my depths—the opening up of new depths, vertiginous swoons on the edges of inner rifts, gaping chasms, whirlpools! She who affects me like a spell-casting diamon, elemental spirit in earthly guise! Who excites my nerves to the searing point, arouses my senses to electric numbness, over-whelms all thought—God! propels me into waking trances which are outside of deliberation, intention, and memory; but that are nevertheless subject to the laws of conscience, under the juris-diction of guilt! Yes, my bewitching beauty propels me into rea-son-suspending trances, then I emerge from them: who's to blame? Who bears the responsibility for whatever unsociable act I may have committed while under the influence of the trance? Ha! Note what I said: 'whatever unsociable act'! Why am I still more than willing to suspect the worst? Does such willingness point to buried sins? to guilt struggling to see the light of day, il-luminate those sins, demand that justice be done? Or is it, simply, random self-torment for the purpose of adding drama to life? But, if so, then why must this drama-mongering always place me in the position of attempting to argue myself out from under the bur-den of fabricated crimes, supposed outrages? One would assume that these suspected crimes can't appear from out of nowhere; that there's a substantial reason why they're able to so effortlessly van-quish ease of mind! If these crimes are merely fantasies for the purpose of inner preoccupation, then certainly the routine would have worn thin and become a bore by now, with the result that I'd be casting about for other subjects! Inner dramatic acting's obvi-ously a means of adding intensity to experience, prolonging in-terest in existence; so why, then, can't it be recast in the form of an aspiration to love? Why can't it veer towards yearnings to at-tain to achingly beautiful states of bliss? Why? God, but my un-ease won't depart! The cackling taunt, as if on account of something being well-informed concerning unpleasant qualities and inclinations of mine of which I'm ignorant, persists! The inner jab, as if on account of something seeking to proclaim distressing truths pertaining to my behavior to the world, persists! Efforts to dispel my uncertainty concerning the missing intervals of my memory—illuminate the primary cause of my fear! are as futile as the first time I attempted to do so! Ha, and I've run in these iden-tical thought-circles nearly every day for far too many blurred days to count and still haven't managed to get beyond self-con-

tradiction, cleverness which crumbles the foundation upon which
it rests! The chance of so much as hoping for a solution to the riddle being perpetually propounded by my memory is being perpetually postponed! So I ask: why bother continuing to attempt to
think myself out of my situation? Why go on and on and on only
to find myself at the starting gate once again—over and over, yet
again?"

I became sensible of having forcibly rubbed the palms of my
hands against the rough stones of the wall, scraped and cut them.
I was subsequently holding my hands up to my eyes, detecting
the vaguely darker lines which denoted the scrapes, while aware
of a stinging sensation; and also aware that the act of curling my
fingers towards the base of my hands, by contracting the wounded
folds of skin, increased the sting. So why, then, was I continuing
to curl my fingers and induce the pain? commencing to rapidly
open and close my hands in order to maximize the pain?

"Ha," it dawned on me, "I've roughly caressed the jaggedness
of this granite for the purpose of recalling myself to myself! I've
deliberately cut my palms so as to break the hold of futile circle-
thought, reintroduce myself to linear cause and effect! And now
I form tight fists in order to exacerbate the discomfort of the
wounds—an act which further yanks me from unproductive speculations, assists in restoring me to external stimuli! But what stu-
pidity! Enough of it! These wounds are real! The danger of
infection is real! I'm sure the city-grime—exhaust and incinera-
tor residue, God only knows what else—which clings to these
stones has intermingled with the blood of these cuts, and... What
was I thinking? Ha! That's the point: I wasn't thinking, I was fleeing from thought-overkill! I've replaced inner preoccupation with
the priority of attending to my hands as soon as possible! I've...
But, God! When will it stop? Windows kicked in, passersby in-
sulted and taunted with the aim of inciting them to anger, this
present self-mutilation! It's all the same! It's all a grasping for
straws of the outer world to prevent myself from drowning in the
inner! It's all on account of wishing to deflect my attention from
the heart-stabbingly beautiful face which shimmers on the screen

of my dreams whether I be asleep or awake, results in tenseness of the muscles, grindings of the teeth, throbbings of the temples—the face which destroys all calm, perpetuates unease, relegates me to a soul-constricting life of unending self-accusation! But, no! I refuse to... Yes, I insist that I refuse to succumb to the lash of circle-thought again; that... But I've got to do something about my hands! There must be a faucet around here somewhere so people can fill pitchers, water the flowers on the graves of their dear departed; must be a tap for garden hoses, sprinklers..."

I strolled towards the headstones in an effort to locate the sort of main walkway which would be likely to have faucets placed at regular intervals along it and, as I did so, became aware of a light-source which hadn't been apparent in the shadow of the wall—a diffused hint of amber that was streaming towards me from the right side of the base of a small hill, being caught by the dew on the lawn, foliage, and headstones, imbuing all with a slippery sheen. I changed direction, approached the hill, had soon ascended it far enough to note the amber was cresting its top, highlighting the ghostly silhouettes of trees which sluggishly shifted in the nearly nonexistent breeze. But when I reached the top of the hill and was gazing down its far side, the light-source (which I supposed might originate in the vicinity of the type of main walkway I sought) was still concealed: the low headstones which had heretofore characterized the cemetery were, on this new side of the hill, replaced by a veritable forest of tall monuments and sepulchres in the dark narrow alleyways of which the light fitfully forced a mist-hampered passage without revealing its origin.

I commenced descending the hill, was soon surrounded by large rectangular slabs, crosses, obelisks, and sepulchres—some of them twice as tall as myself, all of them seemingly placed haphazardly, as if time had unexpectedly caught up with the original plan, forced newer additions between the older graves several instances over. Here, there, everywhere tomb scraped against tomb; and the passages among them turned this way, that in abrupt angles which were increasingly difficult to follow once the base of the hill was reached, on account of greater crowding. Forest, indeed! The light dwindled nearly to nothing and I was obliged to feel my way with the back of my hands, my palms being turned away to shield their cuts from further irritation. The leaves of the trees and shrubs which crowded the spaces between the monuments swished across my face and throat, imparted an unpleasant slimy sensation, soaked my clothes with their dew. Would the maze never end? I'd turn right, left, encounter an unbroken straightaway of a few yards, only to be forced to sharply angle sideways again: was I going in circles? And why had the light all but disappeared? Was it that the ground on this side of the hill was too low to catch it? or had I veered away from it?

Ah! I banged my shin against a hard object: in glancing down to attempt to discern the extent of the obstruction so as not to strike it anew, I was struck by the fact I could detect nothing at all, not the slightest contrast of shadow with darker shadow. I crouched, slowly extended the back of my right hand, encountered a section of metallic tubing: a slight thrill of joy shot through me as my fingers followed its cylindrical coldness upwards, traced the circular outline of a faucet. Ha! I'd all but forgotten what I was searching for but it hadn't mattered because it had found me. Soon I was gingerly clasping and unclasping my hands in soothing icy water: the initial sting quickly departed, semi-numbness took its place. There was also the satisfaction of knowing I was following medically correct procedure—flushing away grime, preventing infection: the slightest thought in one's favor goes a long way when the general tone of them is overwhelmingly forbidding!

Be that as it may: I continued to hold my hands under the cold stream of water, occasionally venturing to lightly rub the fingers of one over the palm of the other to assist with dislodging whatever impurities might be lingering among the wounds—a task aided, no doubt, by the local anesthesia of the numbness-imparting temperature of the water. Before long, however, this same temperature became overwhelming in its effect: discomfort approaching pain commenced to displace the numbness. I was put in mind of the fact that not a great deal of flesh sat between the fronts and backs of my hands—the discomfort was this small width of flesh announcing a warning: something akin to frostbite might occur if I held my hands in the icy water for too long. I consequently removed them. At first, they stung with greater fury: for ten to twenty seconds there was a throbbing ache centered at their backs, almost as if they'd been struck; then the ache became a sensation of tightness, as if their skin was contracting; but, lastly, there was a pleasing influx of humming, almost reckless, warmth: what's the explanation of the latter? Is the warmth a case of one directly experiencing the temperature of one's blood, because one's flesh has been chilled enough to provide a contrast to it? Not that it matters: it's simply that I passed a brief interval in suchlike idle speculations while vaguely aware I was brushing the damp detritus—pine needles, rotting leaves—from the landing of an adjacent sepulchre, seating myself thereupon.

Once seated, I stared at my hands—watched as the ghostly outlines of my fingers, thumbs, and palms steadily became discernable against the backdrop of near-blackness. Near-blackness? Not so: I became aware of the thin crescent of moon which hovered to the side of the gentle sway of a large pine's towering spray; of the splash of stars across the sky. Why hadn't I noticed the moon and stars previously? Had clouds obscured them? Curious: there wasn't, as far as I could determine, a cloud in the sky: had high altitude winds dispersed them within the past few minutes to reveal the heavenly bodies? Whatever the case, I became conscious of a pleasant stir of nerve-tingles in response to the discovery; conscious of a muscle-massaging inner sigh, tone of relaxation...

Yes, the stars were there: twinkling in the dark vastness above the diffused city dust glow of the lower sky, drawing my gaze upwards with my thoughts following. "Ha, here I am," I was saying to myself, "wandering in a cemetery after scampering about the city after fleeing my apartment, and how pointless and silly it seems when I see the stars obliviously sparkling on the far side of more distance than one could travel in a billion lifetimes; and when I think, in turn, of the greater distances beyond these stars;

of the stars visible from them, and on and on! What? I'm in thrall to attraction accelerated to the point of obsession—permitting myself to be knocked about, disoriented, reduced to fear? doing this when the stars blaze in the horizonless empyrean, mock finite vistas, jeer at the experiences we undergo on earth? The vanity of it! To suppose that what we consider trouble or conflict or tragedy is anything besides a childish preoccupation with inconsequential happenings on this speck of, relatively speaking, nearly invisible dust on the endless span of dark space within vaster expanses of dark space within more! Ha! I gaze skyward, and it's like I'm not here anymore! I run my fingers across the skin of my cheeks and the sensation of my fingers on my skin and the sensation of my skin on my fingers becomes lost in the distances above, begins to seem like something imagined, less than an incident in a half-remembered dream! Yes, I begin to feel like a mirage which disappears in direct proportion to the degree I approach it! And so I ask: what's this business of being under the influence of an obsession which scatters my thoughts, sears my nerves, brings about episodes of blinding dread? What are thoughts? What are nerves? What is dread? How, I ask, is it possible for me to be convinced enough of my existence to manage to imagine phenomena such as tension, irritation, unease? Where's the substantiality? Yes, the stars shimmer in the expanses above and still more stars shimmer in the expanses beyond them, and suddenly it's like my body's a random congregation of particles which have united in the illusory activity of persuading themselves they're in possession of the thing known as life! What is life? A variety of equally random electric bond which holds the randomly congregated particles of my body together? an isolationist impulse of that same electric bond which persuades itself it's in possession of the things known as consciousness, individuality, personality? What is this activity that I'm presently engaged in? What is thought? Is thought merely a by-product of the electric bond of life—an alternating current which endlessly repeats itself, ceaselessly begins at its ending point, pointlessly whirls in its own limited sphere of imprisoned perception? What is imagination? Is imagination the alternating current of thought transposed into outlines and colors? And what causes the outlines and colors of imagination to arrange themselves into patterns which bring about unsettledness, yearning, need? What is this endless spinning in explosive self-absorption on account of being teased and flayed by shapes of light? What's the purpose? Ha! A body, a living being! It's as if a living being's an accumulation of particles which exists for the purpose of bedeviling itself! But, again: what is bedevilment? How can things such as bedevilment, desperation, and terror exist in this world where nothing's actually known; where knowledge is but the artifice of assigning invented values to assorted phenomena and contriving to organize, memorize, and communicate them; where, indeed, there's no distinction between invented and real because the urge to impose distinctions is, in itself, a failed-in-advance attempt to assign states of permanence to an illusion? Pleasure? Pain? What's the difference? Yes, the stars twinkle against the blackness, and all sensation and emotion—preferences, aversions! dissolve in the apprehended expanses! And, if it comes to that, who—what? is apprehending those expanses? Expanses? The space my body displaces? What's the difference? And what is this moment? What is yesterday, tomorrow? What is this business of measuring time? Time?"

I became aware that the breeze, formerly sluggish to the point of nonexistence, had picked up; that a steady gust was winding its way through the narrow passages between the monuments and tombs, gathering speed at the corner near where I sat, bathing me in what was perhaps the first chill of approaching autumn. But, although I was dressed for summer weather—wearing nothing but lightweight cotton—the cold became invigorating tingles the moment it touched me—tingles which resembled warmth rather than frigidity. And as I continued to stare at the stars the sensation of falling out from under my senses, dissolving in the vastness of the perceived distances, was heightened by the breeze-imparted tingles: I was, indeed, but a gathering of particles shimmering in the open air, as ghostly and unseizable as light flickering on running water...

I found myself standing, commencing to walk. And it was curious: whereas previously I'd been obliged to blindly grope my way among the tombs with outstretched hands as my only reliable guide, now I made my way not only without their assistance but with ease. Suddenly my feet were capable of detecting, via telltale variations in the surface tone of the ground, the existence of a twisting pathway of mossy stepping stones; suddenly my eyes were capable of detecting the same stepping stones on account of a small amount of illumination—just enough—which seemed to emanate from the air itself, as if its gaseous molecules were rubbing together and the consequent friction produced a faint glow. Somehow, in my star-inspired state of mental disembodiment, my senses were sharper: my footfall felt more, eyes saw more, ears heard more. What did my ears hear? They distinguished the muffled acceleration of engines, honking of horns, raising of voices in the unbroken hum which originated from the city outside the cemetery walls—sounds that reminded me in a discreet, almost subconscious, manner that I was strolling on an island of stillness surrounded by bustle: it was almost as if these sounds were the fragmented memories of a dream I'd had long ago.

But what I soon realized I was most aware of were the outlines of the tombs and monuments against the sky—the slabs, arches, crosses, obelisks, and statues which foreshortened the horizon, surrounded me on all sides with jagged beauty like that of wave and wind sculpted rocks on a remote shore. And from an apprehension of the higher portions of the grave markers, my attention wandered to their foundations: an alteration in awareness no doubt assisted by the fact that I, in turning here and there, had come to a place where the light I'd previously seen and lost had reappeared again, brighter than before.

I found myself in an open area which was reminiscent, on a smaller scale, of a town square. On three sides of this mini-square were the fronts of sepulchres; on the fourth were large monuments interspersed with conical evergreens; in its center was a backless stone bench situated below the extensive canopy of an ancient pine. I seated myself on the bench, watched the light enter the

square at its right corner, flow about the gingerbread whorls of
the eaves of the sepulchres, flicker among their layered arches,
delve within the iron grillwork of their doorways, die in the darkness of their interiors. "Ha," I continued in my recent vein of
thought, "if the stars in the vastness above force impressions of the
transience of life—dreamy ungraspability of life—illusory solidity of life—then what of the dear departed among whom I find
myself? Yes, they were alive once, as I am now. They were in possession of fleshly bodies, in thrall to the tension of their muscles,
surge of their blood, crackle of their nerves; endlessly driven by
the same to seek out the caresses and kisses of others—athirst for
reciprocal love-glances, shared need, mutual oblivion in transports of attraction! But where are they now? What's become of the
eyes which knew the joy of gazing into the eyes of the one they'd
daydream about for hours when they were apart? what's become
of the lips which knew the delight of seeking warmth, excitement,
satiation at the mouth of the one who hummed in unison with
them, tumbled in the undertows with them, wave-crashed and
blazed with them? of the hands which lovingly stroked jittery skin
into flushes of contentment, tongues which adoringly licked soft
necks? Yes, what's become of them: *they are dead!* Dead? God!
How inconceivable that in the cold unfeeling lifeless soil below
these markers are caskets containing the inert residue of these
magnificent beings who were once in possession of breathing
flesh, bloodstreams, and nerve nets; who once knew what it was
to become alert and purposeful on account of bright-eyed beauty;
once knew what it was to surrender to surging euphoria, tumble
out from under themselves in procreation's bliss-bestowing current! But now it's gone: healthy radiant skin, urgently pumping
blood, thrillingly intent nerves all rotted to formless black glue,
brittle cakes of bacteria-gnawed dust! How is it possible?—possible that this, the hand I hold close to my face, will someday be
indistinguishable from the dirt at my feet? I look at my hand: what
a miracle it is! The long slender tapering fingers which tremble
and pulsate with the life-force; the soft layer of skin which is
bonded to the bones by taut muscles; the veins through which

oxygen-rich blood flows to nourish the muscles and skin. I curl my fingers: the bones of each swivel in their sockets in perfect synchronization, the nails of each touch the base of my palm simultaneously; and, also, jabs of pain appear due to the fact this movement agitates the wounds on my palm. What a miraculous system of transmission! The command to curl my fingers issued by thought which is electricity racing the length of the latticework of nerves between my brain and hand; and the resulting discomfort of the wounds which sends dissonant pulses racing in the opposite direction of the initial command along the identical avenue back to the brain to warn of danger! What master craftsman assembled this incredible union of flesh, blood, and electricity? And why go to such trouble if it's as fragile and transient as it is? God! A so-called long life is less than an eye-blink relative to all which has and will pass, an infinitesimally small dot of a blip on the time-graph! And just one instance of wrong-place-at-the-wrong-time—one falling roof tile, one car jumping the curb, one thug on a kill-for-kicks spree—and: life's gone, irretrievable! One's entire record of experience—the body which endured it, senses which gathered it, thoughts which ordered it, memory which stored it—is instantly relegated to the worms, as if it never existed in the first place!"

I'd already risen to my feet, commenced walking towards the corner of the square from which the light was issuing. Upon reaching it and continuing a few yards down a fairly wide straight pathway of rectangular stones, I emerged from the area of large grave markers and detected a row of gas lamps in the near distance, the white-amber flame-jets of which were visible above a level expanse of waist-high tombstones. I accelerated my pace and a minute or two later was standing on a well-maintained loose gravel walkway wide enough to admit the passage of a car. Young maple trees and gas lamps were situated at regular intervals, alternating with one another, on both sides of the walkway: the cheerful glow of the lamps was flitting among the fluttering leaves of the trees.

I glanced down the shorter length of the walkway and perceived an arch which surmounted iron gates, doubtless open during daylight, that lead from the cemetery. On both sides of the
gates were large seated stone figures, not difficult to climb, which
were nearly as high as the cemetery wall. There, then, was my
way out of the cemetery when I was ready to return to the city. For
the time being, I wasn't willing to trade the peace and quiet of
this private walkway for the crowds outside, abandon the conversation I was having with myself. "Yes," I resumed while turning to stroll down the longer length of the walkway, "the stars
agleam in the far reaches of the firmament and the dead decayed
to dust in the ground: I would think they'd put matters in perspective! Afraid of a woman? In thrall to an obsession which takes
all, gives nothing in return? How, when I'm able to gaze above
and dissolve out from under myself? How, when I'm able to consider the vitality gone to ashes below and understand the fragile
gift of life isn't to be squandered? Yes, I'm perplexed in earnest:
how is it possible for my bewitching beauty to unremittingly grip
me from the inside out, claim every moment of waking consciousness for herself, create an increasingly unbridgeable gap
between my present tortured existence and former carefree life?
No, I don't understand why I'm unable to extract the claws of this
unhealthy preoccupation from my feelings; why she, of all the
women in this city (women I formerly enjoyed at will, caught and
released with ease), should be the one and only inhabitant of my
fancy; why the mere fact of her existence inflames me such that
all other means of engaging my attention are erased from possibility; why the awe, dread, unshakable mood of ominousness on
her account!"

Before too long I was aware of having reached the end of the
walkway, where it widened into a large circular area of the iden-
tical gravel bordered by the same gas lamps and maples. A semi-
circle of stone benches was in the center of this circle; they
flanked a crescent-shaped plot of soil seeded with an unfamiliar
variety of flower which, excepting a few isolated ragged red blos-
soms, had wilted into tattered brown. The thought of sitting did-

n't occur to me and I began to pace in circles about the benches and flowerbed while continuing to keep company with my thoughts: "But we never fully know what we're about—why we're behaving as we are—do we? And as regards myself: is this soul-gnawing attachment what I secretly desire? Is it, in actuality, a beneficent windfall of shudderingly vivid struggle following a childhood, adolescence, decade of adulthood spent in unproductive ease? Of course, that's how I initially viewed it! I recollect all too well the manner in which I advertised it to myself: 'Life-affirmation via sanity-straining extremes of sensation! My special means of flirting with the limits of endurance, awakening the survival-instinct, experiencing more of intensity than I would've otherwise suspected was possible in this life!' Fine words, indeed! An impressive manifesto! But now I'm running for my life, and I don't care a jot for self-transformation via intensity of sensation! I no longer have the luxury of attaching fine phrases to this instance of obsession which has leaped clear of all comfort zones, become a baleful fury at my heels! One must occasionally be allowed to believe oneself capable of distancing oneself from trepidation, dread—occasionally be granted a token interval of respite! On the other hand, earlier today (Ha, earlier today: how deceptive time can be! Earlier today already seems as far away as last month!), when I awakened in my all but forgotten apartment... There's no denying there was a sense of having reached safe-harbor following unheard-of tribulations—certainly I was overcome with something resembling the ground-kissing thankfulness of mariners of old after a life-threatening voyage was over! And tonight, despite the inner grating which hasn't ceased to afflict me, intimate of unpleasantness to come... I can't deny there's an element of satisfaction in the thought that I'm wandering alone at night in this cemetery while surrounded by civilization, undergoing an experience very few people ever get to undergo! I do, indeed, occasionally reach some version of safe-harbor! Not for long, it's true: wild water never stops churning nearby—always pulls me to sea anew! but..."

I was now pacing back and forth in an overlapping line, no longer having the patience to go in circles—was vaguely conscious of executing the about-faces at each end of the overlapping line with emphasis, as if they were physically enacted exclamation points, while continuing to harangue myself: "Yes, life's precious and isn't to be taken lightly, wasted! And I've undoubtedly tasted more of life on account of this obsession's intervention than I would've otherwise—far more! And should this obsession happen to permanently submerge my reason; should all thought be dashed to splinters in a savage inner clash, engulfed in shrieking night; then it will still certainly be true that I've managed to wring the quality from life, been vouchsafed a degree of vividness of experience which my previous existence of comfort deprived me of, and... But why am I dictating a eulogy? Ha! More drama made possible by the selfsame obsession! That's right, I'm being permitted to compose my epitaph as I pace under the stars in the dead of night in a deserted cemetery that's surrounded by thronged city sidewalks: another unique experience courtesy of the boundless munificence of this attachment which has altered the course of my life! But all of these unique experiences—this night's waking blackout of not above two hours ago; the insomnia-fueled overindulgence—perceptual and affective extremes—of the past two or more months; the flirtations with madness, immolation-rehearsals: yes, truly very impressive and something to be proud of, assuming I'm ever again allowed to feel I'm able to willfully direct the course of my life! But, if not? If I at last knuckle under, find myself atumble in wave after wave of sensation too forceful to mentally negotiate, withstand? If... But, no! I refuse to spin in circles again! Anything can be asserted regarding the nature and significance of a given person's unique collection of life-experiences; then the opposite can be asserted with an equal amount of assembled facts and rational organization to support it! Which just goes to show that it's neither vouchsafed us to comprehend why we do the things we do to feel the way we feel nor to comprehend the implications of those feelings; that there's no convenient bundling up of motivation and experience in tidy little packages of the pathetically ineffectual tool known as thought! Only circles endlessly doubling back on themselves! Ha! Only the inevitable return to a mention of the circles! Only the inevitable command to myself to drop the matter, shut up!"

I willed myself to cease pacing, sat on one of the benches. The wilted flowers were before me, rattling in the breeze. About me were the young maples, their leaves fluttering in a rapid succession of light and shadow as they alternately faced and turned away from the illumination of the gas lamps. And beyond the lamps and maples, what had previously escaped my attention, was the back of a church which was framed on both sides by the cemetery's enclosing wall. Prompted by this discovery, I made a conscious survey of my surroundings—a survey which revealed that the circular space of gravel was an empty parking lot, doubtless for the convenience of the pastor and other minions of the church. Also, I perceived that a narrow path of stones led from the far end of the parking lot through a plot of grass to steps which rose to a door on the right side of the church. I glanced upwards and was astonished at the extent and height of the church's spires; astonished, further, when I recognized them as being those of St. _____, a well-known landmark. Yes, of course the cemetery was attached to St. _____! How had the fact escaped me? I couldn't help but laugh: there, right before me, were the spires I knew so well from the city's side of the wall! I'd been stomping about the cemetery as if it was located in a neighborhood I'd never been in before, oblivious of which streets surrounded it on its several sides! Yes, I knew where I was, all right: I was within three blocks of my bewitching beauty's place of residence!

"God!" I exclaimed while leaping to my feet. "I haven't been idling about, as I thought, in a far-flung section of town! I've been as good as in front of my spine-igniting beauty's building the entire time! My wanderings and musings in this cemetery? Nothing but procrastination—me working up the courage to knock on her door! And, of course, I have to knock on her door—facing her is my one and only option! Whether I'm fearful or not, wish to flee or not: all worthless window dressing, self-deception! Bottom line: my present situation of unceasingly being under her influence no matter where I am or what I'm doing, having my emotional life infiltrated to such a degree I'm frequently unable to detect any remaining aspect of myself, is unendurable and can't continue! The only possible exit is exposure to her physical presence in the hope that I'll be able to apprehend her human qualities and, in so doing, dispel the unsettling aura which imagination has conferred upon her. Yes, by all rights, the more I see of her with my eyes—as opposed to with my mind's eye—the less her fancy-exaggerated features will have a hold on me. And if I were to speak to her, hear her replies? or touch her, grasp one of her hands? Oh, if only I can! If only I can communicate with her person-to-person—apply brakes to all impulse-acceleration, dissolve the dread! Yes, certainly chinks will begin to appear in her armor as a consequence of exposure to her corporeal presence; certainly she'll begin to seem as whimsical, vulnerable, approachable as any other woman! It's inevitable, isn't it? But what if it isn't? What if exposure to the sound of her voice, instead of providing me with a concrete impression to fasten upon for the purpose of grounding myself in rationality, becomes a new stirring quality for my fancy to embellish, whip into more sleep-murdering waking dreams? What if the act of touching her, instead of associating her with physical solidity and enabling me to assign finite limitations to her, opens up hitherto unexplored avenues of the imagination, flings me into more somnambulistic conscience-bedeviling intervals of recollection-eluding time? Ha! Speak to her? Touch her? Who's to say that the sight of her won't instantly render such things as impossible as flying via a flapping of my arms? Who's to say that I'm not on the cusp of another desperate double-month of...? Oh, God forbid that I am! But if I am? Well, worse than my present situation isn't much different: both are unendurable! So what will become of me? I'll know when I know!"

What was I doing? What was I looking at? Simple questions, indeed! Questions that people generally answer with ease; that generally require little pause for reflection before an answer is given! "I'm reaching into my pocket for bus change," replies someone to the first. "I'm watching the delivery man fill the dispenser with the early morning edition," replies someone to the second. Simple questions, simple answers! What was I doing? What was I looking at? No ready reply to either is forthcoming! Mostly, I recall a renewed onslaught of duress on account of realizing how close I was to my bedeviling beauty's apartment; recall standing there stunned, as if with mouth agape and eyes wide—uncontrollably shaking. Did I sit on the gravel in the center of the parking lot, recline onto my back, dazedly lie there for a spell? An angle of view of the spires of the church which returns to memory would seem to warrant such a supposition: spectacular flutings of stone soaring upward at the back of my head, seeming to pierce and merge with the starry vastness of the sky, bring it close to my outstretched fingers that are flexing as if seeking to grasp the distances: was I lying on my back or standing with my head tossed back? Ha! As if it matters!

Sometime later I was strolling towards the right side of the church, where it joined with the cemetery's enclosing wall. Yes, recollection informs me that I pass through the row of maples and gas lamps, step onto lush grass above which is a wooden trellis thick with ivy, the broad leaves of which all but obscure the sky. A steady breeze stirs the leaves of the ivy to whisper and the whisper seems to be further away than it actually is, a reverberant muffled swishing as of waves hitting shore on the other side of an expanse of dunes. I advance to the end of the trellis, where a comparatively low portion of the wall, about seven feet high, appears before me. I extend my arms upwards to gauge the distance between my reach and an overhanging eave of the church. I then leap, am grasping the eave with both hands while pawing at the wall with my feet, progressively bringing them towards the top of it. Pain emanates from the wounds on my palms as I grasp the eave and I grit my teeth against the pain, will myself to disregard it. After all, I must climb over! And soon, somehow, a leg is slung over the top of the wall; soon I'm seated on the wall, examining its street-side, noting the descent is greater by at least a yard. Moments later, I'm hanging over the edge of the street-side of the wall from my chest down with the bulk of my weight supported by my arms. I propel myself outwards with a thrust of my shoulders and feet, drop to the lawn below. Ah! The pain in my palms, from having grasped the eave, is flaring again—I've doubtless scraped them again! I'm wringing them against the air, pacing in tight circles, cursing under my breath with clenched teeth. But, quiet! Quiet! Not four or so yards away, on the other side of the spiked iron fence, are passersby on the sidewalk. I'm shielded from view by the shadows and low-dipping branches of this large oak, but quiet! The blazing stings of my reinjured palms have subsided, are slight stabbing pulsations now: I've got to clean my hands again, locate a restroom, any place with running water. But, as to how to get out of here... Yes, over there, a gate of the same iron grillwork and spikes as the fence but lower, only as high as my chest: I need to creep up to one of the gate's pillars, conceal myself behind it, wait for this cluster of people to pass—for their chatter to become indistinct. Ok, now peer over the gate to make certain the coast is clear: damn! Lone individuals, on both sides of the street: it mustn't be as late as I thought it was, must still be fairly early; or... Well, how do I know? It could just as easily be well past midnight... At any rate, check again: no one in sight or sound! Ok, quick! Insert a foot here, atop this crossbar; now grasp the spikes, but—careful! don't aggravate those cuts again, use fingers only! Good, now pull upwards, then bring the other foot to the higher crossbar, between the spikes—then bring the first foot up further, and over! Ha, back on the sidewalk again; in the streets again; en route to my bewitching beauty's place of residence again! My hands? Forget them! I'm sick and tired of futilely flailing in diversionary tactics, procrastination: I only want the encounter to be over and done with, sooner than soon!

*   *   *   *   *

My next solid recollection is of sitting on the landing of my bedeviling beauty's building, with my back to the entrance. I hadn't, as far as I know, attempted to locate her apartment; therefore, I couldn't be certain if she was home or not. So why, then, was I firmly convinced she'd soon be dropped off by another car? Ha! Another car? I was doubtless harking back to the car in which, months ago, I'd glimpsed her for the second time and that had discharged her at this building, thereby revealing her place of residence. Yes, a supposition had taken root in my thoughts and, regardless of the flimsy foundation of the said supposition, I was acting in accordance with it: I was persuaded that she'd been obliged by work responsibilities to remain late at the office; that she'd completed what she needed to do and was being driven home by a coworker; that before long the coworker's car would halt at the end of the walkway I was facing; that she'd emerge from the car and I'd be face to face with her again, bracing myself to endure the onslaught of her eyes!

How soon would the car appear? When would its passenger door swing open, reveal her nerve-scattering beauty to me again? When would the car's interior light be illuminating the electric equanimity of her presence, shimmering in the cascades of her hair? When would she be stepping from the car onto the sidewalk, straightening herself, flinging her hair into the breeze? When would she be turning towards the walkway, taking steps in my direction? When would I again be gazing into the eyes which hadn't ceased to haunt me from the moment of my first encounter with them in that cafe?

Yes, I was sitting there: no car had, as of yet, appeared. And of course, because the matter of a car discharging her was a spontaneous fabrication of my fancy, there was virtually no likelihood of it happening. Nevertheless, I was already behaving as if it actually was happening—beginning to picture her on the sidewalk, undergo an alarmingly sharp hint of the authentic experience! Yes, suddenly she's at the end of the walkway, with the breeze flattening the folds of her dress against her slender figure in the streetlight's amber glow; suddenly I'm being unsettled by the forceful emanations—thought-warping insistence! of her presence, whirled into gasping disorientation by the pull—emotional undertows! of her center of gravity; suddenly I'm... Oh, I jerk my head downwards to avoid meeting her eyes with mine, stare hard

at the steps at my feet while aware that the landing's dissolving
out from under my hips; that I'm teetering to one side, grasping
at the handrail to steady myself—what handrail? The iron becomes rubber in my hands—becomes airy feathers in my hands—
turns to mist, blows away! I seek to rally myself, hold my ground:
I don't want to flee, lose this opportunity to face off with my obsession—don't want to be an imagination-harried wanderer of insomnia-altered streets again! I'm watching, seemingly from far
inside myself, as my head jerks upwards—as I seek to locate her
eyes—lock stares! in the blurriness of the air! But my head's vibrating too violently for me to be certain of what I'm seeing...

"No!" I silently shouted to myself while pinching my thigh.
"No!" I was shaking my head to rid it of the involuntary vibrations, vigorously blinking to clear my eyes—finally opening them
wide, focusing upon the walkway before me: *nothing!* She was,
indeed, not there! She was, indeed, nothing but a mental mirage,
something fancied to life! So why, then, were my muscles tense
to the point of yanking at the sockets of my bones? Why was I
breathing deeply and rapidly, grasping my ankles, scraping them
with my nails? Why was every nerve in my body a flaring ember
singeing my skin from the inside, tying hot knots of unease in my
chest? "No!" I repeated while shuddering at the thought of the effect of an invented phantom upon me, struggling to move my
limbs on my own, independently of the twitches of panic...

I was sitting there: orange light was emanating from the lobby
of her building—streaming through the glass of the door at my
back, flickering and dancing on the steps and landing, creeping up
my legs and arms, causing me to wince! How unbelievably de-
luded—stupidly hubristic! I'd been to believe myself capable of
awaiting my seizure-inducing beauty at the entrance of her building! It was as if live wires were being jabbed into my skin, fed underneath its surface—snaking throughout me, attacking from all
directions with a steady shock! Yes, the electricity was wining—
hissing! in my ears; it was rapidly accumulating, leaping from
me—overflowing! into the open air! God! The instant the elec-

tricity entered the air, it bent and twisted it into opaque jelly—suffused the orange light with shadows, smothered it in gloom!

I ask: how is it possible to experience claustrophobia while outside, in the open air? How is it possible for open air to acquire the appearance of melting gray glass upon which splinters of light are wildly twisting? And the distortion of depth-perception, games being played with objects! Listen: the building-fronts on the opposite side of the street were suddenly closer than the railing within hand's grasp—looming against my face, slapping at my eyes! at the same time that the railing was curling away, hovering somewhere in the air to the left and right, disappearing in the pyrotechnics of light! I sought to counter this sensory havoc—yank myself deep inside myself, still my nerves, deaden thought: wailing sounds, as of a high wind, roared about me; discernable pressure, as of the air acquiring solid density and weight, surrounded me on all sides! Suddenly the impression that I was being stared at by a hostile something interposed: yes, it was a fact that every nuance of feeling which was evident upon my face or in the tone of posture of my body was being closely observed, ruthlessly categorized, mockingly analyzed! It was as if the steps, pavement, and buildings were laughing at me! As if the breeze, light, and air were taunting me! As if every discernable object was bearing down on me, seeking to hammer my thoughts into an unbroken yell!

And then, amidst my erupting panic, a single crystal clear thought: the *stare*! What was staring at me? Who was staring at me? Who besides the source of all upheaval, my beautiful nemesis! Yes, it sprang into my head, shrieked!—that she was, at that very instant, rounding the corner of the block; that she was watching me while advancing with measured, implacable step; that she was enraged, determined on emotional violence—dead set on grinding my nerves into spent embers, reducing me to a gibbering wreck!

"No! No! No!" I silently yelled while yanking myself to my feet, descending the choppy—zigzagging, rising and falling! steps, negotiating the tilting walkway with stuttering jerky strides, half-running down the sidewalk as if being shoved! Yes, again in the streets and with not a moment to lose, as she—my succubus, fury! wasn't far behind me, and was closing the distance between us with the sure aim of a long-buried thought, memory one's fruitlessly endeavored to overcome, expel; memory that resurfaces with a vengeance, not to be given the runaround—obscured by sexual excess, insomnia, and imagination-life! any longer; memory that's insistent on being given due respect—confronted, come to terms with! regardless of one's consent, whether or not one's prepared!

I was frantic-walking while all too aware that her eyes were stabbing at my back, prodding icy dissonance into my nerves, causing my legs to shake to such a degree I was teetering to the left and right, at risk of losing my balance! But I couldn't slow my pace, stop; couldn't permit her eyes to gain on me, better focus their assault! What to do? How to escape? I turned onto another street, ran outright to the corner—turned again, ran again... I vaguely recollect an interval during which the blocks were fairly crowded; an interval of glances of surprise, flickers of alarm, on the faces of those I sped towards in passing; exclamatory gestures, swift step-aways; animated chatter, distant laughter; late night kiosks, wind-snapped banners, sidewalk cafes; taillight glows on window glass, slurred views of vehicles streaking towards me and away; and with neon shooting up the sides of buildings at the black sky, street lamp orbs pulsating on puddles in the gutters, dull gray pavement playing dead!

I recall leaving the crowds behind, finding myself on a deserted avenue—the leaves of the trees which lined it were flashing green, amber, silver according to the fretful flittings of street lamp light. Then more sprints to the ends of blocks, turns, sprints... I began to lose my breath, slowed to a walking crawl with my blood beating in my temples: I had no idea where I was, wasn't able to care.

Had I given my beautiful bedeviler the slip? lost her piercing eyes in the populated blocks I'd rushed through, become impossible to keep track of and follow in the crowd? Ha, hope is ever ready to surge forth to comfort, but hope isn't known for reliably reading situations accurately—false comfort's seldom beneficial! Some situations require caution stacked on top of caution, steadily maintained vigilance and suspicion, the unwillingness to relax! I was distressed and infuriated in equal measure on account of being too winded to run: too far from her prodding eyes would never be far enough! Where was I? In some sort of warehouse district: the cobblestones of another time were visible below the worn and neglected pavement of the present; unwashed windows infrequently relieved the gray monotony of the low buildings; all was overspread with dirty mist, dim ocher light. I was dragging the fingers of my right hand along the warehouse-fronts, awaiting the moment when I'd be able to run again...

But, then... Oh, suddenly it seemed to me... No! There was no seeming about it! It was a fact that she—my rapacious phantom, fury! was standing behind me at the end of the block, below one of the street lamps, bathed in its dark gold light! Yes, I could feel her there—a gray-black silhouette surrounded by bronzy bright-ness, like a brand burned onto a patch of well-tanned skin; could feel her vengeful accusing angry eyes stabbing at my back again, shooting needle-pricks up my neck, gripping my head in a vise of throbbing heat! I was still laboring for breath, utterly drained of physical stamina, but I had to run—had to! I jerked forward as if jolted by an electric prod, firmly believed—for an instant! that I'd be dashing down the street again—God! suddenly—like a bird knocked down by a gale! spun towards a building—flish, flash! glimpsed my reflection in a window switching off, on—getting larger, smaller, larger! before tasting sickly nausea sweetness, watching sight turn to black!

I've no idea for how long I was unconscious (several minutes? an hour? longer?) before I opened my eyes to discover myself on my back, with one foot trapped under the thigh of my extended other leg: an uncomfortable situation which I did nothing to alter. I simply remained motionless while making an assessment of my physical state, with next to no reaction to the assessment—in-forming myself it was as if every muscle in my body had been re-

peatedly struck, bruised; that I was in no better shape than a ship-
wreck survivor who's withstood hours of swimming in choppy
water, been washed ashore in a condition of aching stupefaction.
I was aware of wishing to extract my benumbed foot from beneath my sore thigh, rearrange my body in such a manner as to
minimize discomfort, but also convinced that what little strength
would be required to do so had been sapped from me by my ordeal and that I had no choice but to resign myself to my situation.

Perhaps I fell unconscious again—once, or several times; or
perhaps I didn't: the murky sky at which I was staring didn't strike
me, in my spent condition, as being very different from the inside
of my eyelids when my eyes were shut. Therefore, in theory, my
eyes could have been closed without my being aware of it or remained open when I believed they were closed: lapses of attention? waking entrancement? unconsciousness? What's the
difference if one's not only too exhausted to relieve physical discomfort, but too exhausted to actively perceive it as being physical discomfort? And so again: as to whether or not I slipped from
consciousness for assorted intervals or was drifting unawares in an
open-eyed trance... But why am I splitting these hairs, seeking to
ascertain the precise frame of mind I was in during the interval of
immobility? All that matters is that I eventually became aware
sparkles were congregating in my chest, pulsating in a vaguely irritating manner; aware vitality was beginning to assert itself
against the violence it had suffered, flicker and crackle back to
life...

Following the first moment of my awareness of reemerging
energy, there was no longer any question either of slipping into
unconsciousness or wondering if I unknowingly did so; in addition, I suddenly knew I was able to move again. I pulled my right
foot from below the thigh of my left leg, shifted my weight from
my right hip and shoulder—evened the weight of my body against
the pavement—but remained on my back. I now noticed drizzle
was falling so slowly it seemed to hang suspended in the ghostly
yellow light; now noticed my clothes were damp, that moisture
had gathered into droplets upon my face, that the pavement was

dusted with a silvery sheen; now noticed the street was deserted, that the only traffic noise was a muffled hum originating from other areas. Concurrent with this increased awareness of my surroundings was an awareness of the preposterousness of my situation: what was I doing flat on my back on a sidewalk in a warehouse district on a chilly, advance taste of autumn, night? wearing nothing but a lightweight shirt and pants, spent and sore with insane exertion on account of...? On account of what? God! A lightning shaft as good as shot through my thoughts: I'd been stalked, pursued, forced into a fainting fit by a phantom! A phantom? fabrication of my fancy? Oh, suddenly my resurgent vitality was tensing my muscles, rasping at them like fiery claws; suddenly it was flaring outward to my fingertips and toes, pounding expanding heat into my head, bringing on a panic-attack!

"No, for God's sake, no!" I heard myself yell (whether silently or aloud, I know not) while quivering—shaking, jerking! on the pavement! Who was I? What was I? Ha, will I be believed? Alone and cold and forsaken by any impulse to cling to the person I once was and certainly was no longer, I began to believe that she—my bedeviling beauty, vengeful fury! had slipped inside me, infiltrated my body; yes, that it was she who was gathering herself at the center of my chest, winding my muscles into tight excruciation, shooting through me in a firestorm of fear!

Yes, that's why my breath-breaking beauty was nowhere to be seen! That's why her eyes were no longer maliciously glowing nearby! She'd—it's a fact! taken advantage of my fainting fit— helpless unguardedness! to slip inside me (via the pores of my skin?) like a ghost, disembodied diamon! She'd taken up residence in my sinews, bloodstream, and nervous system! She'd done so with the aim of delving to the roots of my awareness— displacing my personality, destroying all memory of my life-experiences, consuming consciousness until only a burnt cinder remained!

Yes, that's the fancy which seized ahold of me, made me impervious to my aching exhaustion, forced me to my feet; that's the fancy which flogged me into a frantic zigzag dash on the wet

pavement, set me to running as fast as I could! Ha, hope is ever
ready to surge forth to comfort and is often one's last lifeline, a
necessary—despair forestalling! mental prop! I hoped to counter
her inner assault, expel her! Somehow, as long as I continued running... Perhaps I'd reach a level of physical exertion euphoria
which was stronger—more emotionally dense! than she was! Perhaps I'd become too overheated to comfortably inhabit, sweat her
out! But—God! the tops of the buildings were curling towards
one another above me, descending, pressing oppressively close;
the silver of the dew-dusted pavement was whipping upwards,
slapping at my eyes, darting blinding brightness inside them!

Shimmering pavement? Reflected light? No! It was she—my
bedevilment, dread! explosively pulsating within me, filling my
eyes from the inside out with the unholy light of sensory overload! And I was running! Ha! To what purpose? She was below
me, above me, on all sides; within me, without me; where I'd just
been, where I was now, where I'd soon be! Am I being comprehended? What I'm talking about is a violence of being confronted,
opposed—a focused fury of hostility, rage! which was present in
every avenue of perception and emotion, all facets of my personality! Yes, the sensation of my hereness—being among the ele-
ments, inhabiting space and time, the very feel of myself in my
own flesh: it was the dreadful impression that all of creation had
become sick of me, and no longer wanted me in it; that existence
itself wanted to disown me, destroy all evidence of anything I'd
ever done, make it as if I'd never been born!

God! Of all the fancies possible for a predatory imagination to
seize upon, subject me to! What was the cause of such a fancy?
Why would it occur to me I was unworthy of life, too vile to be
abided by existence? It was my bloodcurdling beauty who was
responsible: she was systematically turning my every thought
against me! Yes, first grasping my nerves in a parasitical vise—
saturating them with gloom, paralyzing them with dread; then
forcing my thoughts to compliment them! But again, why? Why
the rage, thirst for vengeance, on her part? Why the relentless pursuit, as if I was Orestes and she a fury risen from the underworld?

Ha! As if I was possessed of the ability to reply to such questions—as if I was able to formulate them in the first place! As if such questions are representative of anything other than an omnipresent mood of ominousness that I'm translating into words in retrospect! Did I want to live or did I want to die? God, I never would've believed it possible to fear to such an extent! Unease was clinging to and erasing the facades of the buildings pressing in on me; turmoil was glowering in the glares of gold on the pavement; mental breakdown was pulsating in the darkness of the doorways! The glittering flutings of drizzle in the dim air suggested bejeweled death shrouds: they sinisterly rippled in the breeze, descended towards me as if with intent to wrap me tight until I could neither move nor breathe! The breeze was the wheezing whispery urgency of deathbed confessions: it seemed eager to exult in bygone perpetrations of heinous crimes, cram my ears to bursting with repellent slithery cackles! Every shadow was a stalking ghost, dead thing fretfully flitting, wringing itself in rage at being too immaterial to seize ahold of me, inflict pain! And myself still running despite the fact I was certainly still suffering from the aches and bruises I'd sustained from my fainting-fall; despite the fact there was certainly little, or nothing, remaining of my regular store of stamina!

Yes, phantoms were shouting the pursuit and I was the quarry! What to do? Where to turn? I reached the end of the street, all building fronts suddenly disappeared: open space took their place, rolled to my left and right, rose and fell like large swells in mid-ocean. I stepped forward a few yards, came to a standstill. A standstill? Did I dare? Ha! I'd reached the periphery of the city, was standing on a dividing strip of grass in the center of a wide avenue. The avenue separated the city from the hilly park I was facing— a large park which, on the other side of its hills, bordered the river.

What a miraculous medicine open spaces can be! The non-building-blocked vistas before me were instantly rushing through my veins and nerves like a swift stream, washing me free of claustrophobia—all sensation of being hounded by phantoms, occupied by a hostile spirit! As I've said, my tribulations were inescapably associated with the crowded jumble of concrete at my back: dashing into this open area was like awakening in cheery daylight, with birds twittering, from a bad dream! Presto! Sighs of relief in place of nightmares!

I found myself slowly turning around and around while gazing at the sky, savoring the sight of the no longer threatening—now beautiful! silver spangles of the drizzle: they were gently ebbing back and forth to the rhythm of the breeze in a somehow comforting, beckoning motion. Beckoning motion? Speaking of beckoning... I ceased turning about, was again facing the park, regarding the two massive brick pillars which framed its entrance—was bringing to mind the soothing lawns, flowerbeds, and trees on the other side of those pillars...

Yes, the park was an invitation, all right! The city at my back harbored nothing but unhealthy associations, hostile stimuli! I didn't possess a single untroubling memory of it! Breeding ground of so much struggle, panic, trauma! Alarm lurking in every abrupt twist of a shadow on litter-strewn sidewalks; neon which ignites one's veins, sparks jagged stutterings in one's nerves, explodes into blind fear! Too many insomnia-fueled tastes of imminent psychic collapse! Too many frantic pacing sessions in stark white rooms—futile attempts to acquire equilibrium by fleeing those rooms, dashing outside! Ha, the outside which is never really outside—which is nothing but twisting entangled mazes of streets hemmed in by grimy architecture, interrupted views, blocked horizons; nothing but renewed prod, sting, overload; nothing but desperation-reinforcing claustrophobia—an endless reenactment of being backed into corners, attacked!

I turned to face the city, observed the higher residential and business structures which rose beyond the buildings of the warehouse district—observed the melancholy tinge of dark amber light which suffused all, smothered all, suffocated all—and was seized with an overwhelming desire to never return to it. Yes, that was the solution: I'd physically remove myself from the scenery which brought uneasiness to my thoughts, panic to my nerves, hysteria to my imagination; above all, I'd reduce to naught the chance of encountering she who'd infiltrated my existence, banished emotional stability—the remotest chance of attaining inner quietude! from my life! No more self-flagellation—baitings of breakdown! on account of the impossible endeavor of seeking to confront her, solve an unsolvable mystery! Perhaps in another location, far away—on an unpopulated coastline, via the rejuvenating cheer of sea and sand... In such a place would my depth-convulsing beauty's picture slip from my mind's eye, dissolve from memory? would all unnatural excitement vanish like an exorcised spirit? would every trace of perceptual distortion disappear as if it had never existed...?

Yes, yes! How fortunate I was to have ended up on the periphery—salvational outer boundary! of the city! My instinct for self-preservation hadn't, after all, entirely deserted me! I turned about to face the park again—glanced up its hills of lush vegetation, thought of the ferry on the opposite side of those hills where they descended to the river—and instantly had a plan of action: I'd spend the remainder of the night in the park, catch the first ferry to the other side of the river in the morning, and keep on going without looking back! I'd never set foot in the scenes of the past several months' disturbances again! Good riddance to the city, my bewitching beauty, and psychic havoc!

But, God! In the small amount of time—or so, at least, it seemed to me—that I'd taken to hit upon my self-resurrectional plan of action, the drizzle and sluggish breeze had turned into the heavy rain and high winds of a fierce thunderstorm! Yes, suddenly thick sheets of rain were battering my face, ricocheting off the pavement like shattering glass—slanting across and obscuring the scenery, obliterating all sense of being surrounded by open space! How precarious—willing to depart! relief of mind is! Or, rather: what a farce safe harbor is when the sea inside oneself only subsides to gather itself for a renewed onslaught of crashing breakers! In short, the storm outside me reignited the storm within: uneasiness gripped my ribs with electric claws, viciously swirled! By the time I entered the park I was dashing again, panting with panic, flinching as if in anticipation of a seizure's strike...

So much for an equilibrium-restoring plan! The strident emotions were vengefully reclaiming the ground they'd all too temporarily lost, scattering all possibility of ease of mind to the winds of the storm! In addition, upon gaining the park... God, I remembered that the park was actually very much a part of the city I'd thought of fleeing! Ha, talk about desperate hope distorting the facts! When I'd been standing on the traffic island in the center of the avenue it had somehow seemed to me I was gazing across a great distance at the twin pillars of the park's entrance—that the park was a safely removed place of refuge where my city-associated experiences would cease to exist; but the park—despite its considerable size—was in fact surrounded on all sides by the city, which resumed on the opposite riverbank! The supposed ferry to freedom? It was alternate public transportation, a means of bypassing the bridges and underground transit! And, as if that weren't enough, I also realized that the warehouse district I'd just exited—right over there, across the avenue! wasn't more than six blocks from my bedeviling beauty's place of residence! I'd been racing in circles, doing nothing but create the illusion of distance traveled, since leaving her doorstep!

Too much disheartening information at once! My legs turned to rubber, buckled; my head pounded, reeled! I slipped on the rain soaked grass of a hillside, was on my hands and knees, starting at the sight of dozens of black wings which were swooping close, darting hither and thither, in the mist-enshrouded amber of the park's gas lamps—wheeling in time to the wailings of wind, screechings of gust! Wings? Were they alive? Attacking? Did I yell? Slap my cheeks? And then I realized the wings were but shadows cast by the storm-slapped branches of trees in the unceasing flicker of lightning; realized I was flittering in and out of phantomland again!

The park a refuge? Ha! I'd been tricked into leaping from the frying pan into the fire! I jerked myself to my feet, turned towards the twin pillars of the exit with the aim of beating a hasty retreat, returning to the alleys from whence I'd emerged; that is, turned towards where I believed the pillars to be... Where were they? I could see nothing but the same dark shapes menacingly flapping in clouds of rain-churned mist; see nothing but the jagged outlines, flailing branches, of trees and shrubs—branches which seemed to be pointing accusing fingers, waving frantic warnings! I was turning around and around as I desperately sought to race this way, that! Seeking to run? I couldn't see clearly enough to do anything besides haphazardly stumble, repeatedly slip to the ground! But I had to run: tight grating friction was writhing all about me, in the claustrophobic absence of depth perception! I could feel the friction approaching, closer and closer, in every slippery vaporous shadow; every slithering patch of darkness in depressions of the hillside; every swipe of the gale-tossed tree-tops against the lightning-slashed sky! Yes, I had to get out of there, escape the sensation of being seized and squeezed by the air!

"Please, for God's sake!" I heard a tension-cracked voice whimper as I laboriously advanced up the incline of one of the larger hills, approached the dark billowings of foliage at its crest. "Please... Oh, why can't you let me be—allow me a moment's quiet! Why..." The voice died in an anguished stammer as I reached the dense canopy of a huge oak, ducked to pass beneath the ground-approaching weight of the ends of its branches. Upon passing below the branch-ends, crawling three or so more yards, and standing I found myself inside a veritable cathedral of gnarled limbs and layered leaves which excluded the rain and wind, was comparatively silent. A gas lamp was within the oak's canopy, on the other side; its direct light was blocked by the oak's massive trunk. I was staring at the base of the trunk, recoiling at the sight of someone sitting with their back to it on its opposite side, facing the gas lamp; yes, the other's feet were just visible, extended into the sparse wisps of uncut grass...

I was recoiling? At first, yes; but then something—a long-buried, unfamiliar inclination—gave me pause: I who'd been steadfastly avoiding others for weeks, and considered myself unfit for social interaction; who hadn't spoken to anyone heart-to-heart for... Listen: the accumulated burden of the past three or so

months, the virtually nonstop state of inner seizure they represented, combined with the fearful tumult of this particular night;
plus the prospect of there being no relief from my condition on the
near or far horizon, merely infrequent teases—the mocking semblance—of such... I just didn't care anymore, was no longer able
to wonder whether matters would become worse than they already
were; nor able to be apprehensive of appalling others, causing
them to retreat in disgust or fear. But to the point: I unexpectedly
found myself, for the first time in God only knows how long, de-
sirous of communicating with someone—chatting amiably, con-
fiding sincerely. And no, I've never felt that misery loves
company; I've always been of the opposite inclination, wishful
of keeping to myself when uneasiness strikes, more comfortable
resolving it alone; but, as I've indicated, I was no longer able to
believe any effort at resolution would alter anything. And as for
the other's disposition: was he another night refugee—someone
fallen on hard times, either emotionally or economically? or was
he a thief in hiding, potential assailant? or, quite simply, a well-
balanced individual uninhibitedly surrendering himself to enjoy-
ment of the storm? Again, I was past caring: I just wanted to talk.
So I began strolling to my right and forwards, slowly and not too
close to the other so as to minimize the impact of my presence;
began strolling into the unobstructed swath of the gas lamp's
light...

I'd proceeded a few yards to the other's side of the oak's
trunk, and felt I was now fully disclosed to his gaze. I was awaiting a greeting, or a curse—some sort of reaction. "But what if the
other is sleeping?" a distant-seeming inner voice inquired, adding,
"Doubtless it is so." I waited a few more moments, then struck a
branch with my hand, as if inadvertently, to draw the other's attention to my presence. Still no response. Ok then, I'd slowly turn
and politely call out, announce myself as a fellow night-denizen
coming in peace and brotherhood. Hopefully, the other would respond in kind.

I turned in the direction of the other, was beginning to speak
the words, "Excuse me, sir...," when a sharp contraction seized

my throat, stifled my voice into mute convulsive mouthings! The light of the gas lamp brightened, dimmed, brightened—reeled into flicker-flash! as I staggered on legs of dust—found myself on my knees, gasping as if kicked in the stomach, seeking to yell! I couldn't yell—couldn't make a sound! My eyes, my eyes!—they raised themselves from the spinning ground despite myself, stared at what was propped up against the tree:

Yes, it was she: my bewitching beauty, otherworldly diamon, implacable fury! Her legs—one of them unkindly twisted, bent the wrong way from the knee—were stretched out before her, spattered with mud. Her head was slumped onto, lying all the way flat on, her right shoulder—with a dark swath of carmine, as of a paintbrush stroke, on the tree trunk behind it. Her mouth was dribbling red foam—wide open, as if frozen in mid-scream. And her throat was torn, mangled—as if clawed, chewed!—its blood as if deliberately smeared on her exposed chest, collected in handfuls and flung on it! Soaked shredded dress, bruises, violation! God! Her eyes, her eyes!—they were overlaid with a dull film, unseeingly staring into the nothingness of the air—no surprise in them, no alarm in them, no accusation in them—waxen doll's eyes, stuffed animal's eyes, dead thing's eyes—no light in them, only the gas lamp's light sitting on them—no light but icy light, unfeeling light, dead light—no more magical interplay of diamond brilliance and velvet shadows; no more cataract-swift hints of Creation's most carefully guarded secrets; no more flashes of elevated states of being I'd never attain to! No more!